Heartthrob

Heartthrob

An American Royalty Romance

Robin Bielman

TULE
PUBLISHING

Heartthrob
Copyright © 2019 Robin Bielman
Tule Publishing First Printing, March 2019

The Tule Publishing, Inc.

ALL RIGHTS RESERVED

First Publication by Tule Publishing 2019

Cover design by Lee Hyat at www.LeeHyat.com

No part of this book may be used or reproduced in any manner whatsoever without written permission except in the case of brief quotations embodied in critical articles and reviews.

This is a work of fiction. Names, characters, places, and incidents are products of the author's imagination or are used fictitiously. Any resemblance to actual events, locales, organizations, or persons, living or dead, is entirely coincidental.

ISBN: 978-1-950510-12-2

Acknowledgments

This book is really special to me and I so appreciate the assist from the following awesome people...

Thank you, Greg, for giving my heart a home since we were teenagers. Thank you for your love and support every day. And thank you for talking baseball with me while I wrote this book. You're my walk off home run and I love you so much.

Thank you, Samanthe Beck, for helping me with Chloe. Your brilliant suggestions truly helped make this book what it is and made writing this story even more fun for me. I'm beyond grateful for your friendship and writerly wisdom. Love you, sister!

Huge thanks to the amazing Tule team – Meghan, Sinclair, Jenny, Nicole, Jane, Cyndi, Lee, Marlene, and Helena. I appreciate your partnership, guidance, and patience more than I can say. (Sinclair, your kind words are still on repeat in my head. Jenny, I'm happy I was part of your new-found love for first person. And Helena, your style sheet is the bomb!)

Thank you, Kim Matlock, for your continued support of my work. Readers are so special to me, and you're one of the best. Thanks, too, for sharing the name of your dog with me when I gave a shout out for help. Sammy was the perfect name for Finn's puppy and it makes this book that much more meaningful. :)

Thank you to Social Butterfly PR and especially Sarah

Ferguson for working with me to get Finn and Chloe's story into the hands of readers. You rock!

And lastly, thank you from the bottom of my heart to my readers. Thanks for reading, blogging, reviewing, teasing, and sharing my stories with your friends and followers. I'm in awe of all that you do and forever grateful.

Dear Reader,

I've wanted to write a pro baseball player forever, and I'm so excited to finally bring you Finn Auprince. Baseball has been a part of my life for a long time, starting when my oldest son turned five and I signed my husband up to coach his team. (He continued to coach for fifteen years.) Both my boys are grown now, but our family's love for the game continues. The MLB Network is on in my family room at least once a day, and that's not even during the regular baseball season!

In writing this book, I tried to stay true to the game of baseball, but ultimately this is a romance between Finn and Chloe, so any errors are my own. The Landsharks are a fictional team, designed to give me some creative freedom, but I do make references to actual MLB teams. Along with Finn and Chloe, you'll also meet the extended Auprince family, most notably Finn's brothers Ethan and Drew. Stay tuned for two more books as they each get their happily ever after. Ethan is up next in *Sweet Talker*. Then it's Drew's turn in *Hotshot*. All three of them have stolen my heart, and I hope they steal yours, too.

Thanks so much for reading!

xoxo
Robin

Chapter One
#InjuredList

Finn

UNTIL A WEEK ago I'd say I was the luckiest guy on the planet.

Good family. Check.

Good looks. Check.

Good—no make that phenomenal—job. Check.

I'm the hottest player in major league baseball with sick stats, millions of fans, and the respect of my fellow players.

I'm also the center fielder who collided with the back fence while trying to rob the second hottest player in the majors of a home run in game seven of the World Series. The collision knocked the ball out of my glove. And landed me on my back with a fractured clavicle.

I lost my team the championship. My error allowed the other team to score a run, costing us the game and the series.

Yeah, I know baseball is a team sport, but I'm the captain, and our first trip to the world stage in over thirty years was supposed to end differently. Now, instead of reliving all the glory, I can't get that moment out of my head. When everything went completely silent, fifty thousand plus home fans all holding their breath as I dove for a hell of a hit, determined to rob the other team of victory. I had it, held the ball in the sweet spot of my glove…until it rolled off the leather in slo-mo, a collective groan echoing around the stadium. I'm still not sure if the grumbles were for the dropped ball or my injury, but either way, that sound of disappointment hurt a thousand times worse than the pain slicing through my collarbone.

"Then she unzipped my pants and pulled out my dick, right there in the middle of the restaurant."

I blink back to the present at the word "dick." When talk turns to a guy's favorite body part, shitty memories bite the dust, at least temporarily. "She did what?"

"Nice of you to rejoin the conversation," my older brother, Ethan, says from the other side of the couch. He stopped by to cheer me up with coffee and tales of his latest sexcapades. Beats the time he and our younger brother tried to put me up for adoption. (That's what happens when you're the best-looking and most athletic of the three.)

I rotate my right shoulder, trying to stretch my upper back. The sling on my left arm is a royal pain in the ass. Several more weeks of this is going to kill me.

"Were there any witnesses?" I ask to mess with him. "Or was a magnifying glass used to confirm said extraction?"

"His sense of humor returns. You must be feeling better."

When I don't answer right away he gives me the big brother eyebrow raise, silently telling me to fess up. There's no one I trust more than my brothers, but that doesn't mean it's easy for me to spit out my every worry. Truth is I'm scared as hell. The doctor tells me most clavicle fractures heal themselves without surgery, that three weeks in a sling to immobilize my arm followed by passive range-of-motion exercise, then more aggressive strength training should be all that's needed. This is his conservative plan. The not so easy route for some compound fractures is a trip to the OR to repair the damage. Look, I know it's not *major* surgery, and I'm in the best shape of my life otherwise, but even the possibility of being cut into does things to a guy's psyche, you know?

"Pain's still kicking my ass," I finally say. "Nothing I can't handle, though." What I really don't like is dealing with the constant attention from my family and friends. I wouldn't call myself a loner exactly, but I have no problem being left alone—especially with my injury. Insert laughter here, because having the last name Auprince has afforded me very little privacy since the day I was born. Add in baseball, and let's just say I have to work hard at keeping some semblance of solitude.

"It's only been a week. Give it time."

I lift my Starbucks cup off the coffee table to finish the warm brew. A shot of pain where my neck meets my shoulder reminds me it *has* only been a few days. "Feels like a year. I hate sitting around doing nothing."

"I agree forced time off sucks, but you've been going nonstop for a long time. A little rest might be good for you."

I've heard about this thing called "rest" but unless it's right after mind-blowing sex—in which case rest is necessary before overwhelmingly impressive round two—I want no part of it. I've got one speed: on.

Granted, usually when the season ends, I take a two-week-long break before cranking it up in the off-season and hitting the gym every day with my trainer. But those weeks are not me sitting on my ass, babying an arm.

"Or it might slowly turn me into a couch potato with an unhealthy attachment to socks," I say. To prove I'm already on my way to insanity I prop my feet on the coffee table. I'm wearing a blue athletic sock on one foot and an orange one on the other. I don't normally wear socks without my shoes, but this injury has messed up my internal temperature and my feet are cold.

Ethan cracks up. "It's laundry day, huh?"

I shrug. I think it's Thursday. Maybe Wednesday. Definitely doesn't feel like a Friday. Not that I'm captain of my calendar at the moment. Nope. All my days blend together like my daily kale, pineapple, and almond-milk smoothie.

Jesus, I'm pathetic. It's time to suck up my misery and get back to some sort of routine to keep my body and mind sharp.

"Come to the restaurant tonight," Ethan says. "I'll have your favorite meal waiting."

"Charlotte?"

My brother shakes his head. "My manager is no longer on your menu. She's got a boyfriend."

"Damn. Guess I'll have to settle for a filet then. Thanks for the offer. I appreciate it." I do need to get out of the house. Shower. Shave. But just putting on a shirt is damn difficult when I can only comfortably lift one arm.

The doorbell rings, reminding me our mom said she was stopping by this morning, too. "Hello," she calls out, letting herself in.

"Back here," I return, dropping my feet to the floor and sitting taller. A sharp pain slices through my collarbone. I hiss in a breath, not happy about my brother noticing my discomfort. I don't want the sympathy I see in his eyes. I want to hurl this sling across the room and feel like my old self.

"Hello, darling—darlings," Mom corrects as she enters the family room wearing her customary bright smile and carrying a—

"Is that a puppy?" I ask. Our mom is passionate about animals, taking in strays and fostering dogs for as long as I can remember. She's never brought one here, though.

She kisses Ethan's cheek. "Hey, Mom," he says. "New tennis partner?" He nods to the bundle of fur in her arms.

"Isn't she the cutest thing ever?" she answers then turns to me. "I got her for you. To cheer you up." She extends her arms, the puppy dangling from her hands.

Ethan chuckles. He's finding this morning quite amusing, and probably remembering the time I was five and peed my pants when the next-door neighbor's golden retriever rushed me, only to attempt to lick my face off. "I was thinking about getting him a female to cheer him up too, but one with two legs."

I let my brother's joke that I can't find a woman for myself slide. Is my mom insane? I don't want—or need—a pet.

Especially right now. When I don't reach for the puppy, Mom sits down beside me, cradling the dog in her lap. "I've brought him *appropriate* female company. He doesn't need another ball girl."

I choke on my dignity. I live and breathe baseball. Nothing matters more to me than my career. A nice benefit of being one of the best players in the league is having companionship when I want it. I play by my rules and make that clear to any woman I choose to spend a little time with. Which is far less often than the media portrays.

"Never hurts to have someone give your balls attention," my brother says with a smirk.

"Ethan," Mom reprimands. "You know I don't need details about all the fans your brother likes to spend the night with."

I scrub a hand across the scruff on my jaw. "You do know I'm sitting right here." And the topic of my sex life is one I'd rather not discuss with my mother sitting beside me.

"Anyway," Mom says. "This is Sammy. She was abandoned on the side of the road. She's approximately ten weeks old. A husky, mini Labradoodle mix, we're guessing. When I saw her, I knew you had to have her. I'm worried about you getting bored while you're recuperating."

So am I, but I wasn't thinking *puppy* to remedy that.

"Sammy" looks up at me. Her eyes are an unearthly shade of aquamarine. And sad. Puppy dog eyes right here, folks. The cable-knit fur around those eyes, on her ears, and on parts of her body is beige. The fur on her front paws and circling her very pink nose is white. Who would abandon this adorable animal? She crawls into my lap like she understood exactly what my mom said. I'm so screwed.

"How am I supposed to take care of a dog with one arm?" Not to mention a dog is a distraction I don't need even when I'm 100 percent healthy. I'll come right out and say it. I'm selfish when it comes to my time, and I make no apologies for it. I'm breaking baseball records, focused on breaking more.

"She just needs love," Mom says like it's that easy.

"She needs more than that," I argue, even while I pet her soft fur. She drops her chin on my thigh. *I'm going to snuggle here all day*, her relaxed posture says.

I repeat, I'm screwed.

Mom shifts so she's facing me fully. "I've taken care of everything. All her things will be delivered shortly."

"Her things?" I mentally picture all the equipment and paraphernalia my teammate, Mike, has for his one-year-old daughter. Half the stuff I've never even heard of and would be hard-pressed to know what to do with.

"Yes, you know food, toys, potty-training pads, a leash—everything I could think of."

A wave of panic hits me. "Dogs don't do their business outside anymore?"

Ethan laughs. I glare at him.

"They do, but you have to train them to go outside, and accidents are inevitable the first few weeks."

I run my free hand through my hair. The only training I want to do is with my ass-kicking trainer, Dwayne, back in the gym and on the field. "Mom, this is very nice of you, and

Sammy seems like a sweet dog—" she's resting comfortably on my lap "—but I can't deal with a puppy right now."

"Of course you can," she says with love and optimism and there is no way I can refuse when she's also looking at me and Sammy like we're a perfect pair.

That is until I feel something warm and wet on my sweatpants. With quick reflexes—I am the best center fielder in the AL—I scoop Sammy into my good arm, jump to my feet, and shake my leg out. "She just peed on me," I grit out. Mostly because of the sharp pain radiating through my shoulder blade. Sammy's accident is a common initiation into dog ownership, I assume.

Ethan cracks up yet again. He's laughing so hard, he's holding his stomach.

Mom gets to her feet, too. "Come here, Sammy." She lifts the puppy from me. "Let's show you the backyard."

Fantastic. That could take a while. As Mom walks away, I push down my sweats until they pool at my ankles and then I step out of them.

"It's definitely laundry day," Ethan says, taking in my boxer briefs.

I glance down. I'm wearing my Landsharks underwear. Tiny gray sharks are all over the blue cotton. Every player on the team has a pair or two. "I think you're right."

"Where is Sylvie, by the way?"

Sylvie is my cook-slash-housekeeper-slash-godsend. She's been with me for four years and I'm man enough to say I'd be lost without her. She was a gift from my mom, too. That sounded weird—not a gift exactly. Mom made the introduction because she thought I could use some help when I moved into this house. "She and her family are at Disneyland for two days. It's her grandson's birthday."

I sit back down and look my brother right in the eye. "Want a puppy?"

Ethan grins. "That's funny, but no, little brother, Sammy's all yours."

"What the hell am I going to do with a dog?"

"You don't really need me to answer that, do you?"

"Hey, what about the time I got you field seats for the All-Star Game *and* an introduction to that *Sports Illustrated* swimsuit model? You said you owed me one."

"You never remember where you leave your phone, but you remember something that happened years ago?" He gets to his feet. "Dude, the puppy is yours and the sooner you accept it the better."

"Fine." I know this. Mom doesn't give gifts lightly; her heart is always behind the gesture. She'd be crushed if any of us ever rejected her tokens of affection. Her line of thinking doesn't always coincide with that of her sons is all.

"I'll see you later. Say bye to Mom for me."

I nod then pick up my ringing cell phone. "Hello?"

"Hi, Finn. It's Rena."

"Hey. How are you?" Rena is our team's senior director of Public Relations.

"I'm good. How are *you*?"

"Hanging in there."

"Glad to hear that. We'd like you to come in for a meeting on Tuesday. You available?"

"Sure." No one says "no" to Rena. Not that anyone wants to. She may have a no-nonsense attitude, but she's the best liaison there is when it comes to our fans and charities. Best of all, she treats me like a player, rather than an Auprince.

"Great. We'll be connecting you with a social media manager for the off-season. Be here at ten."

"Sounds goo—wait. What?"

"It's something new we want to try. You've got huge followings on social media, but we want to go next-level. We do that by hiring a professional to take over your accounts, but who will work side by side with you in order to keep your profiles honest and authentic."

"Is this a joke?" I do just fine posting on my own, albeit reluctantly and rarely, and I definitely don't want someone *taking over* anything of mine.

"Not at all," she says, no smile in her tone. "I promise this isn't a bad thing, Finn. Especially with your behavior during the series and your injury. We want to—"

"Stop right there." I don't need to hear that the front office is worried about me and wants to help. In uncharacteristic fashion, I behaved like a dick during a couple of the World Series games. Nerves got the better of me for the first time, enough so that I even mouthed off to the home plate umpire. I'd never disrespected the game before and my reputation took a hit. "I'll see you Tuesday," I say tightly.

We disconnect. First a puppy. Now a social media manager. So much for a quiet recovery on my terms. I tilt my head back, resting it on the back of the couch. I got called to the majors at twenty. Won Rookie of the Year unanimously. I'm the youngest player to reach one hundred home runs and one hundred stolen bases. A two-time MVP. My career batting average is over .300. If I continue at this pace, I'll break records, be a shoo-in for the Hall of the Fame (if I'm not already). Baseball is all I know. All I've ever *wanted* to know.

I've suffered bumps and bruises along the way, but cutting management some slack, I've never acted out or been injured like I am now. Never been escorted off the field by the team doctor. I don't know what to do with it. I'm completely unprepared. There isn't a manual for how to deal with injuries, and even if there were, I'd have a hard time reading it. When everything's gone your way and then *bam*! All of a sudden, the future you've worked your ass off for isn't a guarantee anymore, it takes a huge mental toll.

There are a couple of young, hotshot players in our club itching to take my place if I don't come back strong. No way in hell do I want to be Wally Pipped at thirty years of age. Pipp was a Yankee and the first on his team to lead the American League in home runs, only to be replaced by Lou Gehrig for something minor, and we all know how that turned out.

So, if I have to give up some privacy to a social media manager to keep in good standing with the team, I'll do it. Because no matter what it takes or the sacrifices I have to deal with, I'll make sure I repair any damage to my name and remain the major league's favorite center fielder.

A FEW HOURS later I'm sitting on the hardwood floor playing sock tug-of-war with Sammy. She's fun and terrifying at the same time. My sweet, mellow puppy has decided to show her true colors now that she's here to stay. She's feisty. Energetic. And she's got sharp little teeth. I found this out when she decided to nip at my sock-covered toes until the sock slid off my foot. Victory looked damn cute so I gave her my other sock, too. She's no match for my strength, of course, but I let her win our battles over and over again. When I glance out the floor-to-ceiling window toward the ocean, I'm surprised to see only soft glowing light. Sammy's taken my mind off my troubles for longer than I thought.

I laugh when she tugs the sock out of my hold and falls to the side, her big paws getting in the way of her balance. She shakes the sock vigorously back and forth and looks at me like this is the best game ever and she's eager to play all night.

Then she stops. And takes a shit.

I drop my head into my hand. The latest poop from the life of Finn Auprince?

Puppy: 1

Professional baseball player: 0

Chapter Two
#CursesLikeChickensComeHomeToRoost

Chloe

THIS IS IT. The curse has finally been broken.

I don't even try to contain my smile as I run up the stairs to my boyfriend Leo's apartment. Jittery excitement, the kind you feel right before riding a roller coaster or jumping into the glorious, but cold ocean, has me catching my breath when I reach the second floor. Leo's just returned from a business trip and texted me to come right over. The original idea was he'd pick me up for dinner, but he had a change in plans, he'd written, which leads me to believe he's got something special up his sleeve at his place.

Today is our one-year anniversary.

Twelve months of happy and the kind of contentment I thought I might never find. It's the longest I've been with a guy. The longest I've been in love. I fought it at first, but Leo's height, his handsome face, his sense of humor, made it impossible not to fall for him. That he fell first helped.

I run my sweaty palms down my navy polo dress. I've paired it with my pewter Vans. This is as spruced up as I get, my athletic style one of the things Leo loves about me. My hair is down, peach lip gloss applied, legs shaved and moisturized. If I've read all the signs right, tonight isn't just a dinner date.

Given the time difference between here and London, we haven't had much of a chance to connect while he's been away, but before he left I got the distinct vibe he was ready to go from calling me girlfriend to calling me fiancée. The idea makes me so unbelievably relieved—and happy—that I've tried not to think about it too hard. I don't want to jinx it. We haven't talked about tying the knot specifically, though marriage is something we both want. Kids, too. Leo is amazing with his nieces and nephews. It's another thing I love about him. He has a big family, something I really enjoy.

I pause outside his door. Since my mom passed away twelve years ago, it's been just my dad and me, thick as thieves. We'd been close before she died, but her absence strengthened our bond even more. Back then I hadn't wanted to let Dad out of my sight, terrified he'd leave me, too, so he took me on the road with him during baseball season, homeschooling me when he wasn't on the field to umpire. I may not be able to ramble off all the U.S. presidents' names without an assist (history was my least favorite subject), but I can list every major league baseball team, their division, and the name of their stadium with exceptional ease.

My chest tightens. For eight months out of the year, Dad's whole life revolves around calling balls and strikes and his recent diagnosis worries me. His being alone when I move out of the house worries me.

Of course, I'd think about that right now. We talk through any big decisions. Not that my saying yes to Leo's proposal is up for discussion. But knowing Dad likes Leo makes this a moment I can act on with confidence.

Normally, I'd let myself in to Leo's, but not this time. I don't want to ruin the surprise. I knock twice, in time to the quick beating of my heart.

Leo opens the door wide, his height filling the space. "Hi, Chloe. Thanks for coming over."

Chloe. Not babe. Or baby, as he is apt to call me. Especially after his business trips. His tone is also flat, dutiful, not at all cheerful. A funny feeling invades my stomach because more things are noticeably absent: a kiss, a lifting off my feet, a God-I-missed-you smile. I take a step back. This is not what I'd envisioned for the past hour. This is all wrong.

"Hi," I say automatically. Robotically. Some sixth sense tells me to stay cool and distant. To not grab him and kiss away the sickening vibe he's carrying. This is just some weird form of jetlag. But then my gaze snags on a flash of color behind him. He isn't alone.

"Chloe." My name has never sounded so hurtful.

Our eyes meet again, and this time I notice my boyfriend isn't happy to see me. He's shamefaced.

"Please come in."

I can't. I physically can't. My feet are stuck. If I step over the threshold, my world as I know it will change, and I don't want it to change. Not. Again.

Leo takes my hand. He brings me inside. He closes the

door. A beautiful girl with dark hair and dark eyes, dressed like she stepped out of a fashion magazine, stands up from the couch.

"Chloe, this is Adele."

No offense, but I hate you, Adele.

"I didn't mean for this to happen…" he says.

I stand there, stunned and numb as Leo tells me he met Adele his first night in London and their attraction was undeniable and *blah, blah, blah.*

"I hope we can stay friends," he concludes sometime later. I think it's only been a minute, but I can't be sure.

I hope your penis breaks in half.

"What?"

Oops. Guess I said that out loud. "I hope you have a happy life," I amend, keeping my expression neutral. No way am I giving them the satisfaction of knowing my insides feel like they've been fed through a weed whacker. Then I turn and walk out the door.

Refusing to show people your heartache means when you get to your car and you're alone inside the old, but trusty two doors, you cry like a baby.

I cry until the betrayal is leached from my bones. So, ten, fifteen minutes. I mean it's not like I haven't suffered this unfairness before. I have. *Four* other times.

See, I'm cursed as a good luck charm—for my exes. Long story short (because I'm already down, I don't need to be kicked any harder), every boyfriend I've had has found his one true love while dating me. Yes, *while.* Not after. *During.* It's ironic, really. Cue the Alanis Morissette song. Because as my dad likes to say, *Those boys weren't meant for you.* But it doesn't make it any easier to get dumped. My boyfriend before Leo? We were at a restaurant eating dinner when two women, a mom and daughter I'd come to find out, sat down at the table next to us. I excused myself to use the bathroom and when I returned Tyler and the daughter were talking and laughing—the mom nowhere to be seen. "I've never been drawn to someone so quickly or strongly. I'm sorry," Tyler said to me.

I'd said, "What the fuck?" More to the universe than to Tyler, before I hurried out of the restaurant.

This time, though, is the worst. I wasn't ready to marry any of the other guys. My head falls back against the car seat. "Why?" I say aloud. Why am I the gatekeeper to others' happily ever after? Why does 'I love you' mean I-like-you-until-someone-better-comes-along. It's uncanny, really. Date me and your dream girl will present herself. And never the two shall mix.

I turn the key in the ignition and drive home blurry-eyed. The tears continue to fall, my heart hurting like Leo's poisoned each chamber and the organ is slowly shutting down. Good. Because this is the last time I'm liking, letting alone falling in love with someone. I love my dad. I love my friends. I love my work. That's enough.

The sun is behind the mountains and streetlights flicker on. Twilight is usually my favorite time of day, but right now it sucks. I'm also, I realize, driving the wrong way. I wipe at my eyes, swallow the string of lumps in my throat.

The car beside me honks when I accidentally cut them

off to move into the left lane to make a U-turn at the stoplight. I wave in apology and mouth "sorry." The light turns green. There are no cars coming from the other direction so I make my U-turn. And crash into another car making a right turn. Shit! Isn't this just the cherry on top of a sucktastic day.

Fortunately, neither of us was driving fast. I put it in reverse since I'm the one kissing the shiny white Porsche SUV's side fender then follow the car into the corner parking lot of a fast-food restaurant to check out the damage and make sure the diver is okay.

I get out of the car on shaky legs. The breakup with Leo, and now this, has wreaked havoc on my stability. I see an entire one-pound bag of almond M&M's and some television in my future.

But first I need to deal with this situation. I had a green light, thus the right of way. Meaning despite what it looks like, it's not my fault we collided. (Confession: I had a minor fender bender a few months ago and my insurance went up. I can barely afford the coverage so I can't have another claim against me.)

The first thing I notice about the other driver is his long, muscular, jean-clad legs as they exit the vehicle. Next is his hard-bodied torso and a sling on his arm. Last, but definitely not least, are his surreal blue eyes, brown hair longer on top than the sides, and scruff around his full lips and along his chiseled jawline.

Unbelievable. As if my day cannot get any worse, I've hit Finn Auprince. Major League Baseball's golden boy. He's arguably one of the best center fielders ever. His stats are unreal. On top of that he's American royalty, a "prince" in the media, his family one of the wealthiest and most influential in the world with their hotel empire. His popularity on and off the field is talked about weekly. Which is probably the reason he thinks he's God's gift to all women.

Except this one.

The minute he called my dad a "blind sack of shit" and proceeded to show him up in front of the fans by drawing a line in the dirt with his bat to illustrate the path of the ball off the plate in game three of the World Series, he was removed from my list of favorite players, never to earn a spot back. I was sitting behind home plate. The pitch was clearly strike three. To my dad's credit he didn't throw Finn out of the game, choosing as he usually does to tolerate a player's aggravation and not take it personally.

"Hello," I say.

"Hi." He looks at me funny and for a beat we take each other in. Does he recognize me? I've sat in the stands dozens of times but he rarely looks at the crowd. *Except that once.* When our eyes connected and I stopped breathing. "Uh, are you okay?" he asks breaking the charged silence.

"No." See this gaping hole in my chest? It's where my heart used to be. Oh, wait. He means am I okay from the accident. "I mean, yes. Sorry. You?"

He smiles, flashing his straight white teeth. Smiles like his make birds sing and flowers bloom. And hearts pitter-patter. Good thing mine is dead. I study him. He thinks I'm flustered because of him. Ha! I will not give him the satisfaction of knowing I know who he is. Or being in any way, shape, or form affected by his good looks.

"I'm fine. My car, however…"

I follow his gaze. There's a big ol' dent above the front tire. I turn my attention to my car. The paint is scratched, but otherwise my nine-year-old convertible Toyota Solara—a sixteenth birthday present from my dad—appears undamaged.

"I had a green light," I say, not sure if Finn is implying this is my fault.

"I had a green arrow," he counters.

I frown.

He nods toward the intersection. "You also had a 'no U-turn' sign." He says this lightly. He's not mad in the least, which is reassuring, yet in this moment I'd rather he be anything but nice. I'm in the mood for a fight.

Not only does the sign spell out "NO U TURN" it also has a picture of the black U-turn arrow with a red circle and line through it. Obviously I wasn't paying attention. Not so obvious (I hope) is that I've been crying and I'm not thinking clearly.

"You should still watch where you're going," I tell him.

His eyebrows arch. Playfully. Jeez, he's charming, even under these circumstances. "You do realize *you* hit me, right?"

"I think we hit each other."

"Through no fault of my own."

"Should you even be driving with that?" I point to his sling. The question isn't nice. It's meant to get a rise out of him because…because he's the guy standing in front of me right now and my feelings are hurt beyond reason. Plus, it's the best I can do—I really have no experience fighting. I hate confrontation, and will do most anything to avoid it.

"I'd say it's safer than you driving."

Some sort of huffy sound comes from the back of my throat. "I'm a great driver." Besides my last minor accident and this one.

"I'm not so sure about that. Have you been drinking?"

"*What?* No."

"Your eyes are bloodshot."

I blink like that will clear the redness.

"Allergies?"

"Yes," I quickly answer. From now on I'm allergic to single men. Unless they're gay. Or already a friend. "That's exactly it." I sniffle for good measure. I *am* allergic to shellfish so I'm not totally lying. Although that allergy is life-threatening not heartbreaking.

Finn stares at me. I shiver. Because it's chilly out, not because his fixed look feels like he can see I'm fibbing. It's just his magnetic personality doing its thing.

Which also seems to bring out the responsible side of my personality because I next say, "I guess we should exchange information."

I reach into my car for my purse, pull out my wallet, and slide my insurance card out from behind my driver's license. Finn has his phone in his hand when I turn around.

"I'll just take a picture of your card," he says. My hope that he'll say, *Hey, accidents happen, don't worry about this,*

I've got it, have a good night, dies a painful death in the middle of my chest.

I hand it to him. He struggles to hold on to it with one hand while taking a picture with the other, the sling making it difficult. He also winces, and that's all it takes for me to offer my assistance.

"How about I hold it for you? Or take the picture?"

"Thanks." He gives me back my card, but still battles with the phone.

"It's not easy with one hand," I say with authority. I'm constantly on my phone taking pictures. "How about I do that instead?"

He grumbles, a few cuss words slipping out of his nice mouth. Finn is over six feet tall and probably tips the scales at two ten, so watching him fight with a small electronic device is entertaining. I chuckle. I get it. I'm not one to ask for help either.

"Something funny, Blondie?"

That stops me cold. "You did not just call me that."

"Blondie? I did. I could call you Freckles instead."

He noticed my freckles? I have exactly five of them across my nose. "Are you being cute with me right now?"

"You think I'm cute?" A sly smile takes hold of his face, the kind of smile you can't *not* be enamored with. The kind that constructs butterflies in your stomach whether you want them there or not.

"Going by the North American informal definition of cunning in a self-seeking or superficial way, yes."

Finn's eyes light with amusement. "Did you just quote

the dictionary to me?"

"I did. Got a problem with that?" As you might guess, English was and still is my favorite subject. I'm a lover of words. I use them a lot in my profession and have an uncanny memory when it comes to their definitions.

"No, no problem." He's trying really hard not to laugh. "Webster."

I throw my hands in the air, even though *that* nickname I secretly like. "Do you nickname all the strangers you meet?"

"Just the pretty ones."

"Smooth," I say with a shake of my head. He no doubt compliments every woman he meets. "But overused." I put out my palm. "Hand over your phone. I'll take the picture."

He looks like he's ready to yank the sling off his arm and throw it across the parking lot, but instead he gives in to my request. I put the card down on the hood of my car and snap the photo. After checking to make sure it's a clear shot, I say, "Would you mind letting me know the cost of fixing your car before we go through insurance companies? I may pay out of pocket." I hate the idea of depleting my savings account, but it might be the better option in the long run.

"Sure." His fingers brush mine when I give him his phone back, and a surge of heat charges up my arm. Our eyes lock. Hold. "I should also get your digits then—" he glances down at the photo "—Chloe Conrad."

His saying my name shouldn't make me weak in the knees, but it does. We're no longer strangers, not that he'll remember me or give me any thought beyond fixing his car.

I snag the phone back and type in my number. Then I call myself. My phone rings from the car. "Now I've got your number, too." I never answer my phone if I don't know who's calling.

"Would you like a name to go along with it?"

"That's okay." I hand back the phone.

His blue eyes dance. "You already know it."

"Why would I know it? Are you famous or something?" I turn to go before he can see the truth on my face. "I'll wait to hear from you and uh, sorry about hitting you. I don't think I said that."

"No worries."

I wish. Life isn't exactly going to plan at the moment. At least my next job assignment should be easy. My boss said it was a perfect fit and I'd get the details on Monday.

"Oh, and Chloe?"

I pause before sliding into my car and look at Finn.

"Nice try." He tips his head toward my front bumper and winks. Actually winks! Normally I find winking cheesy, but not when Finn does it. His wink is like a calling card for *let's get naked and run our hands and mouths all over each other.*

Then it hits me. My license plate frame. It says *Baseball…The Perfect Game.* Shit. Can't a girl catch a single break?

"See you around, Webster."

No, he won't. Not if I can help it.

Chapter Three
#BatterUp

Finn

I NOW UNDERSTAND what people mean when they say they feel an instant connection to someone. I can't get Chloe Conrad out of my head. The second her big honey-brown eyes met mine I was drawn to her in such a major way, it scared the hell out of me. She was beautiful, yes, but there was something about her that went beyond simple awareness. I _liked_ her and had this instant primordial desire to claim her like I was Tarzan and she was my Jane.

Insanity is what that was.

And the reason why I won't call her. She is a temptation I don't need or want. I'm focused on one thing and one thing only: baseball. I hope to have another ten years in the game, at least, which means I've got to continue to look out for myself. When I do something, I give it 100 percent, and right now that something is my career. I'm nothing without it.

Not that I planned to call her anyway. When someone asks about paying out of pocket it usually means they can't afford for their insurance rate to go up. At the same time, I got the impression Chloe couldn't spare extra cash to fix what I can repair no problem. She'd probably hate me for thinking that way, but my mind is made up.

I smile. Damn, she was feisty. And pretending she didn't know who I was? Insanely refreshing.

"What are you smiling about?" Mike asks from beside me. On the other side of him is Giancarlo. The three of us are known as a triple threat—our on-base percentages what helped us get to the postseason the past three years. We're sitting in the club conference room waiting for Rena and a couple other marketing and PR team members to arrive. I'm not the only one getting a social media manager. "Good weekend?" Mike arches his brows in the standard you-got-laid-didn't-you expression.

"Not exactly."

"Still in pain?" He looks at my sling and for the thousandth time I want to throw the damn thing away.

I cradle the annoying material with my good arm to adjust my position in the office chair. "Worse. My mom got me a puppy." Sammy has decided she wants no part of her crate, preferring to spend the nights in my bed. I've gotten zero sleep. If I wasn't taking her outside so she could relieve herself, I was worried about rolling over and crushing her. She slept sprawled out like she owned the place, her legs stretched out without concern for my comfort. All of this when she wasn't nipping at my sling. Pain radiates from my neck just thinking about it.

Mike cracks up.

"Why is that so funny?"

"Dude, have you ever had to take care of anything in your life? You do know you need to feed and walk it, right?"

"Shut up."

He laughs again then leans over to tell Giancarlo. Great. The two of them love to give me shit for having the last name Auprince. It's all in good fun, I know, but my life hasn't always been easy. Not by a long shot. Thank God for baseball.

I'm saved from further discussion when Rena and a few others enter the room. The meeting goes off with one hitch—my social media manager is running late due to a family emergency. Extrovert One and Two—Mike and Giancarlo—are thrilled with this new plan to guide their social media presence and take off with their assigned sidekicks, leaving me and Rena to wait alone when the other execs say goodbye.

"Don't look so happy," Rena jokes. "This is a good thing."

I nod. "I know. Thanks for arranging it." I may not like the idea, but I'm a team player on and off the field. I've been with the Landsharks since day one. I'd like to be with them on my last day, too. I regret some of my recent behavior and this is a way to show my remorse and dedication to the team.

Voices sound from the hallway. Laughter. "Good luck with Auprince," someone says with a thick New York accent—Mac, manager of the umpires' clubhouse.

"That must be Chloe," Rena says, getting to her feet.

Chloe? What are the chances…

Damn good because Chloe Conrad fills the doorway.

She's wearing light blue jeans, a body-clinging gray sweater, and a Landsharks baseball cap, and I'm immediately bowled over by her for a second time, surprise and some rare magnetic pull making my skin tight. Our eyes meet briefly before hers dart away.

"Hi, Rena. I'm so sorry I was late."

"Hi. Is everything okay?"

"Yes, thanks."

"Happy to hear that." Rena gives Chloe a quick smile then glances at me. "I was just telling Finn how great this is going to be."

"Absolutely," Chloe says.

"Finn, meet your social media manager, Chloe Conrad. Chloe, this is Finn Auprince."

I stand. "Hey, Webster."

Rena frowns. "We've met," I tell her.

"Briefly," Chloe is quick to add. "And at the time I didn't know we'd be working together. Hi, Finn. It's good to see you again. If you wouldn't mind using my first name, that would be great."

"And if I do mind?"

A grumble I'm pretty sure Chloe didn't want heard slips out of her pretty pink mouth.

"Is this going to be a problem?" Rena asks, her tone stern.

"No problem," I'm quick to say this time. A hardship, yes, because keeping my hands off of Chloe for the next three months won't be easy.

Rena looks to Chloe. "We're good," Chloe agrees.

"Okay, then. I've got another meeting to get to. Finn, Chloe is the expert in this arrangement, so you play by her rules."

"Will do." What else can I say? The Landsharks are my mother ship.

"Chloe, we'll touch base in a few days." Chloe nods and Rena leaves the room.

I sit back down. I can't believe I'm looking at the only woman to star in more than one of my fantasies. "Small world, huh?"

She takes a chair across from me. "Yes, so before we start working together, I'd like to settle the car situation."

"Nothing to settle. We're good."

"Finn."

"It's not a big deal. I probably should have noticed you making a U before I turned, so forget about it. Now tell me, why do I get the feeling you're no stranger around here?"

Indecision mars her soft features before she relaxes into her seat. "Thank you."

"You're welcome."

"I've been around baseball my whole life. My dad is Casey Conrad."

I rub my free hand across my jawline. "Shit." Casey is the home plate umpire whose face I got up into when I didn't like his call. The major league umpire crew is a tight group and over the years, players get to know them. I'd never had an issue with Casey before. He's one of the most respected veteran umps there is. But that day, in game three of the World Series, we were down by two and I'd snapped. I regret drawing lines in the dirt to show him up. The ass that day wasn't him, it was me.

"Yeah, I was there for your little tirade. For the record, it was definitely a strike. McNeal lit up the radar gun all night and with a WAR of 5.6, you should have at least swung on the pitch."

Jesus Christ, this girl knows baseball. I'm tempted to ask her for the definition of WAR, but then I'd definitely lose my mind and probably drop down on one knee and propose. That I even thought that last part means there is something wrong with me. Yes, the soft, melodic timbre of her voice makes me forget the pain in my collarbone. And yes, she radiates some kind of angelic light to go along with her confident attitude. But since when am I blindsided by a woman?

"Not my best moment."

"We all have bad days."

"Yeah? Tell me about one of yours," I say to deflect. I'd much rather talk about her.

"Not today. Today I'm here to tell you about the job I was hired to do. For the next three months, I'll be responsible for curating your brand. I'll monitor, moderate, and respond to your followers, arrange and manage partnerships with other brands, and create and post shareable images and videos. I'd love to strategize with you, but if you prefer I take care of everything, I can do that. That doesn't mean you're off the hook. You're our biggest asset so that means I'll be taking lots of pictures of you. We'll work the injury angle, baseball, your favorite stuff and your family if you're cool with that. People want to keep getting to know the real you so we're going to give it to them. Every couple of days I'll track our traffic and note what content is working best. We'll use those analytics to grow your audience. Rena tells me you have accounts on Instagram and Twitter. Can I ask why you're not on Facebook?"

Business Chloe is hot AF, FYI. "My time is limited and I like the other two better."

"Fair enough. Social media can be a time suck and a lot of people don't particularly like being in a fish bowl. We can definitely leverage those accounts to engage existing users, enhance their loyalty, and gain new followers." She glances at her phone. "Are you free for the next couple of hours? I sort of arranged an impromptu lunch with Mike and Giancarlo."

"Sort of?"

"I did."

"First order of business, then, we need to sync up our calendars. I've got an appointment with a veterinarian at one o'clock." I could ask Sylvie to take Sammy to her first appointment, but 1) that's asking too much, and 2) I want to do it.

"Is it time for your rabies shot?" A tug on Chloe's lips accompanies her lighthearted tone.

"Funny, but no. I need to take my new puppy in."

Chloe's eyes widen in surprise and delight. "Are you serious right now? Because that totally trumps lunch today. Pets and athletes are social media gold. Is it okay if I tag along?"

I get to my feet. "Sure. Let's go."

She taps out something on her cell as we walk through

the hallways toward the parking lot. "What's the puppy's name?"

"Sammy."

"Aw. Boy or a girl?" she asks while still typing.

"Girl. My mom gifted her to me last week. She thought I could use the company while I'm healing." I open the door for Chloe to exit the building before me. She brushes my sling, and I inadvertently hiss in a breath.

"Sorry!"

"Don't be." The last thing I want is her walking on pins and needles around me. "I'm fine."

She pauses to look at me like she's thinking about whether or not to pursue the topic of my injury, then says, "Have you posted any pictures of Sammy yet?"

"No."

"Great." She resumes walking. "We'll start there."

"I'm parked this way." I wait for her to turn. "Why don't you follow me to my house and we'll go together from there?"

"Um…maybe I should just meet you at the vet."

"Worried I'm about to lure you to my lair and you won't want to leave?" The truth is I don't invite anyone outside my family and close friends over, but I imagine she'll want to see my home eventually for work purposes.

She points at me with a quick flick of her wrist. "You should be so lucky." As if she's said something wrong, she drops her chin to stare at the ground. "What's your address?" she asks a moment later, her phone at the ready. "In case we get separated."

I watch her type in my response. We part ways and an hour later she's following me through the gate of my Malibu property. If she's impressed by what she sees, she doesn't say anything, only lifts her face to the overcast sky and breathes in the ocean air.

A beach girl. I mentally add another item to the list of things I like about her.

I open the front door and we're immediately met by Sammy. She runs toward us but her big white paws slip on the hardwood so she skids in our direction like she's sliding into home plate.

"Safe!" Chloe says, kneeling down to pet my dog. Sammy's entire body shakes with excitement. She licks Chloe's face. "Oh my God, you're the cutest thing ever. Your fans are going to go crazy over her, Finn."

I'm going a little crazy over my social media manager. *Safe?* It's like she's in my head.

Chloe picks up Sammy and follows me into the living area. The large open floor plan includes the kitchen, family room, dining area and two fireplaces.

"Hey, Sylvie," I say to my housekeeper. She's cleaning off the kitchen counter having recently made her famous meat loaf by the smell of it. "This is Chloe Conrad, the social media manager the team hired for me."

"Hi." Chloe tries to extend her hand but her arms are full of squirming, happy puppy. "It's nice to meet you."

"You, too." Sylvie wipes her hands down her apron. "It looks like you've made a new friend."

"I have." Chloe rubs noses with Sammy. "Haven't I?"

She puts Sammy down on the floor, picks up the plush toy near her foot and tosses it across the room. Sammy gives chase. "I love dogs. I never had one growing up."

Sammy fetches the toy and brings it back to Chloe. Chloe throws it again.

Sylvie laughs. I frown.

"What?" Chloe asks.

"Sammy never just drops her toys for me. It's always a tug-of-war."

Chloe shrugs. "She obviously likes me better."

"You think?" Never one to be outdone, I get down on my knees and pat my thigh with my good hand. "C'mere, Sammy."

Sammy runs right into my chest, her skill at putting on the brakes obviously in need of work. Sharp pain lances through my shoulder blade, but it ebbs once Sammy rights herself and licks my chin. I rub the soft, thick fur behind her ears. "Hey, girl. How about we show Chloe how you fetch balls outside?" I may have gone a little crazy at the pet store over the weekend and bought a few dozen soft baseball toys to throw around. Sammy's yet to catch one midair, but I'm confident we'll get there.

Since my dog is a genius, she already understands the word "outside" and runs over to the sliding French door. When I get to my feet, Sylvie's left the room and Chloe turns her phone in my direction. A picture of me and Sammy fills the screen. "What do you think?"

"I like it."

"Great. Can I get your logins and passwords?" At my

raised eyebrows, she follows with, "I signed a contract with the Landsharks and those types of things are kept in complete confidence. I thought we'd start off with posting together so that I can get a feel for what you're comfortable sharing. After that, you should follow my direction. If at any time you want to pull back, we can. Rena paired us for a reason, though, so I hope you'll trust me."

I stare at her.

"Is there a problem?"

There's that "P" word again. I scratch the back of my neck like that will get rid of my apprehension. I've learned the hard way that trust is something earned, not given. And I'm not fond of being told what I *should* do.

I also need to change my password before I give it to her. I don't think she'd appreciate *baseballstud69*. My younger brother, Drew, is the techie in the family and created my accounts. He thinks he's hysterical.

"How about we take some pictures today, and tomorrow I give you that info?"

"I understand. I did spring it on you."

"Appreciate it."

Sammy barks.

"Come on. Looks like we're keeping someone waiting."

We walk past the pebble pool, rose garden, fruit trees, and large grassy area. Chloe stays quiet, one eye on Sammy, the other on our surroundings. When we round the corner, she gasps.

"You have a baseball field."

"It's not regulation size, but it does the job."

She jogs into the outfield, Sammy nipping at her heels. The field ends at the edge of the bluff, the Pacific Ocean a massive backdrop. Chloe looks over her shoulder at me—damn she's pretty. "This is insane," she calls from the short perimeter fence along the rim.

I reach her side. On a clear day, the view is unparalleled. She stretches her neck, her chin jutting out, in order to peek over the fence line. I've got a good six to eight inches on her so I casually follow her line of sight. Stairs lead down to a flat dirt area for collecting "home runs."

"You have a crag so balls don't fly into the ocean. That is brilliant. Do you fetch them yourself?" The question is full of amusement. She thinks I don't.

"Actually, I do, Webster."

She side-eyes me. I'm not sure if it's because she doesn't believe me or because I called her Webster. Neither bothers me. She'll discover soon enough I always speak the truth. And when it comes to her nickname, she's stuck with it whether she likes it or not. I don't go around nicknaming just anyone.

"Okay, Hotshot Center Fielder, let's see you and Sammy in action."

We turn back to the field. Sammy's baseballs are scattered all over the diamond. I grab one, wave it at Sammy so she makes eye contact with the toy, then toss it. "Fetch!"

Sammy chases the ball down, puppy teeth picking it up. She runs back toward me, dodges left and scampers off, her understanding of the game a work in progress.

"You need treats," Chloe says. "To reward her with."

"Right. I keep forgetting that." I grip another ball, get Sammy's attention, and throw it. Repeat. If nothing else, Sammy loves shagging balls and keeping them away from me.

The arm motion dumps sizable tension on my collarbone, but the discomfort is nothing I can't handle, not when I'm breathing in the scent of fresh-cut grass and sea and have a smart, beautiful woman next to me.

We play for a good ten minutes before Sammy drops to her belly, tuckered out. I sit beside her, rub her back. Chloe snaps some pictures. "It's time for a ride in the car," I tell Sammy. She's unfazed.

"Unless you need my help, I think I've got enough for today." Chloe scratches the top of Sammy's head.

"Your help?"

She glances at my sling. "Taking her to the vet."

I know she doesn't mean anything negative by it, but I'm irritated nonetheless. The damn sling isn't debilitating, not when the rest of my body is in peak condition. "I don't need you." I regret my gruff tone the second our eyes connect. The spark I saw earlier in hers is gone.

"Understood." She backs away.

"This isn't easy for me," I concede. "So I may come off as an ass sometimes."

"*May?*"

This girl isn't about to cut me any slack. I push to my feet with a smile on my face and switch tactics. "Have dinner with me tonight." The request comes out of left field. I'd blame it on my injury but I have a fractured clavicle, not a concussion.

"What?"

"Dinner. You and me."

"Like a date?"

I can't remember the last time I had an actual date. Making it official with Chloe feels like the right thing to do. "Yes."

"Um…" She blinks rapidly. With her jaw slightly ajar, she rubs two fingers along her plush bottom lip. My jaw opens in response and I suck in some air. Her mouth is sexy as hell.

My ego takes a hit as she continues to contemplate me like I'm the Landsharks's mascot, not their most valuable player. "Tough question, huh?"

"No, It's just…I can't."

"Have plans already? Tomorrow then."

"What makes you think I have plans and not a boyfriend?"

"Do you?"

"Not that it's any of your business, but no."

"Webster—" I pause to give the name time to settle in "—we're spending the next three months together. If you get to be all up in my business, then I get to know about you, too."

"No, you don't. You're my assignment. I'm not yours."

"Is that a challenge?" I'm a hundred times more competitive than the next guy. It should also be noted I hate to lose. What pro athlete doesn't right? My desire to win, however, stems from sibling rivalry. Three boys, one brother two years older and the other two years younger. You get the picture.

She huffs. "You're ridiculous." Her golden eyes, though, they glint with curiosity. "I'm not going on a date with you."

"Ever?"

"That's right."

"Because...?" I should be relieved. Working with Chloe will be distracting enough.

She crosses her arms over her chest. "Because I'm done with dating."

I'm not even close to knowing everything about women, but my cousin Meredith likes to unload her dating problems on me—which I'm happy to listen to (mostly)—and she used those exact same words last month. "I see."

"What do you see?"

"Some guy hurt you." I clench my fist against the sudden urge to bash in some unknown guy's face on Chloe's behalf.

"More like guys plural," she mumbles, "but that's beside the point. I'm not going out with you now or three months from now, so let's agree to just be friends."

"Ouch. Friend-zoned so easily."

"That's right, big guy." She takes a few backward steps away from me. "Bye, Sammy!" she says with affection. "Bye, Finn," she says even-keeled. Then she turns. I watch the sway of her hips, the swish of her ponytail.

Despite knowing I'd be better off to let things be, if she thinks I'm giving up that easily, she is sorely mistaken.

Chapter Four
#SeperateTheSheepFromTheGoats

Chloe

I'M IN LOVE. Intense dark eyes. Soft scruff. Lips that can't get enough of me. I could get used to this kind of attention. I can't stop smiling and kissing him back. Billy is freaking adorable. He also makes me laugh out loud. My stomach muscles are getting a serious workout from the nonstop giggling. Not to mention my cheeks hurt from grinning so hard. That he's kissed at least four other women in this room is no matter.

"If you have a goat on your back, stay in tabletop."

Billy the goat (I know, right?) freezes, his ears perk up like he understands the yoga instructor, and then he pivots and hops onto Jillian's back before she changes pose.

I laugh. Again.

Goat yoga is the bomb.

When Jillian's sister said she wanted to throw Jilly's bachelorette party here, I thought, *That's a weird idea for celebrating the bride-to-be.* But this is the perfect place for my lifelong friend. Jillian loves animals. And yoga. We arrived last night, had a delicious farm-to-table dinner, stayed up late talking and laughing, slept in this morning, went horseback riding and apple picking, and now this.

"I think I may need a pet goat," Jillian says from beside me.

We're in a picture-perfect red barn on a piece of beautiful property about an hour outside of Los Angeles. There's sawdust on the floor, haystacks around the perimeter, and a happy hour set up near the barn door for when we're done with the whole *baa-mah-stay* thing. That's goat talk for "namaste." I inwardly chuckle even though I'm not sure that's exactly the sound a goat makes. Sheep *baa*. Goats more like bleat, but it's close enough to crack me up.

We continue to stretch and move through different body postures while Billy and two other baby goats roam around the small barn. The cute distractions make it difficult to relax, but that's what the wine is for afterward.

"Let's move to a belly-down backbend next," our teacher instructs.

I watch our group out of the corner of my eye so I can copy their pose. This is only my second time doing yoga. Jillian dragged me to a class once and not only did I lose my balance a hundred times, I was so sore the next day I could barely move. Hiking is more my speed. Running. Basically, I like to stay vertical.

Instead of stretching like everyone else when I lie on my stomach, I cross my arms and put my head down atop them. For one, I need a breather. And two, no amount of baby goat cuteness is enough to take my mind of Finn. Memories of him are exhausting.

It was bad enough I couldn't stop thinking about him after the car accident. I spent my entire weekend daydreaming and fantasizing about rounding the bases with him. And I don't mean the ones on the baseball diamond. Which granted, helped with the crushing blow Leo had delivered. Finn's decency and sense of humor were exactly what my bruised ego had needed, so in a weird way the fender-bender had been a stroke of luck.

But then to find out we'd be working together on the biggest assignment of my career, with only twenty-four hours to wrap my head around it, turned my life upside down all over again. The last thing I'd wanted was to see him a second time, much less spend three months together.

It doesn't matter that I'd mentally crossed him off my favorites list. Finn, up close and personal, is dangerous. I can deny all I want that I'm not intrigued by him, but the truth is I *like* him. A secret part of me liked him even when he had badmouthed my dad. Standing up for something you believe in is hot.

Loving on a puppy is damn near explosive.

He's just a work assignment. He's not to be trusted, flirted with, or admired.

Tiny hooves press into my shoulder blades, a nose tickles the back of my neck. I close my eyes, grateful for the intrusion on my thoughts, as the instructor says, "And lastly, let's move to meditation pose."

I would, but a baby goat is doing a tap dance on my back. It's soothing and funny at the same time.

"Go ahead and gently move into position regardless of

the goats."

I'm pretty sure the prompt is directed at me so I press up until my cute friend hops down. Then I follow suit, sitting and crossing my legs. There is no place for Finn or Leo in this barn. Today is about friendship and love.

We finish the class with Billy in my lap. My wild berry shampoo is obviously a goat magnet.

"That was so fun," Jillian says, jumping to her feet and then picking up her mat. Her energy level is one of the things I love about her. "Now who's ready for a glass of wine?"

Mats in hands, the eight of us make our way to a linen-covered banquet table while our instructor gathers up the baby goats and escorts them somewhere else for their own reward, I'm guessing. A server is ready to pour us glasses of wine after we each fill a plate of fancy finger foods. Stepping outside the barn, a large round table under an umbrella is set with napkins, silverware, and goblets of water. The sun is mid-surrender behind the mountains. The air is cool. The closest neighbor is at least a mile away. It's pretty wonderful, and Jillian's grin tells me she thinks so, too.

Talk immediately turns to weddings. Here's the thing, out of the eight of us, I'm the only single girl. Four are already married and three will be in the next few months.

"I love that you're going to walk down the aisle to an Alabama Shakes song," Jillian says to Naomi. "Your wedding should be uniquely you. You'll never regret a decision you make from the heart."

"Right?" Naomi says.

"Once a decision is made, I don't go back on it," Gina says. "Otherwise I'll drive myself—and Geoff crazy."

"Your gut instinct is always the best one," Jillian's sister, Michelle, says.

"Unless it's your fiancé's," Naomi teases. "Then it's up for discussion."

Everyone laughs.

"Hey," Jillian says under her breath, her knee knocking mine under the table. "Sorry about all the wedding talk."

"It's okay. I'm excited for you guys."

"I know you are, but you don't have to hear about it 24/7. Especially after…" She trails off, catching herself. She consoled me for hours after my breakup with Leo, insisting he was never good enough for me. After she said I'd dodged a bullet, I told her I didn't want to think or talk about him ever again. Good thing she can't read my mind.

Her attention shifts away from me when her phone pings with a text. "It's Robert." Her eyes bug out of her head. "Oh my God. He says he has a surprise for me and he's on his way to pick me up." She turns her whole body to scrutinize me. "What's going on?"

I glance over her shoulder at Michelle. "What's going on…" I start. "…is your fiancé has planned a pre-wedding getaway for the two of you," Michelle finishes.

Robert is whisking his bride-to-be away to The Surfeit Hotel. The luxury boutique hotel has only been open for nine months and it's booked for like the next two years, but Robert works for Auprince Holdings, the corporation behind the hotel, and was able to snag a couple of nights in one of their suites.

And yes, *that* Auprince. Finn's younger brother, Drew, owns the hotel, his first independent venture, and he's succeeding wildly according to news reports.

"You guys…" Jillian looks around the table.

The gang offers smiles and "have funs" and then the sound of a car coming up the dirt road has Michelle and me getting to our feet.

"We packed a bag for you," I say. "It's in my trunk. Come on."

Jillian hugs everyone goodbye. Last is her sister. "I love you, Shel. Thank you for everything."

"You're gonna love me even more when you see what we packed." Michelle and I share a conspiratorial look. Let's just say the two of us did some shopping at the Hustler Hollywood store.

"You guys are the best," Jillian says before she and I round the barn to my car. As the matron and maid of honor, Michelle and I do make a good team. The sound of tires crunching on gravel gets louder. Robert's car comes into view.

My best friend and Robert have been together for four years. They met at a bar the night we were celebrating Jilly's twenty-first birthday. They'd gotten into a playful and drunken discussion about the benefits of jalapeño juice and that was it. Robert told her he was going to marry her one day. I open the trunk to pull out the small duffel.

"Hey, gorgeous." Robert wraps his arms around his fiancée from behind and kisses her cheek. "Surprise."

She spins to kiss his face and hug him.

I patiently wait for them to break apart by studying the side of the barn. The wood planks are more a rust color than red. There's a round dent in one, the impression about the size of a baseball. I glance around the property. Definitely enough room for a game of catch.

"Hey, Chloe," Robert says once they've come up for air. "Thanks for the assist." He takes Jillian's bag out of my hands.

"You're welcome. Have a great time."

"Give us a second?" Jillian says to her fiancé.

"Sure." He returns to his car, gets inside.

Jilly wraps me in a hug. "Thank you. This was so much fun. I loved every second of it."

"You're welcome." I'd max out my credit card over and over again for Jillian. She's been the one constant in my life since before my mom died. The one friend who kept in touch when I was homeschooled and traveled with my dad during baseball season.

"I'll text you tomorrow."

"No, you won't. Enjoy your getaway and text me when you get home."

"Fine."

I put my hands on her upper arms, turn her around, and then give her a small nudge. "I'll see you later."

Jillian waves over her shoulder on her way to Robert's car, her diamond engagement ring catching the last rays of sunlight and sparkling. "Bye!" Her smile is contagious and the corners of my mouth turn up in response. I keep it there until the car pulls away and I look down at my bare left hand.

THE NEXT MORNING, I walk into the kitchen to find my dad plating blueberry pancakes. It's our Sunday morning ritual. Mom made them when I was young and we keep to the tradition whenever we're both at home. The smell of batter and warm berries brings back memories I'm grateful for.

"Good morning, sweet pea," Dad says.

"Hi, Dad. How are you feeling today?" I grab my ceramic baseball mug out of the cupboard—it's extra-large and I need the additional ounces today—then pour myself some coffee.

"Good."

I note his face appears relaxed, but "good" is always his standard answer. It's frustrating more than reassuring. The man is annoyingly stoic. He hates for me to worry about him. Three months ago he experienced severe headaches, jaw pain, and scalp tenderness. He had to beg off umping a game, something he'd never done before. A trip to the doctor and many tests later, he was diagnosed with a type of vasculitis known as giant cell arteritis. The condition causes inflammation of the arteries in his head, especially around his temples. We hoped it would improve without treatment but the flare-ups continued, indicating his condition is chronic. Last week he scared the crap out of me when he had an adverse reaction to his medication. I'd rushed him to the ER, fighting tears the entire drive. I don't want him to worry about me either.

Thankfully, he was helped quickly and easily, his meds were changed, and I'd only been an hour late to my meeting at Landsharks's stadium.

Dad playfully bumps my side when I turn to open the fridge. "How are you?" he asks.

"Good." Two can play this game. I take out the vanilla creamer. I *am* good. Mostly.

"Glad to hear it."

We sit at the square pine table. The kitchen is the largest room in our quaint three-bedroom house. With a TV on the counter and a bay window above the sink that overlooks our backyard garden, we spend most of our time here. Or at least I do, working on my laptop or phone from this very spot. I pour the creamer into my cup. Once my coffee is sufficiently blond and sweetened, I take a sip.

Dad cuts into his pancakes. I watch him eat a few bites before digging into my own. I like when he has an appetite. He's lost fifteen pounds over the past few months. Further complications from his disease can include blurred or double vision or even blindness. I push away the unwelcome fear.

"What's on your agenda today?" I ask.

"Carol and Ron invited me over to watch the Chargers play the 49ers." Jillian's parents are the closest thing we have to family besides my aunt Becky who lives in New Jersey.

"How much did you and Ron bet this time?"

"Fifty bucks says my Chargers will crush his team."

"Want me to drive you over there?"

Dad's eyes, the same flaxen color as my own, narrow. "No thanks. I told you I'm good."

"Just thought I'd offer."

He sighs. "And I appreciate it, but I promised you I'd ask for help if I need it, and I'll keep that promise."

"I know. It's just sometimes…" I'm still scared to death about letting him out of my sight.

His hand covers mine. "I will never let you down, sweet pea. Not if I can help it."

I nod and get out of my chair to hug him. He gave me his shoulder to cry on after Leo broke up with me. He listened to me prattle on about Finn and how excited I am to have this assignment. (I left out the part about how goose bumps have found a brand-new path over my skin whenever Finn smiles at me.)

And he's right—he's the one man I can always count on no matter what, so I'm not about to doubt him or myself right now.

Chapter Five
#OutInLeftField

Finn

AT THE SOUND of the doorbell, I swallow down the rest of my morning shake in one gulp. If I had to rate this morning on a scale of one to ten, I'd give it a three. That's like a batting average under one fifty. The reason for this low number? My brothers.

"We got it," they call out in unison, practically tripping over each other to get to the front door. Sammy is fast on their trail, her barks of excitement pulling a smile out of me. She's the best buffer to Ethan and Drew there is.

"Uh, hi," I hear Chloe say.

"Hello," my brothers chime before introducing themselves and checking Chloe out. How do I know they're checking her out? Because that's the whole reason they're here, the degenerates. If they make her uncomfortable I will get them back tenfold.

It started the other night at dinner when I mentioned the Landsharks had hired me a social media manager. Ethan and Drew found this fascinating and asked about Chloe. Something must have shown on my face because their next question was whether I'd checked out *her* social media accounts. I hadn't, so they jumped on Instagram.

Drew let out a low whistle. "Dude, she is smoking hot. And she's got over fifty thousand followers."

"Wow," I'd said, the idea she had a large following churning my stomach. *What? Did you think you're the only person who gets to look at her?*

"She's got a sexy athletic thing going on," Ethan said, staring down at his phone. "No wonder you blushed when you talked about her."

"I don't fucking blush."

Ethan glanced up. "Not normally."

"You may have a problem," Drew said, engrossed in his phone screen. "I'd venture to guess the Landsharks aren't her favorite baseball team. Looks like the Angels and Padres rate higher given some of these shots."

I snagged his phone and almost swallowed my tongue. There was Chloe in a tight, V-neck T-shirt wearing a Padres hat. Chloe smiling in the stands like it was the best day ever. Chloe at the beach in a bikini top and white cut-off shorts. Chloe in an Angels baseball jersey at a fund-raising event. I looked more closely. The jersey was number seven. I clenched my jaw. She was wearing Hayden Clemons' jersey, the second-best center fielder in the majors and the guy who hit the go-ahead run to win the World Series when the ball rolled out of my glove.

Is he her favorite player?

Drew easily grabbed the phone back. "I'm gonna follow her."

Great.

"We should meet her," Ethan said.

"No you shouldn't." I don't know why I bothered to argue. It was inevitable they would. If Chloe wanted the real me then that included my family.

"Know if she has a boyfriend?" Drew asked.

I felt my blood pressure rise. Out of the three of us, Drew is the one who prefers to have a girlfriend. He likes to be in a relationship, always looking for "the one." He hasn't found her yet, and is currently single, hence the annoying question.

"She's off-limits," I asserted.

Ethan and Drew exchanged a look before they both grinned like they'd won the fantasy baseball league for the first time. (They've never beaten me and it bugs the crap out of them.)

"Finn and Chloe, sitting in a tree…" Drew sang, off-key.

"Real mature," I'd said with a shake of my head.

Sammy barrels around the corner and into the kitchen with a dog bone almost bigger than she is in her mouth, jerking me out of my recollection. Chloe and my brothers are right behind.

"Hi, Finn," Chloe says.

"Hey. Good morning." The scent of wild berries hits my nose. I think it's her shampoo, not that I've taken a whiff of her hair when close enough or anything. "How was your weekend? You had a bachelorette party, right?"

"It was great. Yours?"

"Not bad." The pain in my collarbone has finally let up

enough to notice. Thank the baseball gods.

Once again Ethan and Drew look at each other like they've won something. "You guys are on your way out, right?" I suggest.

"They don't have to leave on my account," Chloe says, sitting at the breakfast bar. "In fact, I'd love a picture of the three of you."

"We do lend ourselves to making Finn look good," Drew says.

Chloe laughs. "Only good?"

"She's got our number already," Ethan says, taking another sugar-free banana muffin off the plate of muffins Sylvie baked for us this morning.

"Hmm…" Chloe glances around the room. "How about by the fireplace? Could you light it first, though?"

"I got it." Any chance Drew gets to please a pretty girl, he's on it.

It's a cold and dreary November day so it's not a bad idea. What is bad is my mind racing to a picture of Chloe and me sitting in front of the flames, my mouth on hers.

We take a few pictures, Chloe's satisfied smile lighting up the space like she's invited the sun into my home. She decides on the best photo and posts it with a clever line: "Mondays are always brighter from behind smiles." #Auprincebrothers #offseason #triplethepower

Thankfully, my brothers do have jobs to get to and with their curiosity about Chloe appeased—for now—they say goodbye and see themselves out.

"They're nice." Chloe leans against the kitchen counter.

"Relatively," I joke.

"You guys are close. I can tell. You're lucky."

I shift my gaze from Sammy lying under the coffee table and chewing on the bone Chloe brought for her to the woman I want to know better. The clues she shares about her life aren't enough to slake my interest. "Do you have any siblings?"

"No. It's just—" She stops abruptly, catching herself from revealing more. Long, black eyelashes sweep over high cheekbones. Seconds tick by, and then I'm hit with remarkable pools of gold and caramel.

Whatever she sees in my expression, it's enough for her to continue. "It's just me and my dad. My mom passed away."

My stomach twists. "I'm sorry. I didn't know."

"It's okay. It was a long time ago. So—" she claps her hands together, the gesture a means to release us from the unhappy strain "—this morning is all about you and coffee. You do drink coffee, right?"

"Only Tuesday through Saturday."

Her brows knit together.

"I'm kidding."

"Good thing." She moves around the counter. She's wearing a zippered pink hoodie, black leggings, and white Vans. Her blond hair hangs over one shoulder in a side braid. Ethan was right. She definitely has the sexy athletic thing going on. She's also comfortable looking through my cupboards.

I'm comfortable staring at her ass.

"Which is your favorite mug?"

Firm, round cheeks, more than a handful, but I'd need to confirm that with a hands-on approach and—

"Finn? Your favorite?"

My eyes jump up to hers, peering at me from over her shoulder. If she noticed where my attention strayed she doesn't call me on it.

"I don't have one."

"Come on. Everyone has a favorite. That one mug that makes the coffee taste better." She continues her search.

I reach above her, my chest brushing her back and shoulder blades. The soft hair on the top of her head tickles my chin. My arm span stretches well beyond hers to the top shelf, where I locate my most valuable mug. I'd forgotten about it until she reminded me.

Her breath hitches, from our closeness or from the bright rainbow of ceramic colors, I don't know. It takes all my strength to step back rather than bury my face in the slope of her neck and trail kisses along her skin.

She spins around. Neither of us speaks for several moments of pure electricity. I swear we could power Landsharks Stadium with what passes between us.

But as fast as it rippled, it disappears. She studies the mug instead of me. "Did you paint that when you were young?"

"Drew did actually. He made one for me and one for Ethan for Christmas one year. I think he was five, maybe six. He was really proud of himself."

Chloe's head tilts to the side. "That's so sweet you've

kept it."

"I can't take all the credit, or much of it, really. My mom somehow made sure it stayed with me. She's sentimental about the things my brothers and I made growing up."

"You still could have gotten rid of it."

I inspect the mug, a wave of nostalgia washing over me. I've kept this small token of my brother's affection to remind myself of what matters. Despite having more money than we could ever spend, my mom kept us grounded, her humble beginnings never far from her mind. She taught us to value the small things, she didn't spoil us, and made sure my brothers and I always had each other's backs. I blink and reconnect with Chloe, her soft eyes watching me. She's only got her father. As much as my brothers and I give each other a hard time, we'd also jump in front of a moving train for each other.

"And miss out on the opportunity to tease Drew with it?" I finally say. "No way. I'm glad this morning brought it to mind. It's definitely staying out now."

"Okay, so this morning's photo op is for Men and Coffee. They've got several hundred thousand followers on Insta and they've agreed to feature you. I'm not sure we want to use Drew's mug, though. We want to keep the focus on you. I realize I've contradicted myself, but we'll use his gift in another photo."

"I'm yours to focus on however you want."

She grabs a plain white mug then tips the coffee pot, filling the cup halfway. "Let's get a shot of you sitting at the table with your back to the French door."

I take a seat while she moves around the room. She places the mug in front of me. She puts the plate of banana muffins beside the mug, thinks better of it, and returns the plate to the counter. She opens the French door, stands back and studies me, closes the French door. "Do you have a newspaper?"

"No," I say.

Sylvie walks into the room with a laundry basket in her arms. She puts the basket down and then lifts up the potted succulent sitting near the block of knives on the kitchen counter and offers it to Chloe. "Thanks," Chloe says, stationing the plant on the center of the table. "Great idea."

Women have an incredible eye for detail. I've always been intrigued by their ability for quick analysis. If not for my interior designer, I'd still be decorating this house. If not for Sylvie, I'd walk out the door to a formal event with unsuitable shoes and the wrong tie.

"Anytime," Sylvie says before resuming her trek to the laundry room.

"She's nice, too," Chloe says, standing in front of me and eyeing my hair.

"The nicest."

"Is it cool if I muss up your hair some more?"

Chloe's fingers in my hair? Yes, please. I just imagined us naked and her underneath me when it happened. "Have at it."

Her short nails get to work. My eyes try to close but I will them to stay open. There will be no relaxing or enjoying this.

"Better." She takes a step back, scoops her phone up off the table. Pharrell's "Happy" begins to play. "Let's do this."

"You always play music when you work?"

"Most of the time, yes. It's hard not to smile to this song. Now hold the mug in your hand, look at me, and show me those pearly whites."

I do as I'm told. She takes a couple of pictures. "Now take a sip, eyes on me." She moves around the table so I track her. I don't think she realizes she's dancing to the music, her hips swaying, shoulders bouncing. It's unconscious, her seamless movements. Her joy. She likes her job. I know the feeling.

Watching her in motion is a total turn-on and I have to send a mental command to my dick to keep still. I'm wearing pajama pants. There's no hiding my attraction behind the thin cotton. Stiff resistance, man. This morning's focus is on morning joe, not morning wood.

She stops to scroll through the photos. "I think we've got enough here."

"Great." I put the mug down, relieved.

"Let's move to your bedroom next."

"I'm sorry. *What?*" I choke out.

"Wholesome Finn is done. Now it's time for Sexy Finn. I'm not sure which we'll use, but I'd like to have a choice. Posts with shirtless guys get far more engagement."

"You want me to take off my shirt?"

"Yep."

"So, this really isn't about coffee is it?"

She laughs, then gets busy on her phone, hands it to me.

"Take a look."

"Now I get it," I tell her.

"I should have shown you their profile first. Sorry about that. They don't exactly match your brand, but Rena would like to see an uptick in female followers and this is one place to do that."

"You girls are the bosses." I push up from the table, give Chloe her phone back.

"You don't sound happy about that."

The strap on my sling cuts into the back of my neck. Frustration—with my injury, with being put on display, with feeling out of control—gets the better of me and I pull the damn thing off.

"What are you doing?" Worry lines crease Chloe's forehead.

"I can't very well take off my shirt with it on. Come on." I start toward the stairs.

"Finn." Chloe stays me with a hand to my arm. "We're partners, remember? If there's something you're not comfortable with, all you have to do is tell me. I got some great shots of you here that I'm happy to choose from."

I'm mad at myself for being short with her. She's doing her job and she's right, I've got the option to decline. (I think.) Either way, I don't have to be a jerk about it.

"Although..." She strings out the word, letting it dangle like a fish on a hook so I'll take the bait. "I thought a guy like you would love showing off his muscles."

That's where she's wrong. I show off on the baseball field, period. Off the field, I'm far more reserved. I've had enough eyes on me, judging me, to last a lifetime. Rena and the team think in the here and now, though. They don't know what my teenage years were like.

"Especially since Hayden Clemons took his shirt off for Men and Tattoos."

Okay, now she's got my attention. "Did he now?"

"Yep, and he got over fifty thousand likes. Let's beat him."

This is language I understand and am happy to comply with. "When you put it that way…" Sling in hand, I lead us out of the kitchen and to the stairs.

"I forgot the best way to communicate with someone like you is to make it a competition."

"I can think of other good ways." That don't involve speech at all. I push open my bedroom door.

And one day I'll show them to her right here.

Chapter Six
#CoffeeInBed

Chloe

I'M IN FINN'S bedroom.

I'd like to say I thought this through, but I didn't. Sometimes the synapses in my brain misfire when I'm around him and the intellectual properties in my head space out. Do I really need to take this shot in here? No. We could have done this on the couch or leaning against the kitchen counter, but my subconscious obviously decided I should see a shirtless Finn *in bed*, just to be sure we put our best photo forward.

To my credit, a lot of the Men and Coffee pics are between the sheets.

That doesn't mean we have to, though. *Gah.* I'm second-guessing myself. Something I don't normally do.

"You know what?" I say. "We can do this anywhere. It doesn't have to be in your bedroom." Do I sound nervous? God, I hope I don't sound nervous because I'm in his bedroom. Where he does things. Probably super well. Whatever those things are. Not that I'm thinking about those things because that would be weird with him standing right here. *Oh my God, Chloe, stop.*

"Where did Clemons do his?"

I scrunch up my nose. "In bed."

"We should stay put then." He stops in the middle of the room. Finn is a big guy, but he's somehow swallowed inside these four walls, his superstar status brought down to earth. He likes this space, he's comfortable. Which will translate into great pictures. *You know what you're doing, Chloe. Relax.*

"Okay."

The room is made up of cool grays and dark woods. The king-sized bed is unmade, white sheets ruffled under a gray down comforter, and I can already picture him lounging there, smiling for me. Only it's not for me, it's for the thousands of women about to fall in love with him. I look away and step toward the floor-to-ceiling windows that allow natural light to spill into the room. A cozy nook to my left includes a small couch, ottoman, and television. To my right, a bookshelf holds framed photographs and baseball memorabilia.

Outside is a large terrace, beyond which is a perfect view of the ocean. I imagine on a clear day Finn can see Catalina Island.

He comes to stand beside me. "On a clear day you can see for miles."

"I was just thinking that. Did you know the word ocean comes from the Greek word *okeanos*, which means great stream encircling the earth's disk?"

"I do now, Webster."

"Good, because there may be a pop quiz later." I am such

a dork.

"Yeah, what do I get if I pass?"

"What do you want?" I flirt back. I can't help myself.

"A date."

"Sorry, Charlie." I turn away. My dating days are over. Not that I have any delusions about one date with Finn turning into something more, but even a single dinner would be too much with him. I like him. Which means he's destined to break my heart. "I never date anyone who doesn't make his bed."

"Ah, well see that excuse doesn't work on me. Sylvie makes my bed and is slacking this morning."

I push him in the shoulder. "That's worse, Mr. Spoiled."

He flinches. "Ow."

"Oh shit. I'm so sorry! Are you okay? What can I do?"

"Keep two feet back?" he teases, but I still feel terrible. If only he'd kept the sling on, I wouldn't have forgotten myself. "Also, I was joking about the bed. Normally I make it, but with the fracture, I'm taking it easy. I'm actually a little embarrassed you're seeing it this way."

"Don't tell me you're a neat freak."

"Okay, I won't tell you. But playing ball eight to nine months out of the year, you develop a routine and an order to things. Coach doesn't stand for sloppy behavior on or off the field. Plus, my mom taught us it's nicer and more inviting to get into a made bed rather than an unmade one."

"I highly doubt anyone would say no to getting into your bed, made or not."

He arches an eyebrow, setting off a flutter in my belly.

Before he says something playful to poke at the waking butterflies, I add, "Let's get you ready to get in it. Do you need help with your shirt?" It's the least I can do after nudging his bad shoulder.

"Sure."

I have the feeling he'd say yes to help whether he needed it or not. "Permission to approach?"

"Permission granted," he says, eyes shining.

I step in front of him. He's wearing black pajama bottoms and a light green cotton T-shirt and I love that he didn't feel the need to change clothes before I arrived. It won't always work in his favor, but it did this time. "Ready?"

He nods.

I help guide his good arm out of his sleeve first. His skin is warm, his biceps big. And hard. So hard. I think about all the baseballs he's thrown with this arm, the incredible skill and talent. He's won two Gold Glove awards for his superior fielding, a double honor few players achieve. What would it feel like to be tucked under this strong, accomplished arm? Amazing, I bet.

Next, I lift up on my tiptoes to stretch the material over his head. He smells like man and lazy mornings, and I take a second whiff while his shirt covers his eyes. His soft, light brown hair springs back to its sexy, unruly state after I get the warm cotton off. Then I gently slide the shirt straight down his left arm, careful not to bump him in any way.

I toss the shirt onto the bench at the foot of his bed.

"Thanks."

"You're welcome."

"Where do you want me?" he asks.

I think Finn just spoke, but let's be real here. I'm busy inspecting the goods. It's part of my job, and I always give 100 percent to my assignments.

His pajama bottoms hang low on his hips. Low enough for me to see the top of his Adonis belt. The V-shaped muscle is sexy as hell.

And low enough for me to count that yes, he does have a six-pack. His waist is a couple inches narrower than his shoulders. His pecs are cut, his nipples brown and flat. There's no obvious sign of his fracture, his collarbone unmarked. His forearms are corded with muscle. His hands big, his fingers long. I've never seen such a flawless specimen in person before and I have the insane desire to lick him all over. I've never had the urge to do that before.

"*Ahem*," he clears his throat.

Shit. I've been staring at his body like an unprofessional, infatuated perv. "Sorry, just uh, thinking about how to pose you."

"I don't think that's all you were thinking."

I ignore his flirty tone of voice. Also? I don't think he's wearing any underwear. Also, also? I'm starting to sweat. "Is it hot in here?" I pull on the neck of my hoodie. I'd take it off, but I'm only wearing a bra underneath. Note to self: always wear an undershirt around Finn. "Don't answer that. Oh hey, we forgot the coffee mug. I'll go grab it. Be right back!"

I hurry out of the room and race downstairs, grateful for a minute to gather my wits and regain my composure. I'm being ridiculous. Baseball players don't ruffle me. I've been around them forever, and I've had several crushes, but I've never felt the need for a cold shower before. Finn is just an anomaly I didn't expect.

As I pour a little more coffee into the mug, my phone chimes with a text. I pull it out of my pocket. At seeing Leo's name, a sharp ache flares in my chest. He's texted me twice since we broke up to make sure I'm okay, but I've yet to respond. It doesn't take a genius to know that I'm not, so what does he want from me?

> *Hi Chloe. Me again. Could we meet for coffee? I promise I'll stop bugging you after that. LMK.*

I swallow the baseball-sized lump in my throat. How the heck am I supposed to respond? How does a girl talk to the boy who engineered the final barricade around her heart in under two minutes? It's not like we were fighting or didn't get along or had doubts about our relationship. We'd made love the night before he left. I kissed him the next morning, wished him a good trip, and told him I loved him. It was a Tuesday. Ten days later he returns and tells me he's found someone he loves better. Who does that?

My boyfriends, that's who.

Love at first sight bites. Me in particular. In the ass.

Speaking of asses, there is a fine one upstairs. I push Leo out of my mind. He can wait. Today is about Finn. I return to his bedroom and find him looking out the window. *My* view is so far out of the ordinary that I take a sec to appreciate it. Finn's backside is glorious. A piece of art that should be bronzed and placed in the Baseball Hall of Fame.

He must sense my presence because he turns before I tell him I'm here. "C'mere, quick. There're whales."

I put the coffee on his bedside table and jog over to him.

"Riiight…there," he says.

"Where? I don't see anything."

"Scan slowly from left to right and back again, fairly close to the shore, and watch for a break in the surface of the water or a puff of smoke on the horizon."

"Okay." Finn and I are both quiet, like our silence will make it easier to see the cetaceans. I'm not sure which one of us moves first, but our sides touch, and I find myself leaning against him. He doesn't seem to mind, maintaining our closeness, so I relax. "Oh! Thar, she blows!" I declare, seeing a plume of water rise above the surface. I have seen whales along the coast before, but it never gets old.

Finn laughs. "Keep watching. There's a second one."

"Those are blue whales, right?"

"At this time of year, blue or humpback."

"I could stand here all day and watch for them. Growing up, I wanted to be an oceanographer."

"What stopped you?"

"Too much math and not enough writing. One day I hope to write a children's book with ocean animals as my main characters, though. I think that will satisfy the tiny part of my brain that wishes I'd stuck with science."

"Did you know a blue whale's tongue can weigh as much as an elephant?"

"Wow. I did not know that. Are you trying to out pop

quiz me? Because then game on. There are a lot of flashcard facts in my head. My dad Brain Quested me to death while we flew to games when I was younger."

Finn turns, his mouthwatering chest at eye level yet somehow, I manage to keep my attention on his questioning eyes.

"Brain Quest was an educational question and answer game," I clarify. "After my mom died, my dad homeschooled me and so I traveled with him during the season."

"That must have been hard."

"Yes and no. Yes, because I didn't have normal experiences like dances and pep rallies and cafeteria food. No, because being with my dad gave me the security I needed to do well in my studies. Not to mention I got to see so much of our country. Field Trip Fancy Pants right here."

"You learned on the road," he says, sounding almost envious.

"Mostly in hotel rooms and baseball stadiums. Anyway, we've gotten completely sidetracked and your coffee is probably cold now."

"Your dad's a good guy." Finn's voice is low, deep, steadfast. His sincerity so intense it's almost tangible.

"He's the best," I manage to say, appreciative of Finn's kind words. I'm pretty sure he's referring to on and off the field, and his opinion means something to me. "All right, let's get this over with."

"Is my nakedness bothering you?"

"Not in the least," I toss over my shoulder on my way to his bed. I wonder if his mattress is hard or soft. I wonder which side he sleeps on since there's no obvious sign. Maybe he sleeps in the middle.

"Liar," he whispers in my ear, making me jump.

Grrr. He knows way too much about me. "Let's start off with you sitting against the headboard, one leg bent with the bottom of your foot on the mattress and the other leg bent knee down with your ankles crossed, so your legs make an open triangle," I instruct in my best managerial voice.

Somehow, he follows that mouthful of direction, favoring his good side, and propping a pillow behind his back.

"Here, let me help." I shore up another pillow behind him. "Do you want to put your sling back on? It's fine if you do."

"I'm good."

"Okay." I scroll through my phone for Earth Wind & Fire's "Shining Star" and hit play. My song selection earns me an unguarded smile that is as hot as it is genuine. I take his picture then hand him the coffee. "Hold this just under your chin like you're about to take a sip, eyes on me. Perfect!" I snap a few shots. The natural lighting plays off Finn's coloring beautifully. "Now bring the cup to your mouth and take a sip. That's great." My thumb continues to get a workout as I take a bunch more photos. Seeing fatigue settle on Finn's handsome face, I stop to swipe through the pics and discern if we're good.

"Are you cool to do one more pose?" I ask, pushing my luck.

"If you have to ask, what does that tell you?"

"That you're almost at your limit but you'll take one

more for the team." I grin and hurry to position him. "Let me have you hold the cup on your leg here." I carefully bring his arm to rest on his thigh. "Then cross your other arm over your abs and hold on to your elbow. Yes! Like that." I take a step back and bring my camera phone back to my face. His biceps are bulging. It's a heart-stopping thing.

"Now instead of smiling, give me a neutral look like we're strangers and you've just noticed me for the first time but I haven't noticed you yet. Very good." Despite Finn's wish to be done already, he is immensely photogenic. "Lastly, keep your face forward while I walk around the bed to score different angles."

I capture a bunch more pictures, bopping to the music as I work. Once finished, I press stop on the song and sit at the foot of the bed. "That's a wrap. Thank you. How about I buy you lunch for your troubles?" The Landsharks have given me a decent expense account to work with and I plan to use it.

Finn slips off the bed. "How about you join me instead?"

"Isn't that the same thing?"

"Sure, we'll go with that."

I give him a what-are-you-talking-about look before I realize what I just did. "Wait. This isn't a date. Just lunch."

"Agreed."

"So why do I feel like I'm missing something?"

He lifts his good shoulder. "I'll shower and then we'll go."

I continue to sit there, riveted to the hand on the waistband of his sleep plants. Adonis, Adonis, what oh what do you promise?

"I don't mind an audience, but I should warn you, you'll be ruined for any other naked man."

I jump to my feet and then…I crack up. That's the funniest thing I've heard since the curse reared her ugly head for the fourth time. I'm already ruined. Which means I should take him up on his offer. But I can't stop laughing.

Cannot stop.

And from the look on Finn's face, it pisses him off.

Which only makes me laugh harder.

Chapter Seven
#SacrificeFly

Finn

AS FAR AS distractions go, Chloe is the worst.
 And the best.
 I sit back in my chair and watch the beauty that is my grandmother unfold. We're seated at a round table in the middle of Ethan's restaurant, Royal. It's closed to the public on Mondays, so every Monday Grandma Rosemary has lunch here. She's not big on crowds and Chef Louis adores her and is happy to come in on his day off and cook new things for her. She's his guinea pig, which thrills her culinary cravings and scores points for Ethan from both of them. Today's lunch was supposed to be the two of us, but I called ahead to make it three. My grandmother is loving, smart as a whip, and inquisitive doesn't begin to cover her interest in her grandsons. Hence, a buffer is sometimes nice.

"How about a punny LA birthday hashtag?" she says. Like my brothers, my grandma is intrigued by Chloe and has made it her mission for the past twenty minutes to find out everything a social media manager does. That my grandmother understands hashtags and used the word "punny" makes me grin.

Chloe taps her chin in thought. "Hashtag Malibu Barbie—B-A-R-B-I-E—Q, for a barbecue-themed party in Malibu. Get it?"

"Not only do I get it, I think you've just given me the best idea yet for my party next year."

"Aren't you too old to have played with Barbies?" I ask. Nicely. I don't think the toy has been around for eighty years.

Grandma tries to glare at me. Tries because let's just say she's had some help to defy her age and her face doesn't move all that much. "You, young man, can zip it."

Chloe giggles. "Is next year a big birthday?"

"Yes. And we're having a blowout. I'm not privy to the planning, but I shall pass along the Barbie idea because I love the hashtag."

"Are you even on social media?" I ask.

"Not yet, but now that I've met Chloe, I may want to hire her for my next decade." She takes a sip of her Arnold Palmer.

"You don't have to hire me. I'm happy to get you started whenever you want."

I have the same blue eyes as my grandmother and right now hers are gleaming. She pulls her cell phone out of her handbag. "Put your digits in, would you?"

Digits? My grandmother is a riot.

"Absolutely." Chloe quickly types in her name and number then hands the phone back.

My buffer is working out better than I expected. Not

that I should be surprised. Chloe is a natural people person. My grandmother can sniff out bullshit from a mile away and I could tell a minute after I introduced the two of them that she approved. Otherwise she'd be asking *me* all the questions.

"What do you do when you're not social media managing?"

See? This is so much better than her hounding me about my personal life.

"I like to hike, hang out with my best friend, go to the movies, and read."

"Have a boyfriend?"

"Grandma."

She waves me off with her hand. "Chloe can fend for herself."

"No, I don't have a boyfriend. Do you?"

"Girlie, I like the way you think. None of my grandsons ask me about my love life."

"And since one is sitting right here, we should change the subject." Does my grandmother have a love life? Granted, she looks a good ten years younger than her driver's license states, but that still makes her uh, older. She's fiercely independent, has been since before my grandfather passed away, and I've always imagined her happy on her own. With her attention on Chloe it's hard to gauge how serious she is.

"To answer your question, I don't either. I had one great love and that was enough for me."

"You're lucky," Chloe says. It's impossible not to pick up on the reverence in her soft tone. Whoever hurt her did a good job. Recently, I'm guessing.

"Luck had very little to do with it. More like respect, appreciation, and hot toddies. And I don't mean the drink."

Chloe and I exchange a look. I have no idea what my grandmother's talking—oh hell. My grandfather's name was Todd. Before I or my grandmother can share that fact, Louis arrives at the table with our lunch.

"Miso-glazed duck with polenta and kumquat chutney," he announces with authority as he sets a plate down in front of my grandmother. His sous chef places the same before Chloe and me. The presentation is photo worthy, the scent mouthwatering. "And candied sweet potatoes with ginger aioli for sharing." He puts the large side dish in the center of the table. "I'll expect a full report when finished. *Bon Appetit.*"

"Thank you," Chloe says.

"Yes, thank you," I say.

We waste no time digging in. As usual, the food is delicious. Sitting on some prime real estate with an ocean view in Santa Monica, Royal is the hottest restaurant in Los Angeles. Celebrities, dignitaries, and a real prince or two have eaten here. Ethan's worked hard and hired the right people to make it the success it is, and I'm damn proud of him.

Grandmother puts her fork down. "I'm sorry you won't be joining us for Thanksgiving."

I'd been wondering when she'd bring that up. "Me, too."

She shoots me a no-nonsense look. "If that were true, you wouldn't be staying here."

"All right, I'm not sorry, but I will miss you."

"*Pffit.*" She waves her hand in the air. "Do I look like a fool?"

"What's happening at Thanksgiving?" Chloe asks.

"My parents, brothers, and grandmother are spending the week at our house in Hawaii."

She looks at me like I'm crazy. "And you're not going because…?"

"I'm starting PT and workouts with my trainer." Normally by this point in the off-season I'm in the gym every day with Dwayne. One day we'll work on speed. Other days we're doing footwork and agility, heavy lifting, endurance. I'm not sure where we'll start this year given my collarbone is still healing and the doctor has warned me not to do much more than gentle movements with my upper body, but I can't wait to do something. All this rest is killing me.

"Can't you start the week after?" Chloe spoons more sweet potatoes onto her plate.

"Excellent question." My grandmother loves having someone else do her bidding. Maybe bringing Chloe wasn't such a great idea after all. Now it's two against one.

"I'm already behind schedule."

"For a good reason," Chloe says. "No one works harder than you. I get it. But you don't want to end up like Upton. He fractured his clavicle and tried to come back too soon. Ended up misaligning the bone and needed surgery to repair the damage. It took him an extra few months before he was back in play."

"Upton is a pitcher." One of the best.

"He's a reliever, and I'd argue your arm is more valuable."

"This is fascinating," my grandma says. "I didn't realize you followed baseball so closely, Chloe."

"It's my favorite sport."

"Mine, too. For obvious reasons." Grandmother looks fondly at me. "What made it your favorite?"

"My dad." If Casey were sitting with us, he'd see how fond his daughter is of him by the small, endearing smile lighting up her face. She takes a bite of her sweet potatoes, buying herself time, I think, before she decides to tell my grandmother more about her dad, her mom, and her youth. Not since high school has a woman besides my mom or grandmother carved out a soft spot in my chest, but Chloe is doing so with ease.

I pay her close attention, listening for information she may have left out previously.

Sweet isn't a word I'd use to describe my grandmother, yet she says enough sweet things to make Chloe's eyes water. Without thought, I take Chloe's hand in mine. She gives a quick squeeze back before pulling her arm away.

The too brief acknowledgment is a reminder she doesn't want anything from me except my social media accounts.

"You know you could start PT and work out in Hawaii," my grandmother points out, wisely changing the subject back to me.

I know that. I also know an entire week without my family stopping by to check on me is what I need more than anything else. I don't mean to sound ungrateful because I'm not. I love my family.

But they don't always understand my desire for solitude. Ethan and Drew call me self-absorbed, and they're right. I didn't get to where I am in my career by socializing. I got here because I've put in the time and effort, and because baseball is what I'm good it. It wasn't a struggle like everything else in my life, and since understanding that incredible gift, I've worked my ass off every day to be the best ball player I can be.

And now that I am the best (hey, my stats don't lie), I want to keep that distinction for as long as possible. My injury has screwed with that. It's screwed with my head. The sooner I get back into my routine, the better.

"That's true, but I'm staying put."

"You're choosing exercise over your family for a holiday that is traditionally all about relatives and eating way too much turkey and only happens once a year?" Chloe asks.

Yep, this two against one sucks. "This time, yes."

"That's dumb."

I know she means my choice is dumb, not that *I'm* dumb, but it rubs me the wrong way and my entire body tenses. I haven't been made to feel unintelligent in years and I'm not sure why I do now except to think no woman has gotten to me like Chloe has since high school. A picture of my high school girlfriend, Sarina, floats through my mind. Her telling me how amazing I was the day I was drafted, how smart. Only for me to overhear her tell all our friends the next day how stupid I was and if not for baseball I'd be nothing.

My grandmother meets my eyes. She knows lunch is

over. "Grandmother, it was a pleasure as always." I stand, lean over the table to kiss her cheek.

"Please don't rush off," she says.

"I have to. I'll talk to you before you leave for Hawaii."

Understanding clouds her blue gaze. She's always been perceptive, like Yoda, only better and slightly bigger.

Chloe gets to her feet. "It was really nice to meet you, Rosemary. I'm sorry if I've cut your lunch with your grandson short." Seems Chloe is perceptive too.

"It was lovely to meet you. I hope to see you again."

"Will you tell Louis the meal was excellent?" I ask.

"I will. You sure you won't stay for dessert?"

Damn it. I feel terrible for leaving early but distance from Chloe is more necessary at the moment. When my head says flee I'm useless to stop the impulse. "I'm sure."

I make my escape to the reserved parking in the alley behind the restaurant with Chloe at my side. I wish we'd taken two cars. Separation will have to wait a little longer.

"Finn." Chloe stops once we're outside, the click of the heavy black door in some way leaving my insecurity inside. In another way reminding me I can't lock this part of who I am away.

"Yeah?"

"I'm sorry for what I said. I didn't mean anything by it."

"I haven't known you for very long, Chloe, but I'm pretty sure you don't say anything you don't mean." I'm acting like my seventeen-year-old self and I don't like it. What is it about this woman?

She rolls her bottom lip between her teeth then walks to

the car and climbs into the passenger seat. She snaps in her seat belt, crosses her arms over her chest and turns her head away from me to look out the side window. When I struggle to pull my seat belt across my body and lock it into place with one hand, she leans over to help.

"Thank you."

She mumbles something in response and resumes her position.

The first few minutes in the leather seats go by in uncomfortable silence. It's the first time there's been such heavy strain between us, the air thick and uncertain, and I'd rather miss batting practice than feel this bothered. *Huh.*

"I said what I said because I was jealous," she says softly, her face still turned away from me. "Not of Hawaii, but because you have your whole family, Finn, and a lot of people don't."

People like her.

Shit. I took what she said personally when it had nothing to do with me. Talk about an ego problem.

"It's just me, my dad, and my aunt Becky. She's a pediatrician and lives in New Jersey so we don't see her very often. I didn't mean to make you feel bad and I'm not explaining myself so you'll feel bad for me. Please don't. Sometimes I just don't know when to keep my mouth shut." She turns her head to look at me. "So, we good?"

"If you accept my apology for being a jerk about it then yeah."

"Done." She rolls her head so she's staring out the windshield.

Dark clouds continue to blanket the shore in colorless light. Despite the dreariness, surfers dot the water to our left, sitting on their boards until a large enough wave comes for them. Right now, the sea is placid so they'll be waiting a while. Patience will eventually pay off. Much like it does when a baseball player is up to bat.

"Your grandma has a lot of spunk."

"She does. I'm surprised you didn't ask to take a picture of the two of us. Hashtag favorite grandson."

The corner of Chloe's mouth crinkles. "Ethan and Drew might have something to say about that."

"Exactly. By the way, thanks for fielding all her questions."

"She's the cutest Nosy Parker I've ever met."

"A what?"

"The British informal definition is an overly inquisitive person. I bet that's part of what keeps her young. She's always questioning and learning."

"Webster, Webster, Webster. It's more like she's always in everyone's business."

"He says with affection."

"Well, yeah. You met her. It's impossible not to love her even with her wise and powerful gift for prying."

"She's like a nosy Yoda."

I almost get whiplash when I turn my head to stare at her.

"Only with much smaller ears and fewer wrinkles," she rushes to say, thinking incorrectly that might not be the nicest description when it's spot-on. "And beauty. Your grandma is still stunning, but something about her reminded me of Yo—never mind. I'm going to stop putting my foot in my mouth now." She slips her phone out of her purse and swipes up.

"Don't ever stop talking, Webster." *Unless you're up for putting something else in your mouth.* Yes, my mind went there.

"I'm going to remember you said that."

"Please do."

"Hey, our posts are kicking ass. You've already accumulated over ten thousand likes on your coffee pic and it's only been two hours. The one with your brothers is at nine K."

"What are you doing?"

"Scrolling through the comments. Do you want to help respond now?"

"Definitely. It doesn't get more authentic than me, right?"

"A lot of them don't require any detailed engagement beyond a thanks or thumbs-up since they're compliments like 'I'll take one of each' or 'good morning indeed' but @instawithjulie asks, 'Which one of you is the funniest?'"

"Funniest-looking is Ethan, don't you think?" I say.

"That's perfect." Chloe taps out the comment, I'm assuming verbatim, her fingers moving a hundred times faster than mine do when I'm on my phone.

"@baseballblondie wants to know how you're feeling."

"Better every day. Thanks for asking."

"@heather95 wants to know where Sammy is."

"Hiding under the coffee table."

Chloe and I continue back and forth for the rest of the drive. We make a good team, one I appreciate more and hate less as she effortlessly manages my accounts. She has no idea how much easier she's making my life. I don't normally respond to comments, not because I don't want to, but because I don't have the time it would take me to do so.

Peeking at her out of the corner of my eye, the distance I sought from her earlier is gone. Instead, this magnetic pull I can't defuse gathers more heat and I suspect I'm headed toward heartache.

Chapter Eight
#StepUpToThePlate

Finn

FRIDAY MORNING FINDS me toeing off my sandy running shoes with a satisfied grin on my face. While a run on the beach is still a couple of weeks away, I did a ridiculous number of squats on the water's edge. The high reps equal fantastic fatigue in my thighs. A job well done. A balm for my troubled mind and spirit. My muscles will probably tell me I'm a dumbass for going hardcore the day after the team doctor gave me the okay, but I don't care. Leisurely walks with Sammy haven't been enough.

I look down at my dog. I'm pretty sure she's wearing a satisfied grin, too, having done multiple reps of stop, drop, and roll like a preschool champ.

We enter the house through the French door. She takes off for her water dish. I lift the hem of my shirt to wipe the sweat off my brow.

"Where's your sling?"

The question, not to mention the voice, makes me jump. I drop my shirt to find Chloe sitting at the breakfast bar. Her laptop is open, her phone is beside it, and she's got her hands wrapped around Drew's mug. Behind her sits a fresh pot of coffee. Next to that is my smoothie. Sylvie makes it better than I do and she must have decided to take pity on me this morning.

"Good morning to you, too."

Chloe puts down the cup. "Good morning, Finn. How are you? Sylvie let me in, I hope that's okay."

"It's fine." More than fine, really, but that's only for me to wrestle with. I move around the counter to pick up my green beast of a drink.

"Sylvie told me you got the go-ahead to exercise your lower body. Do you get to burn your sling now, too?"

"That's not a bad idea."

"Want me to get some matches?"

"Nah. I think I'll use it for tug-of-war with Sammy. The two of us can work out some aggression over it." At the sound of her name, Sammy jumps up onto my legs. "Sit," I command. She obeys so I grab her a treat. "Good girl."

"Look at you two," Chloe praises.

"These treats are training crack."

"Have you tried one?" She reaches for the bag and takes out a soft lamb puppy bite.

I catch her wrist in a slight panic. She's not going to eat it, is she? "What are you doing?"

She sniffs the treat. "Hmm. Not bad."

"Not bad? Have you tried one before?"

She eyes me with mischief, but puts the dog food back. "Oh, that's right, Mr. Baseball Superstar with his gross green drink. You probably don't touch anything that's bad for you."

Not true. I've touched her and she's definitely bad for me. In the best possible way according to my fantasies. I take a step to the side to put a little more space between us and change the subject. "What brings you by this morning?" I haven't seen her since lunch on Monday. She's been managing me from afar, she's assured me, not that I'm worried about it. I'm just along for the ride. And according to a phone call with Rena, that ride is off to a good start on the freeway of fandom.

"Surprise! Read this." She turns her computer screen toward me. "I was so happy about it, I had to come show you in person."

I'm not sure what I'm looking at. When I make no move to read it she says, "Huffington Post picked up the story I wrote about you for Trend Chaser. This is fantastic exposure, Finn." She rolls the mouse over a picture of me in my Landsharks uniform, clicks, and an article pops up.

I'm frozen.

"What's wrong?" she asks. "I promise I only wrote good things," she teases.

My pulse quickens as I squint at the screen, the words scrambled and jumping around in a dizzying pattern. The typeface is confusing, the letters bunched together. My head starts to ache, the thought of focusing on any kind of text soul-destroying—after pushing myself until my leg muscles burned, I'm too worn out to concentrate on reading.

"Finn?" Chloe's gentle tone is laced with concern.

I hate it. I hate her worry. I hate being caught unaware

like this. She can take her surprise back where she came from and go home. "Email me the link, will you? I need to shower." I don't wait for her to respond. I don't dare look at her. I don't say thank you when I know I should. Smoothie in hand, I stride out of the kitchen and I don't stop until I reach my bathroom where I plan to stand under a hot shower until it turns cold.

Chloe

I HAVE NO idea what just happened. One minute, Finn and I are joking around and the next he up and leaves the room like I've committed some major sin against him. I didn't tell him about the article sooner because he doesn't have to know every detail of my job. He didn't hire me, the Landsharks did, and it's safe to say when I'm not with him, I'm still working on his behalf.

"What is his problem, Sammy?" The cutest puppy on the planet doesn't bother looking up from gnawing on the new bone I left for her on her dog pillow.

"She's yet to answer any of my questions either," Sylvie says, startling me when she walks back into the room. The woman has serious ninja skills. I never hear her coming or going.

"Can I ask *you* the same question?" I say on impulse.

Sylvie leans a hip against the counter. Her dark hair is pulled into a bun, her soft, round face is free of makeup. She could pass for forty even though I think she's closer to sixty. Kindness exudes from her, and has since the moment we met. "What happened?"

"I showed Finn this article I wrote—" I nod at my computer "—and he brushed it off with barely an acknowledgment and zero thanks. I don't need his approval or praise, but a little gratitude would have been nice. He left the room like he couldn't get away from me fast enough. This is what Rena and the team want from me, but ultimately I want Finn to be happy with what I'm doing, so if he has a problem with something he needs to tell me so I can bring it up to the powers that be." I'm rambling, but keep going. "I get that he's been in the media spotlight a million times, and he might be tired of it, but I've researched previous stories on him, and I wrote something different. He could have at least read the first paragraph or something."

"May I?" she asks, turning my laptop toward her.

"Sure."

While she reads the article, I wash out my coffee mug and place it on the drying rack then scroll through stuff on my phone. I'm not sure if Finn's quick exit implied I should leave or wait for him to come back downstairs, but I'm leaning toward going. This is the second time his mood has swung fast enough to give me whiplash, and I have no idea what to make of it. I'm used to seeing him composed and ultra-confident on the baseball field, like nothing can touch him.

"You're a gifted writer," Sylvie says a few minutes later. "This was a smart and thoughtful piece and you should feel proud of yourself."

"Thank you," I say with heartfelt appreciation.

"If I may speak on Finn's behalf, I think he'd agree."

I frown. Meaning he won't bother to read it himself? Not that he *has* to. I wanted him to, is all. To see what I'm capable of. To see what an impact I can—and want—to make on his behalf.

Finn's fancy iPhone rings from across the counter. It stops. Rings again. Sylvie walks over, glances down at the screen and picks it up. "Hello, Liza."

Finn's mom.

"I'm good. You?"

I quit out of the internet, close my laptop.

"Yes, as usual your son is nowhere near his phone." Sylvie glances at me. I mouth *in the shower*. "He's upstairs and when I saw your name I wanted to make sure everything was okay… Tonight's gala, yes I'll remind him… His date?"

My chin drops and I study my knees. Finn has a date tonight? I mean, of course he dates. He's a sports celebrity after all, and along with his brothers, the three of them are the most eligible bachelors on the West Coast.

"Rosemary mentioned his social media manager, Chloe?"

I jerk my head up. Sylvie looks both surprised and delighted. I'm not sure what to make of that.

"She's right here actually. Would you like to ask her yourself? Sure. Hold on." Sylvie hands me the phone. "Finn's mom."

"Hello?"

"Hi, Chloe. This is Liza. It's nice to meet you, albeit not face-to-face."

"You, too."

"We'll make it official when I see you tonight. I do hope

Finn mentioned the gala this evening and that you'll be joining him?"

"Umm..."

"He forgot to tell you."

"I think he might want to attend by himself."

"And be subjected to unwanted attention from all the single women?" She laughs. "Doubtful. He likes to leave that to his brothers. I'm guessing it slipped his mind is all, so if you could let him know we'll see you both by eight o'clock, that would be great."

"I'll tell him, but—"

"Thank you, darling. Oh, and please remind him it's black tie. Goodbye." She hangs up before I can decline her invitation. I stare at Finn's phone, unsure how I feel about this. On the one hand, Finn doesn't have a date. *Yay!* But on the other hand, his plus-one is me. *Boo!* That my feelings are so mixed up when it comes to him is proof I should stay away.

A Friday night anything with Finn is asking for trouble. My safety zone is daylight hours. Things change when stars twinkle in the sky. Defenses are lowered. Romantic notions can overrule a girl's self-reliance and determination to keep her distance from the male species.

"You're still here," Finn says from the bottom of the stairs, his vexed tone accompanied by a deep wrinkle bisecting his forehead.

On second thought, it will be easy to hang out with this jerkface after the sun goes down. "Gosh, how does any girl resist your charming personality?"

"Is that my phone?" Mr. Grumpy asks. His prickly temperament is unfortunately offset by how attractive he looks with wet hair and a clean-shaven jaw. Not to mention how delicious he smells.

"I just spoke with your mom."

"You did what?"

Sylvie sidles up next to him. "I suggest you take a chill pill," she says.

I press my lips together so I don't laugh.

"Two things you need to know," Sylvie continues. "Chloe is on your side and she is trustworthy."

Finn stares down at her. Sylvie is petite in size, but it's obvious she's a giant when it comes to holding his respect. That she sang my praises is something I will honor in return long after my three-month contract is up.

"Listen to her and talk to her." Sylvie squeezes his arm then leaves the room.

"Thank you," I call after her. I try not to get choked up. I wish I had a motherly figure like Sylvie looking out for me. Although, I guess I just did.

"I'm—" Finn and I start at the same time. "Go ahead," I say.

"I'm sorry. I was rude to you, and you didn't—don't deserve it."

"I'm sorry, too, if I made you uncomfortable in some way."

He walks around the breakfast bar, lifts Drew's mug off the drying rack and pours himself coffee. His palms dwarf the handmade cup and I picture him at age seven or eight drinking hot chocolate with hands much smaller.

"So, you talked to my mom?" He leans against the counter, cool and casual in light blue jeans and a white waffle-knit Polo shirt that molds to his well-sculpted muscles.

I remind myself I'm immune to muscles and stay focused on his face. Not that that view is any easier to deal with. "Yes. She told me about the gala tonight."

He frowns. "She wants me to be there?"

"She wants *us* to be there."

"Us?" He ponders that, his eyes roaming around the kitchen like one of the shiny stainless-steel appliances will spit out a formal invitation addressed to Finn Auprince and Chloe Conrad. "Are you available?"

"I think it would be rude of me not to attend now." I mentally check off the clothes in my closet. Do I have an outfit fancy enough to wear? That would be a big fat no. But…I do have my bridesmaid dress for Jillian's wedding. She'll kill me if she finds out I wore it before my official maid of honor duty, so I'll just be sure she doesn't and be extra careful.

"Plus, this is a good chance for me to capture some pictures of you all dressed up in a tux. You own one, right?"

"Yes."

"Do you know who designed it?"

"Tom Ford."

"Oh my God. That's great. I know one of his social media managers and will reach out." I pull up Whitney's contact info on my phone. "The TF following is huge and if we can get you on his IG page that would be incredible." I start a text to Whitney, but a Twitter notification pops up, snagging my attention. Someone has decided to get nasty with regards to my article on Finn.

"Chloe, about earlier…"

"Mother trucker."

"Excuse me?"

I lift my head. "Sorry. That wasn't directed at you. Some asswipe has unknowingly decided to go into Twitter battle with me. Give me a minute." I don't normally engage with people who have their heads up their butts, but I don't like the comment about Finn. At all. And if you mess with someone I care about, then you mess with me.

"Someone is fighting with you on Twitter?" Finn asks, now in position to look over my shoulder and read the tweet. "Or me?"

> **Replying to @FinnAuprince @ChloeConrad1 @HuffPost**
> Saying he works hard is laughable. Entitled, pompous, stupid rich dude born with privileges 99% of the population don't have is more real. He is not greatness helping others. Get off your fucking soapbox.

"Okay, so technically you, but since I'm managing your accounts and it's in regard to my article, I'm going to respond. Just one tweet to put this jerk in his place."

> **Replying to @baseballoriginal82 @FinnAuprince @HuffPost**
> No one gave Finn Auprince anything. He earned it, and I stand behind my accounts of his accomplishments. My sources are credible. His stats don't lie. Talking ill of

someone you've never met makes you the ignorant one. #sharekindness

"There." I lay my phone face down on the granite countertop. "I feel better now. Why do people get off on saying mean things? I hate this part of my job. Dealing with scuzzballs who don't care about anyone but themselves."

"Scuzzballs?" Finn's voice is full of good humor. The sound makes me happy. He read the tweet and he's chosen to tease me about my dad's favorite name for jerks.

"That's right." I straighten my back. "Feel free to use it whenever you want."

He smiles at that. The kind that says he'll never use the word but he will think about it and when he does he'll think of me. "Thanks for standing up for me."

"It's my job."

"Is that all it is?"

I'd hoped to hold off on this moment of truth. At least until the polar ice caps melted. "No," I say softly.

"Then I'd like to explain about earlier."

Chapter Nine
#HitAndRun

Finn

STARING DOWN A Cy Young winning pitcher who throws a hundred mile an hour fastball is easier than opening up about my dyslexia. I learned from a young age to hide it. Confused as to why I couldn't read like Ethan, and later on like Drew, I was afraid my mom would be mad at me if she found out. When I refused to read to her over and over again, she used my favorite thing against me: baseball. I immediately confessed to my failure after that. She hugged me tight and told me I wasn't a failure, that success was measured in many different ways, and she loved me no matter what. But just because my mom knew, didn't mean I was comfortable with anyone else knowing.

"I reacted poorly to your article because it's difficult for me to read," I say, proud of myself for sounding matter-of-fact.

"I get it," Chloe says with her usual team spirit. "It's like actors who can't watch themselves on the screen. It's weird reading about yourself."

"No, that's not it." I run my hand down the leg of my

jeans. "I'm dyslexic."

I'm not sure how I expect her to react, but an immediate look in her eyes that reminds me of respect more than anything else hits me in the middle of the chest and my remaining defenses evaporate with nothing more than the release of a deep breath.

"I didn't know that."

"Not many people do." I sit on a barstool, my thigh muscles screaming to give them a rest.

Eyes locked on one another, the thrum of energy that is always there between Chloe and me intensifies. She knows my secret, knows my weak spot.

"Finn." Reverence mingles with gratitude, her voice a comfort I'm growing addicted to. "It's nothing to be ashamed of, you know. God, if anything you should feel incredibly proud of your accomplishments."

"I do."

"But?"

I don't want to have a full-on discussion with her. This is my least favorite topic of conversation and yeah, I'm not sweating at the moment, but I could be soon. I come from a family of accomplished men and women who graduated from top universities with masters and MBAs, and because I'm the only one not working for the family business in some way, it's often difficult to consider myself worthy.

"You know," she says, filling the silence. "Baseball is 90 percent mental. The other half is physical."

We grin at each other. I'd venture it's the biggest smile I've worn in a long time. That Chloe has tossed out a Yogiism to shred the remaining unease in the pit of my stomach cements her place on my shortlist of people I can trust.

"Seriously," she says, "most people don't realize how clever and shrewd baseball players have to be in order to be successful."

"We are an intelligent bunch," I agree.

"And millions of people have difficulties with learning. You're not the only one."

"I know that, too." I run a hand through my damp hair. "But I am in the minority when it comes to my family tree. I've been under a microscope since the day I was born and while my family never made me feel ashamed or unintelligent, I didn't want any more unwanted attention. So much of my life has been public; certain things I needed to keep private. Growing up wasn't easy. I struggled in school and was made fun of. People I thought I could trust turned out to be two-faced. No one cared about me. They cared about my status, off the field and then on it.

"When I was drafted right out of high school, that was my ticket to freedom. From a girlfriend who used me and said cruel things, friends who didn't understand me, and my own doubts about my intelligence. I couldn't read well, but I could hit a baseball and field better than any other eighteen-year-old in the country."

"So you put your dyslexia in a box and sealed it away."

"Basically, yeah. When I can take my time and my body is well fed and strong, my threshold for confusion is pretty high, so I do okay. When I'm stressed or overly tired the scale tips away from my favor."

"I'm a stressor for you," she says with sweet concern.

"Sometimes. But that's okay." *Because you also drain all the tension from my body.*

"That's good since you're stuck with me. I won't, however, ambush you again like I did this morning."

"I'd appreciate that."

"I appreciate you telling me more about yourself. Thank you."

"You're welcome."

"You didn't read the nasty tweet, or my response, did you?" she asks without judgment.

"I caught a word or two. The upside to all this is very little of what is printed about me, bothers me."

"I don't want you kept out of the loop, though, Finn. Let me know how I can keep you informed of things without bothering you."

"You're doing fine. Best social media manager I've ever had." I wink at her. "You eat breakfast this morning?" I ask, ready to move on. I pull a pan out, put it on the stove.

"You cook?"

"Don't sound so surprised." I look over my shoulder at her. "But don't get your hopes up too high either."

"So, eggs?" she asks with confidence.

I point a spatula at her. "Not just any eggs, Webster. You in or not?"

"Since all I ate this morning was a chocolate chip cookie, I'm in." She slides off her stool and sits on the floor, beckoning for Sammy. Settling in to stay.

I'm really glad I didn't scare her off earlier. "A cookie is not the best way to start the day, you know."

"Neither was seeing your face, but I'm continuing on."

I don't need to turn around to know she finds herself funny. I can feel her smile on the back of my neck. I also know she's attracted to me even though she doesn't want to be. Her zings are her way of protecting herself. But she can pretend to make light of the pull between us all she wants. Her flushed cheeks and gently parted lips tell a different story. As does the way she defends me on social media.

She murmurs nice words to Sammy. When I glance at them, Sammy is curled up in Chloe's lap, her head hanging to the side in total bliss as Chloe rubs her back.

"It smells good," Chloe says, catching my eye.

"You want toast with your eggs?" I return to my task.

"Sure. So, the gala tonight. It's for charity?"

"Yes. Every year my family partners with The Humane Society to bring awareness to the association's causes and recognize the organization's leadership."

"Where is it being held?"

"At our downtown hotel. I'll pick you up and we can go together."

"That's okay. I'll meet you there."

I open my mouth to argue, then stop myself. I don't like it, but I'll respect her wish. It isn't an official date so I can't very well insist I take her. I could, however… "How about I send a car for you? Traffic on Friday nights sucks." I set two plates of food on the kitchen table.

Chloe gets to her feet, leaving Sammy to trot to her dog bed. "You don't need to do that. I've driven in plenty of LA traffic."

"Still, I'd like to, given you were unexpectedly roped into attending the event."

"Wow. This looks good." She sits at the table. "What is it?"

"The famous Finn Scramble. Eggs, spinach, mushrooms, mozzarella cheese and secret spice."

"Mmm. I like things spicy."

"Do you now?" I ask, my voice dropping an octave as I fill a couple of glasses with water.

"Get your mind out of the gutter, Auprince."

I join her at the table, my thoughts constantly circling the drain when it comes to her. "I don't know. I kind of like it there."

And from the faint blush on her cheeks, I'd say she does, too.

Chapter Ten
#Heartthrob

Chloe

AT THE SOUND of the doorbell, I panic. I just got out of the shower. How the heck can the car be here already? Yes, I showered for longer than usual. And yes, I closed my eyes for a minute—or five—to touch myself to images of Finn, but unless Father Time is up to some funny business, I've got at least another hour to get ready for the gala.

I wrap a robe around myself as I hustle out of the steam-filled bathroom to check the time, a little angry with myself for giving in to Finn's car request. *Remember why, Chloe. You're saving money on gas and valet parking.* Raise your hand if you hate pumping gas as much as I do. And I could buy at least two dozen shredded chicken mini quesadillas—not in one day, mind you—from Taco Bell for the cost of hotel parking in LA.

The doorbell rings again and I stub my toe on the bed post. Grumbling curse words, I half limp to the front door. The clock on the wall assures me my visitor isn't the driver, but I'll look through the peephole to see who's dropped by. It might be Mrs. Medby needing to borrow a cup of brown sugar again. (I keep a bag just for her.)

I'm glad my parents taught me never to open the door without checking to see who it is first, because at the sight of Leo standing on the porch, I want to pretend I'm not home. My body freezes. I stop breathing. If I'm silent and don't move, maybe he'll walk away. He's dressed in a suit and his hair looks like he's run his fingers through it a few times, which means he probably drove here straight from work.

"Chloe, can I talk to you?"

I jump back. He must have noticed a shadow behind the peephole.

"I know you're home. Your car is in the driveway."

Or there is that.

Looks like I can't avoid him any longer without making this even weirder. I tighten the knot on my robe and open the door. "Hello."

"Hi," he says. One little word in his affable tone and I wish I'd been selfish enough to walk away from the door. "Can I come in?"

No! I hate you. I don't want you here. Too bad I can't blink and make him disappear.

With reluctance, I shift to allow him entry. "I guess so."

"Thank you." He steps inside my house like he's done a hundred times before, only this time his presence hurts. "Is your dad here?"

"No. He's at dinner with a baseball buddy."

Leo takes a seat on his favorite side of our well-loved buckwheat-beige fabric couch. I sit on the opposite end. He checks out my painted toenails then slowly lifts his gaze to meet mine. "How are you?"

"Okay."

"You going out tonight?" Can he smell my Pretty as a Peach foaming sugar scrub? The one I rub all over my body on special nights out.

"Yes."

He looks bothered for a split second before he says, "I won't keep you then. I just wanted you to know I never cheated on you with Adele. I don't think I made that clear before."

I scrunch up my nose. "Excuse me? You said it was love at first sight, blah, blah, blah."

"Yes, but I never touched her. Not until after you and I broke up. I wouldn't do that to you."

My blood starts to boil. He's claiming they didn't even hold hands? I don't believe it. "Correction. *You* broke up with me. And what you're now saying is you had an emotional affair, which can be argued is worse."

He shakes his head. "No. Maybe. Shit. I wasn't looking to meet someone else. I loved you, I really did, but I took one look at Adele and an actual bell went off in my head that told me she's the girl I'm supposed to marry. How could I ignore that? I didn't mean to hurt—"

"Stop. I don't need to hear any more. The fact is you did hurt me. And I'd appreciate it if you left me alone from now on. If this is what you needed to say to feel better about yourself then fine. Mission accomplished. But if you're looking for my forgiveness, that isn't going to happen."

"I don't want you to hate me, Chloe. I still care about

you. I want us to be—"

"Friends? That's not going to happen either."

He loosens his tie. Pain is etched around his eyes. "I'm so damn sorry."

"I know." I do. Leo isn't a bad person. None of my exes are. They simply found women whose souls mated with theirs. I'm like the Angel of True Love or something.

"This wasn't your fault. You didn't do anything wrong."

I fist my hands. Is he for real right now? "I know that! You wronged me, Leo. This is all on you and I don't want to see or talk to you again." I jump to my feet. "It's time for you to go."

He doesn't move as fast as I'd like him to. Finally, he reaches the door and steps outside. "You're amazing and there's someone out there for you."

I shut the door in his face. I'm vibrating with hurt, anger, and an unhealthy dose of how-dare-he. In all my twenty-five years, I have never been this upset with another human being. He doesn't know about my curse, so for him to even imply I was guilty of something is completely insensitive. Tears prick my eyes, but I refuse to shed any more for him.

Never again. I am never giving my heart away again.

I walk back into my room ready to crawl into bed and watch romantic comedies for the rest of the night when I remember I have a party to attend. *Ugh.* I could text Finn I'm not feeling well—because I'm really not—but then I stop, square my shoulders and tilt my head in heavy-duty thought. What better way to get my mind off Leo than to dance and drink and eat cake? Surely, there will be cake.

Tonight, I'll dress up and pretend to be someone else for a little while. Tonight, I'll be Just Chloe, not Cursed Chloe. I'll celebrate with the rich and famous like it's 1999. Heck, who knows? Maybe I did dodge a bullet with Leo. Maybe he secretly hoards fingernail clippings or belly button fluff. We did spend a lot more time at my house than his. He probably has a stash somewhere and now *Adele* gets to deal with it. I laugh. I just realized Adele rhymes with hell.

My maid of honor dress hangs over the back of my closet door. The sleeveless, floor-length champagne-colored gown has a crepe bodice, flowing tulle skirt, and open back, or T-back detail, if you want the exact wording from the bridal shop salesgirl. Basically, it shows off my shoulder blades. It's the prettiest thing I've ever owned.

I blow-dry my hair, use my curling iron to add big curls, then gather it into a low chignon. Without Jillian to help me with makeup, I'm left to my own devices. That means tinted face lotion, mascara, and my peach lip oil, which is a ChapStick and gloss mashup that leaves my lips shiny and plump. I stare at my reflection in the mirror and smack said lips together.

Lastly, I slip into my dress, slide my feet into the matching pair of satin pumps, and throw a few essentials into the one and only clutch I own. It's black, but black goes with everything, right?

This time when the doorbell rings, it's my driver. His name is Benjamin. He escorts me down the walkway then opens the rear passenger door of a sleek town car. I slide into the leather seat and almost cheer out loud when I see there is a minibar. With chilled champagne.

"Is this for me?" I ask Ben once he's in the driver's seat.

"Yes. Mr. Auprince wanted me to let you know to enjoy it if you'd like."

"I'd like," I say. "Thank you."

Ben smiles at me in the rearview mirror. "Have a favorite music station?"

"Anything is fine." I pour myself a glass of bubbly while Ben turns on the radio. Jazz music plays through the speakers. It's not my go-to, but my dad loves jazz and plays it often when he's home. "You like Miles Davis?" I ask, recognizing the trumpet sound.

"He's one of my favorites," Ben says.

"My dad's too." I raise my glass in the air. "To great musicians."

Traffic is terrible. So terrible that I have time to drink not one, not two, but two-and-a-half glasses of the best champagne I've ever tasted before we arrive at the hotel. I'm tipsy, but thankfully the peanut butter sandwich I ate before getting into the shower has absorbed some of the alcohol.

A valet opens my door. Ben wishes me a good time and says he'll be ready whenever I am to drive me home. "Okay. Thanks," I say, wondering how he'll know when I'm good to go. Then I decide tonight is about being carefree and Benjamin is my carriage driver. He'll magically appear after I've eaten cake and before the clock strikes midnight.

Running a hand down my gown, I attempt a graceful walk into the hotel, but the combination of heels and champagne equals more bull in a china shop. I forget all about my inelegant amble, though, when magnificence greets me inside the lobby.

And I don't mean the furnishings. I mean Finn.

All-star center fielder, brother, son, grandson, puppy owner, whale watcher, egg maker, and the hottest tuxedo-wearing man I have ever seen. Black slacks. Black jacket. White collared shirt with black buttons and a black silk bow tie, oh my. My breath whooshes out of me. My knees go weak. (I had no idea that was a real thing until this second.) If Chris Hemsworth and Henry Cavill had a love child, he would look like Finn Auprince.

This is not an exaggeration, people.

Total heartthrob.

"Hi," I say, and manage to sound halfway normal.

"Hi. You look gorgeous." Finn gives me a thorough once-over, his appreciative gaze setting off a powerful string of tingles down my spine. "How was the drive?"

"It was good. Thank you for arranging it and for the champagne."

"My pleasure." He gives me his arm. "Shall we?"

I wrap my arm around his, grateful for something to hold on to. Lucky that something is him. He ushers us into a ballroom that is both opulent and simple in shades of gold, red, and plum. Chandeliers with large glass globes bathe the room in white light. Tables are set with crystal and towering floral centerpieces. A band plays soft music in front of a large dance floor.

"Can I get you a drink?" Finn asks, steering us toward the bar.

"Sure." It appears everyone else in the room has a glass in their hand. Including Grandma Rosemary, who sees us and excuses herself from a group of people.

"Chloe, it's good to see you again."

I smile. "Good to see you, too."

"Hello, Finn."

"Grandmother." He kisses her cheek. "You look stunning this evening. Can I get you a refill? We were just headed to grab something."

"No, thank you. I'm fine sipping this one until it's dry." She puts her hand to the side of her mouth like she's about to tell us something top secret. "Incoming at twelve o'clock."

Finn and I turn. I've seen pictures of Liza Auprince, but in person she is larger than life. A force of nature in a tall, slim, elegant package. Her face lights up when she sees her son. "Finn, darling, you made it. I wasn't so sure I'd see you." She wraps him in a hug, squeezing him without thought to her pale yellow Grecian-style gown. This is a woman who would gladly wrinkle for a loved one, and I instantly like her. "And you must be Chloe. It's lovely to meet you in person."

"Likewise."

"I hope my son is behaving himself for you."

"Oh, he is. He's been a great client so far."

Liza beams at him. "How are you feeling? I see you've taken the sling off. Was that with doctor's permission?"

"Yes, Mom," he says a bit disgruntled. It's very cute. "I'm feeling stronger every day. How's everything here? It looks fantastic."

"Thank you. Your father and brothers are in a huddle with the mayor over at the silent auction table in a bidding war to win a Pedego. Once that's decided, I'll be much more relaxed." Something catches her eye over my shoulder. "Excuse me a minute, would you?"

"What's a Pedego?" I ask.

"An electric bike," Finn tells me.

"Excuse me, too," Rosemary says. "Betty White is waving me over. I'll see you two a little later." Yes, *that* Betty White.

"Maybe," Finn mumbles under his breath before putting his hand on my lower back and escorting me to the bar.

"Are you planning an early escape?" I ask, ignoring the heat that erupts on my lower spine from his palm.

"What would you like to drink?" he says rather than answer my question. "More champagne?"

"Yes, please."

The bartender nods and fills a flute with golden bubbly. Finn orders a light beer. We step away and end up at a high-top cocktail table to stand around. It's a great spot for people watching. I take a stuffed mushroom off the tray of a passing waiter. Finn accepts a crab cake from a passing waitress.

"Would you like one?" he asks me.

"No thanks. I'm allergic."

"To crab?"

"Shellfish."

"Thank you," he says to the waitress to move her along before he puts the crab cake down on the table.

"It's okay if you want to eat it. I don't mind."

"Hypothetically, if I was to eat it, could I, say, kiss your cheek in thanks for coming tonight?"

"Umm…" I down my champagne, suddenly very thirsty. Standing next to Finn when he looks so gorgeous and smells like heaven and says the word "kiss" is more than a mere mortal like myself can handle. "Probably." I glance at his mouth for a quick second. "But I don't think we should test that theory." Because Finn's lips anywhere on my body is a bad idea.

His gaze dips to my mouth and back up. "Agreed," he says.

I relax. For a second there, I thought he was flirting and that is also a bad idea. I wait for him to eat the crab cake. I look at the appetizer, back at him, at the appetizer, back at him, silently giving him the go-ahead to chow down on it already. Instead he takes two filet kabobs from yet another server.

Oh, boy. Talk about a silent message. My head spins. From the idea that Finn wants to kiss me—I mean, why else wouldn't he eat the crab cake? He obviously likes them. And from the champagne deciding to party with my brain cells.

He hands me one of the kabobs. "You're not allergic to beef, are you?"

"Not your beef." Oh my God. I can't believe I said that out loud. I almost poke myself in the eye with the kabob trying to recover. "I mean, not yo beef." Shoot me now! "Yo." I make a gesture with my arm across my body like I'm some hip-hop artist.

Also, I now cannot get the picture of that little old lady on the fast-food restaurant commercials saying "Where's the beef?" out of my head.

Finn grins so hard, a dimple pops up on his left cheek.

"Yo, Chloe," Drew says, arriving at the table and saving me from further embarrassment. He's flashing nice white teeth, too, and I want to throw my arms around him in thanks. Before I can, though, Finn moves between us.

"Hiya, Drew," I say around Finn's broad shoulders.

"Hi, Drew," Finn says.

"Hey, Finny. Nice penguin suit," Drew says back.

The brief greetings are full of brotherly love, both men clearly happy to see the other even though it's also clear they like to give each other a hard time.

"Chloe, it's great to see you again. How are things with this guy?" He thumbs over at his brother. "And please speak freely even though he's standing right here."

I giggle. "Things are fine."

"Fine? Bro, you need to up your game." He tosses an impish smile at Finn that morphs into a flirty one when he meets my regard. "When you get tired of hanging out with *fine*, make sure you find me, okay?"

"Okay." Drew wears his designer tux with much more ease than Finn and is so easy on the eyes I think mine might roll out of my head. *This is your brain on too much champagne talking.*

"You got something on your shirt," Finn says, pointing to the middle of Drew's chest. Drew looks down and Finn lifts his hand to catch his brother under the nose.

"Damn you," Drew says with very little heat.

"Every time," Finn says to me with a smirk.

A server walks by with a tray of shot glasses, each one filled with bright blue liquid and decorated with a lime wedge. "Hey, thanks." Drew takes three, placing one in front of each of us.

"What is this?" I ask.

"It's a Bazooka Joe," Finn says. "Our dad has loved the bubble gum since he was a kid so this has become his signature party drink. You in?"

"Sure."

"Cheers." Drew lifts his glass. Finn and I follow suit and the three of us clink Bazooka Joes before tossing them back and then banging our glasses on the table.

"That tasted exactly like the gum," I say before I wrap my mouth around the lime to curb the sweet flavor.

"Yeah," Finn agrees, making a face. Poor guy. I'm guessing the drink is too sugary for his pro athlete taste buds.

Finn and Drew talk for the next couple of minutes but I have trouble keeping up with the conversation because I have definitely exceeded my alcohol limit. I smile and nod like I'm paying attention when really, I'm dreaming about a big juicy hamburger (damn you, "where's the beef") and french fries.

A man stops to say hello, introductions are made, and then he and Drew stride away. Elbows on the table, I cup my chin in my hand and look dreamily at Finn. "Your nickname should be Kissy Face, not Prince of Thieves." His team nickname is a play on his last name and the fact that he constantly robs batters of hits with his phenomenal catching skills.

"*Really?*" He leans his elbows on the table so we're more eye level.

"Uh-huh. Oh! And instead of black lines under your eyes, you could put lips."

"That would go over well with my teammates."

"Riiight?"

"No," he says kindly, realizing I'm dead serious. At least I think I am. "They'd laugh their asses off."

"And call you Funny Face instead?"

"You're cute under the influence."

"Are you implying I'm not when I'm not?" I release my chin and stand taller, accidentally knocking my clutch off the table. "Oops."

"Not at all," Finn says, bending to pick up my purse and the spilled contents. He hands me the bag, my peach lip oil and my phone, which is lit up with a text from Leo.

I let out an irritated breath as I shove it back into my bag. "What does he want now?" I mumble.

"Problem?" Finn asks with concern.

I wet my bottom lip with my lip oil. Finn watches, mesmerized it seems, by the glossy brush and the way I'm moving it back and forth. *Huh.* I do an extra swipe for his benefit and when finished say, "No. Not really. It's just my ex-boyfriend."

"Is he bothering you?"

Elbows back on the table, I palm my cheeks. My head feels too heavy for my little neck. "You're so handfum."

He frowns, which makes him no less handfum. "I mean handsome. Silly 's' and 'f' mix-up."

"I understand."

"Because you're a smarty marty," I tell him.

"Oh-kay. I think it's time we get out of here." He makes sure my clutch is securely closed, palms it with his big, strong hand, and then links his arm with mine.

I look up at him. "No, no. You can stay. I have Benny."

"Ben—?" He shakes his head in amusement. "Benjamin will appreciate being relieved of his duties. Besides, you're my early escape."

"Are we gonna be sneaky about it?"

"Yes."

I lean against him. "Good, cuz that bubble gum bazooka'd me right over the edge and I don't wanna embarrass myself."

Finn brings me closer. "No worries. I've got your back." He leads us out of the ballroom unnoticed. *Phew.*

"Wait!" I untangle myself from his warm body. "I need a picsssure of you for Tom Sord, I mean Ford."

He looks around. Oh yeah, we're being sneaky and don't want to get caught. "Over here," he says, gathering me by his side again. I like his hold. More than I should. He brings us to an alcove hidden behind a lavish floral display sitting atop a shiny round table.

"Make it quick, Webster." He hands me my clutch.

I retrieve my phone without incident. When I go to snap the picture, though, Finn goes in and out of focus and I pray I got at least one decent shot. "How about a selfie, too?" I give myself a mental pat on the back. Even drunk, I've got some wits about me. Finn can see clear enough to take a good photo. Our fingers brush when I hand him my phone and a shock makes us both jerk in surprise. We laugh it off.

"I like your laugh," I tell him.

He takes two selfies of himself, one smiling and one smoldering. I'm pretty sure both will melt the panties off thousands of women. "I like yours, too."

"Know what else? Don't answer that. You don't know."

"Know what?"

"That I'm cursed." Wow, I spewed that rather easily. Finn is like Captain Spill My Guts.

"What are you talking about?"

"Buy me a burger and frenchy fries and maybe I'll tell you."

Chapter Eleven
#DrunkOnFinn

Chloe

"THESEARETHEBESTFRENCHFRIESIHAVEVEREATEN," I SAY with a mouthful of potato deliciousness. Finn and I are sitting in his car in the parking lot of a drive-thru diner in Hollywood, takeout food in our laps. I'm glad to see my baseball player eats burgers and fries once in a while. If he'd ordered a salad I may have had to switch him for Giancarlo. Just kidding.

"I'm happy you're enjoying them," Finn says. "So, about this curse…"

My head falls back against the seat. "I was hoping you'd fuhgeddaboudit." Apparently when I'm drunk I also try and talk with a New York accent.

"I could, but I've got some indirect experience with them so maybe I can help. I'm not superstitious myself, but I have teammates who are and believe they'll be cursed if they don't do certain things."

He has a point. And maybe a fresh perspective will help with the wretchedness that is my love life. "Promise not to think it's crazy?"

"I can guarantee you I've heard crazier." He turns and casts an understanding gaze on me. "I promise."

I take another bite of my burger. I've only confided in Jillian and my dad about this. And they both think it's not me. A twist of fate, wrong guy, terrible timing—those are the descriptions they like to use. "I'm a reverse good luck charm. Every time I fall in love my boyfriends end up meeting the loves of their lives and drop me like I'm hot."

Finn fights a smile.

"This isn't sunny. I mean funny."

"I know. So, they drop you like it's hot—" one corner of his mouth quirks up "—catching you by surprise?"

"Yes."

"That sucks."

"Tell me aboudit."

Another quirk. "It's happened every single time?"

"Uh-huh." I pop a fry in my mouth. "This last time was the worst, though. Leo broke up with me on our one-year anniversary. I thought he was gonna proposition me. I mean propose to me. Instead he introduced me to Adele."

"The singer?"

"Yo funny."

He laughs lightly. "I could say the same to you. So, this is why you don't want to date anymore?"

"Yep. I'm done with men. Not this burger, though, so no more talking." My cheeks burn from confessing something so embarrassing and hurtful. To be put in the same awkward position several times must mean there is something wrong with me, I don't care what my dad and Jillian say.

Finn obliges my request, finishing his food before I finish mine. I'm nearing the end of my hamburger, stuffing my face, and so engrossed in eating, that I don't have time to stop the special spread from dripping out the bottom of the bun and landing on my dress. Normally, this wouldn't be the end of the world. But not tonight. I look down to find a giant pink-orange splotch on the bodice of my gown.

"Oh my God. Oh my God. No!" I drop what's left of my burger into the paper bag holding my fries then gather up some napkins. What do I do? What do I do? I don't want to accidently rub the sauce into the delicate material. I lightly dab at the stain, trying to soak it up, but I make it worse instead. "Shit!"

"Hey, it's okay." Finn's soothing words are not what I need right now.

"It's not okay." Tears build behind my eyelids. "This is my bridesmaid dress for my best friend's wedding. I'm the maid of honor and I've ruined the dress. She's going to hate me. Then she's going to kill me." I lick a napkin then wipe at my chest some more because the stain *has* to come out. *It has too.*

Finn takes hold of my wrist. "Slow down there. I'm sure it can be cleaned."

"What do you know about cleaning?"

"I'll have you know I did my own laundry in high school and if I can get dirt and grass stains out of my baseball pants, I can help with that stain on your dress."

I sniffle. "That is totally different. We can't put this dress in the washing machine. Look at it."

"I have been. All night."

His cerulean-eyed disclosure burrows under my skin. The air inside the car grows heavy, Finn's admission turning our discussion into something else entirely. Something I'm finding harder and harder to ignore.

Thankfully, he breaks the heady atmosphere when he says, "Are you done eating?"

I simply nod, the back of my throat clogged with emotion.

He collects our trash and jumps out of the car to dispose of it. On the return he says, "Buckle up. We have a dress to save."

A single tear slides down my cheek as I watch him drive out of the parking lot. I'm a drunk, emotional mess and Finn has my back like he said he would. I want to climb over the center console into his lap and kiss him with our lips pressed firmly then softly, and my tongue stroking his until we're both breathless. Then I want to do it a thousand more times.

I don't of course. I force my gaze out the passenger window and fight to keep my suddenly heavy eyes open.

The last thing I remember thinking is I should have skipped the champagne and waited for cake.

I ROUSE FROM sleep surrounded by warm and cozy sheets that smell like the ocean and firewood. I snuggle in deeper, the soft pillow cradling the side of my face like a cloud of feathers. I think I'll lie here for at least another hour or two. It's been forever since I've slept in, and after the Burger Incident—my eyes fly open as everything about last night comes barreling back to me. Or, almost everything. This is not my bed. I lift the sheet and glance down my body. This is not what I usually sleep in.

I bolt upright, pain spearing through my skull. Looking around the room I venture a guess I'm at Finn's house. Muted light fills the space through a giant window left slightly ajar, an overcast sky in the distance. Straight in front of me is a wood-burning fireplace, small embers glowing yellow and orange.

The bed is big. The armoire in the corner is, too. There's a doorway that leads into a bathroom.

I take another peek at myself. I'm wearing an extra-large Landsharks T-shirt and my underwear and that's it. *Think, Chloe, think.* How did I get here? How did I get like this? Did Finn undress me? Did I do my Magic Mike impersonation and do a striptease for him? Mortification slams into me. I don't see my dress anywhere, but on the nightstand is my clutch. I quickly grab my phone.

Jillian picks up on the second ring. "Hey, are you okay?" Her groggy voice tells me I woke her up. Shit. It's seven a.m. On a Saturday.

"Hey, sorry I woke you. Go back to sleep and I'll call back in a couple hours."

"No, it's okay." Sheets rustle and then Robert's muffled voice checking on his fiancée travels over the phone line. "Go back to sleep," she tells him. "Chlo, hang on a sec…all right, I'm in the bathroom now. What's up?"

"Are you peeing?"

"You know I have to go first thing when I wake up. What's going on? How was the party last night?"

Where to start? I give her a quick rundown—champagne in the car, champagne and a shot at the gala, spilling my guts to Finn, eating burgers and fries—but leave out the part about wearing and saucing my bridesmaid dress, then say, "And now I'm in Finn's guest bedroom and I have no idea how I got here."

"That's not so—"

"Clarification: I'm half naked in bed in Finn's guestroom."

"Ohhh," she says, and I can picture her eyebrows raised in excited interest. She's been to baseball games with me and has seen Finn in action. When I told her I was working with him she started planning our wedding and getting pregnant at the same time. She's ridiculous like that. "Half naked how? No top? No bottoms?"

"I'm wearing a shirt of Finn's and have my panties on." I wasn't wearing a bra with my dress so that piece of lingerie is unimportant.

"Pretty panties or no-one-will-see-these kind?"

"Pretty." My bridesmaid dress demands it. *Where oh where is my dress and did Finn get the stain out?* A vague memory floats through my mind. "I just remembered something! Oh crap."

"What is it?"

"I think I invited Finn to your wedding. You know, since

I'm dateless now." I fall back onto my pillow. "God, I ran off at the mouth like it was a marathon. How much can I tell Finn before I take off my clothes and slide into bed. Please remind me never to drink champagne again."

"Maybe *he* took your clothes off?"

"Not helpful," I grumble.

"Sorry, but here's what I do know. You are a fun, smart, kind person and there's only a fifty-fifty chance you pulled a Magic Mike."

"Gee, thanks."

"What are best friends for? Really, though, don't worry about it. Just talk to Finn this morning and ask him what happened."

"I will, but…"

"But what?"

"What if he saw me in my underwear?"

"Then he's a lucky guy."

"It's pretty unfair that I didn't get to see him in his, though."

"Or you don't remember seeing him in his."

"I'm pretty sure I'd remember *that*. Seeing him in nothing but his pajama bottoms is ingrained in my brain, remember?"

"I also remember you asking me to talk you off any foolish romantic ledges."

I sit back up and cross my legs in my lap. "Exactly! So, go… Hello? Jillian?"

"I'm here. Not talking. Because oh my God, Chloe, if Finn Auprince wants to get jiggy with you, get jiggy with him."

"Gah! Please don't reference yours and Robert's sex song ever again."

She giggles. "Well then please have some no-strings-attached fun. I get that you're off men, but rebound sex can be very good for the soul."

"Says the girl who has never had to rebound. And you're presuming Finn would want to do with that me."

"Does Finn have a penis?" she asks in her no-nonsense tone. I roll my eyes. "Stop rolling your eyes and answer the question."

"Yes, Finn has a penis. And from what I can tell, it's spectacular."

"Thank you," a deep, decidedly unfeminine voice says into the room. I fumble the phone in horrified surprise.

"Jesus, you scared me." I bring the phone back to my ear. "Jilly, I gotta go. Bye!"

Finn stands in the doorway, leaning against the jamb with his legs crossed at the ankles, in black pajama pants and a plain white T-shirt. His hair is tousled, his smile is devilish. He's holding a glass of water in one hand and something too small to see in his other. My phone pings with a text. *ARE YOU OKAY?* Jillian asks. I quickly text back, *Finn is here! Talk later.*

"Can I come in?" Finn's first-thing-in-the-morning voice is deep and raspy and my body perks up.

"I guess, but you may not want to get too close. I could punch you for eavesdropping on me."

He walks into the room. "In my defense, I wasn't. I only got to the door for that last part."

I cover my face with my hands. "We are not discussing the elephant in the room."

"You mean the anaconda, don't you?"

I drop my arms and seeing Finn's waggish expression I crack up. A split second later, he's laughing with me. We laugh for I don't know how long, but it's nice and cuts through my embarrassment.

"I was coming to bring you some aspirin," he says, arm extended, when we finally catch our breaths. "Thought you might have a headache this morning."

He passes me the glass of water and two tiny white pills. I could hug him. Instead, I down the meds. "Thanks." I put the glass on the nightstand, the cold drink soothing my dry throat.

"Want me to go? It's early and you're welcome to sleep as long as you'd like."

"Actually, if you could fill me in on a few things from last night, that would be great." I scoot back to lean against the upholstered headboard.

"Suffering from a few memory problems this morning?" He walks around the foot of the bed to join me on the other side, propping a pillow up behind his back.

"Unfortunately. Please tell me I didn't do a striptease for you to get out of my dress."

"That was an option?"

"Oh, thank God," I say under my breath. Not that I would necessarily mind Finn seeing me partially naked, but I'd rather it be because *he* wanted to get my clothes off me. I do have my pride.

"Do you have a side profession I don't know about?"

I give him a side-eye. "No," I say firmly. "I've just been known to dance my way out of my clothes when I'm drunk. Now, on to more important matters. Is my dress okay and how did I get out of it?"

"Your dress—"

"Step by step please."

"What's the last thing you remember?"

I think about it, the evening growing clearer as I concentrate. "I do remember agreeing to come home with you." I peek at him. "*Because* you promised to help with my dress." I reach up to twist my hair in my finger and find it's still in a chignon. A messy one, I imagine. "We came inside and…and went into the laundry room. You gave me a clean shirt to put on, left the room, and I got undressed." I let out a breath. Digging into my memory bank is exhausting.

"That's all I've got," I finish.

"That's because you fell asleep literally standing up. I carried you up here and tucked you in. End of story."

"I can't believe I don't remember that. And hold up. You carried me? Finn! You're not supposed to be lifting something as heavy as me."

"It wasn't a problem."

If he's hurt himself because of me I will add Oreos to his smoothie or something. I get up on my knees so I can take a good look at him.

"What are you doing?" he asks.

"Checking you out. Your shoulders look even. I don't see any bump on your injured side." I gently touch the area that was fractured. "Does that hurt?"

"If I say yes, will you kiss it to make it better?"

My heart rate gains momentum as we stare at each other. I'm afraid to move. Half of me wants to jump off the bed and keep as far away as possible from him. The other half, though, wants to climb into his lap and kiss every single part of him better. He's teasing, but the mischievous glint in his eye, like this is a dare he hopes I take, reminds me of the underlying attraction between us.

I pick option number three and hold my position on the middle of the bed. "If I say yes, will you agree to whatever social media scheme I have up my sleeve for today?" I don't have a plan for today, but it was the first thing to pop into my head and being crazy good at my job, I can think of something on the fly.

His brows arch in retaliation. *Game on.* "If I say yes, will you show me your five favorite pictures on *your* Instagram page and tell me why?"

That isn't at all something I expected him to ask. I can't keep the smile off my face. In my profession, it's always about my clients. It feels nice to have interest in me even though I previously told Finn he didn't get to automatically know about my life. "If I say yes, will you share a brownie banana split with me?"

He doesn't miss a beat and fires back, "If I say yes, will you play Operation with me?"

Again, he's surprised me. I think he means the game I played as a kid. "You want to play doctor with me?"

"I do have an outstanding bedside manner."

"I guess you did bring me aspirin."

"In all honesty, it helps with hand-eye coordination so I include it as part of my off-season routine. The problem is, no one likes to play it with me."

"You do know you could play it by yourself, right?"

"It's better with someone else."

"Meaning you like the competition," I state. Finn plays to win, every single time.

We stare into each other's eyes like perhaps we're in the middle of a competition right now. It is, sort of, but it's one with no loser, this exchange of things we'd like from each other fun for both of us. I lean forward so I'm on all fours and press a kiss to his collarbone through his shirt, conceding to this man because I want to.

Before I can back away, he catches my chin with his thumb and finger, tilts my face up to his. A foot, maybe less, separates our noses. My blood catches fire waiting for him to make another move. Slowly, he inches forward, giving me time to pull free. Little does he know, the house could be falling down around us and I wouldn't move, the tug toward him on some cosmic level I'm powerless to ignore.

His lips graze mine lightly at first, a barely there brush that nonetheless melts me on the spot. He kisses one corner of my mouth, then the other, before he settles in fully, adding a touch more pressure. He moves against me with care. Appreciation. His lips are soft, yet strong, and taste minty fresh. Someone brushed their teeth this morning and for a moment I panic, worried I have terrible breath, but if that's the case, Finn gives no indication it's bothering him.

He must sense my momentary worry because his hand moves up to cup my cheek, to keep us securely connected. My eyes flutter closed as I fall under his possessive and unrushed spell. I've never been kissed with such care, like I'm a precious piece of art and he's my master. His confidence glides through me. The kiss remaining chaste yet so hot my skin prickles with excitement.

I hum against his mouth, ready to break the seam and slide my tongue alongside his. He makes a low guttural sound that turns my nipples into hard, aching points. He's ready, too.

"*Ruff!*"

Our foreheads bump as Sammy barks her way into our private heaven and jumps up onto the bed. Finn draws back on a groan, his eyes shining with desire.

As much as I didn't want the kiss to end, it's for the best. My brain on Finn is completely scrambled. I fall back onto my haunches.

Sammy cuddles right into Finn's lap like she did not just interrupt the start of something good.

"To be continued," Finn says.

"To be determined," I'm quick to say back in an attempt to keep the upper hand. From the cocky look on Finn's face, I'm not sure he buys it. "So, about my dress?"

"It will be good as new later today or tomorrow."

"Really?" I'm so happy I could kiss him. *You just did.* Yeah, and now that I know what it feels like I'm in major danger of not-so-accidentally falling face first onto his mouth. "But how?"

"Trust me to take care of it, okay?"

"Okay." I hop off the bed, careful to keep my butt covered with Finn's shirt, not that I need to worry since it hangs to the middle of my thighs. "Thank you." I pad over to the fireplace, the embers barely glowing now. "Thanks for everything."

Finn comes to stand beside me, his arm skimming mine as we watch the dying fire. "So, Operation and breakfast?"

I inwardly smile. "If breakfast is brownie banana splits, then yes."

Chapter Twelve
#ExtraInnings

Finn

I CAN'T REMEMBER the last time I took a day for pure fun and nothing else. Granted, every day I'm on the baseball field is fun. But it's pressure-filled enjoyment. I'm in the zone to perform at the highest level possible. Letting my teammates and the fans down is unacceptable, and so while I love every second of it, I'm also constantly held accountable.

Today, I've broken every rule in my off-season handbook and it feels better than I thought it would. I didn't work out, not that I'm up to speed there, but I'd planned to do some form of exercise daily since getting the okay. I didn't drink my smoothie. I didn't put protein and healthy fats into my body.

Instead, Chloe is running my Saturday with carefree precision. After having the necessary ingredients for brownie banana splits delivered, we made the sundaes and then ate them while I kicked her ass in Operation. She's a good sport, and laughed at herself more than complained. I think she needs this day as much as I do after the spill on her gown, and I admire her seemingly effortless ability to relax and enjoy herself.

She is most definitely a distraction at the highest level, but right now I don't give a shit because she also affects me in ways that can only be measured by the pounding of my heart and the spring in my step. After the kiss we shared this morning, where sparks singed the skin on the back of my neck, I'm more determined than ever to win her over. She isn't cursed. Is there some bad luck involved in her situation? Sure. But there are equally staggering coincidences out there. For example, Giancarlo has this weird knack for meeting girls named Lexi. He didn't think much of it at first, bringing them home or to his hotel room for his usual one-night-only thing, until he pieced together that after being with "Lexi" he fell into an inexplicable slump that lasted until he "broke the curse" by hooking up with someone else. Now, if there's even a Lexi in the same room as him he hightails it out of there.

"She caught it! Did you see that?" Chloe says, throwing her hand up for a high five.

I smile and slap her palm, my hand so much bigger than hers. My skin rougher. She's soft edges and warm curves and if I'm not careful, she'll find me with my tongue hanging out like Sammy's so often does around her.

We're at a park near her house, tossing a ball in the air for Sammy to catch. I drove Chloe home to change clothes (not that I would have minded seeing her in nothing but my T-shirt all day, but there are kids around), and then we headed here. That she suggested we hang out rather than have me drop her off took half a second for me to agree to.

Being with her is more interesting than spending time alone, and oddly more comforting. I steal a moment to enjoy being in the present and nowhere else. The sun is shining, the temperature comfortable, and the smell of dirt and grass hits me with welcome familiarity.

Sammy runs back to us with the ball in her mouth and drops it at Chloe's feet. Chloe rewards her with a tiny treat. "Good girl," she says, kneeling to take Sammy's face in her hands. "You are the best puppy." Chloe looks up at me. "Want to hike up the trail now?"

"Sure." She could ask me to hike through quicksand and I'd say yes.

I put Sammy's leash back on her and we walk toward the trail opening. We're halfway across the open field when a NERF football hits me on the side of the head. The foam toy bounces off my temple.

"Joshua!" a boy, maybe nine or ten shouts to a younger version of himself. "Watch where you're throwing. Sorry, mister." His eyes go wide as he takes me in.

Joshua jogs over. "Sorry," he says to the ground. I think the apology is for me and not the grass blades, but I get it. I was a shy kid, too. "Can I pet your dog?"

"Josh," the other boy warns.

"It's okay," I say, getting down on my knees so I'm kid level. "Sammy is friendly. She will probably lick you, though. Is that cool?"

"My brother had surgery on his heart and our mom said he has to be careful about germs so I don't know," the older boy says.

His heart? Jesus. No kid should have to go through any kind of surgery, let alone an operation on a vital organ.

"What's your name?" Chloe asks him.

"Jesse."

"Hi, Jesse. Hi Josh." She bends down. "I'm Chloe, and this is Finn."

"We know," Jesse says. "He's our favorite baseball player."

Josh pets Sammy while peeking at me. "I have your jersey at home," Josh says quietly.

"Thanks, bud. I appreciate that."

"It was mine, but I gave it to him when he was sick," Jesse says. "He dropped red Jell-O on it, though, so now it has a stain."

Josh sits on his bottom so Sammy can cozy up to him. She's remarkably calm, sitting in his lap and letting him stroke her back. I expected licks to his face, but it's like she understood Jesse's worry for his brother and kept her tongue to herself.

"I dropped food on something special of mine too," Chloe says in comfort, but I know she's nervous about her dress. Until she sees it, she won't believe it's been cleaned.

After she fell asleep in my car on our way to my house last night, I called my cousin Meredith. She's a dress designer and has contacts all over the city for clothing emergencies 24/7. I've been assured the stain will be removed. If not, Mere knows where to get a new one ASAP and I'll replace it before Chloe's any the wiser.

Josh gives Chloe a small smile then goes right back to

focusing on Sammy.

"Is your mom or dad nearby?" I ask.

"We live across the street," Jesse says. "So, our mom sometimes lets us come play by ourselves. She watches from the window or the front door a lot, though. We're not supposed to talk to strangers, but you're not a stranger. Plus, I have this." He pulls a whistle out of his pocket. "It's super loud."

"I was thinking I could bring you both new jerseys if you want."

"Really?" they say at the same time, their eyes lighting up.

Josh is quick to once again drop his attention to Sammy, though, who is in dog heaven. Apparently, Josh has the magic touch. His pets go from head to tail with a steady stroke that rumples Sammy's thick fur and has her eyes drooping shut.

"Absolutely," I say.

A woman jogs toward us, a concerned expression drawing the corners of her mouth down. "Hey, guys," she says slightly out of breath. Her gaze zeroes in on Josh.

The young boy looks up, guilt written across his face. "Hi, Mommy."

"Julie?" Chloe says.

"Chloe? Oh my gosh, hi."

"I didn't know you lived around here," Chloe says before turning to me and adding, "Julie works—" She falters like she spoke too soon. "She's an RN."

I search Chloe's eyes. She's holding something back and

it bothers me. A lot. I want her to trust me. To talk to me. More than I've ever wanted any other woman to. Hell, normally I'm fine with as little conversation as possible.

With Webster it's different.

"Did you two go to school together?" It's a dumb question. Julie looks much older than Chloe, but I'm trying a vague approach in hopes she'll confide in me.

"No." Chloe searches my face for something. While she does, I count the freckles across her nose. *One, two, three, four, five.* Five tiny beauty marks for a girl who is gorgeous inside and out. "Julie works at my dad's doctor's office."

That's a normal thing. We all have doctors. Unless it's a specialty doctor. My mind races back to meeting Chloe in the Landsharks conference room and her tardiness due to a family emergency. Shit. Is Casey Conrad sick?

"These are your sons?" Chloe asks Julie, swiftly changing the subject away from her.

"Yes. Jesse and Joshua."

"They're adorable. This is my friend, Finn."

"Nice to meet you." I shake her hand.

"You, too. My boys are big fans of yours. Whose puppy?" She kneels down to rub Sammy behind the ears.

"This is Sammy, Mommy. She's Finn's and she didn't lick me, but she likes me anyway."

"I tried to tell him…" Jesse trails off.

Julie stands and draws Jesse into a hug. "It's okay. Puppies are very hard to resist."

"She's pretty good at playing catch," I say. "You guys want to throw the ball around with her?"

"Can we, Mom?" Jesse asks.

"Sure."

The boys take turns throwing Sammy the ball and the three of them run around the field, cheering Sammy on and clapping when she makes a catch midair. I'm not sure the boys notice, but every time Sammy returns the ball, she drops it in front of Josh.

"Jesse mentioned Josh had heart surgery," I say, hoping Julie will elaborate.

"He did, yes. He was born with a congenital heart defect, but didn't show any symptoms until a few months ago."

"He looks great," Chloe says. "Is he cured?"

"We're not sure," Julie says softly. "He has what's called aortic stenosis, which means his aortic valve is too small and narrow for blood to travel through easily, and so the heart has to work harder. Over time the added stress weakens the heart. The surgery repaired his valve for now, but if scar tissue forms, he'll most likely need more surgeries as he grows.

"He's really been a trouper. Never complains. Follows the doctor's instructions. And Jesse's been very understanding." She takes a shaky breath. "I think I'm having a harder time than anyone."

Chloe gives Julie's arm a squeeze. "That's understandable. I think you said your husband is in the medical field too?"

"Yes, he's a medical device rep. He's always on call since he goes inside ORs when the devices are needed and used, which is why he's not here at the park with the boys."

I watch the kids play with Sammy with a twinge in my chest. My learning difficulties growing up were nothing compared to Josh's medical challenges.

After a few more minutes, Josh walks over to us. Sammy notices and immediately stops chasing the ball Jesse threw to follow Josh instead. "Mommy, I'm tired."

"Okay, sweetie. Let's go home. How does some hot chocolate sound?"

"Good."

Julie lifts Josh up to hold him in her arms. "Thanks for letting me play with Sammy," he says to me.

"Anytime," I say, knowing that's not exactly true since I don't live in the neighborhood. I will, however, keep my promise about jerseys and bring Sammy with me when I deliver them.

Jesse says thanks and goodbye, too, and then the three of them walk home. Sammy sits perfectly still at my feet watching them go.

"It's got to be so hard having a sick child," Chloe says from beside me. "When my mom was sick, I asked her if she could give me the disease instead. I wanted to help her. I wanted to stop seeing the grief in my dad's eyes."

I find her hand and lace my fingers with hers.

"She told me absolutely not. For one, she said, wanting me to understand, cancer isn't something you can give someone else like a cold or a fever. And two, no parent ever wants to see their child unwell. She told me I was her greatest gift and she loved me with all her heart and as long as I was healthy, she was happy."

"She sounds like a great mom."

"She was."

Julie and her boys disappear behind the front door of a single-story house painted beige with a large front window and a swing hanging from the tree on the well-kept lawn.

Grateful Chloe is still holding my hand, I ask what hasn't left the back of my mind. "Is your dad okay?"

She stiffens. It kills me, as I'm left wondering if she doesn't want to talk about it in general, or doesn't want to talk about it to *me*.

"It's okay if you don't want to tell me," I say, taking the high road. *Don't make this about you, dumbass.* "Just know I'm here if you need someone to confide in." I'll gladly share her burdens if she'll just open her heart and let me in.

"I don't." Her voice, whisper-thin and fragile, touches a place deep inside me. "No offense."

"None taken." I am absolutely offended.

Which means I'm in this deeper than I thought.

Chapter Thirteen
#ThroughThickAndThin

Chloe

I SIT AT one end of the rectangular table in the conference room of Media Management Corp LA for our weekly meeting and large content planning session and try to stay focused on the ideas being passed around rather than the text I received from Finn this morning.

Good morning.

Yep, those two little words are all he said. But now all I can think about is that he thought of me when he woke up and took the time to tell me. I've stared at the text no less than five times, yet to come up with something to text back. The simple consideration is teeming with *more*. Because the fact is we're no longer just working together. We're developing a relationship outside of the Landsharks, and looking across the table at my coworkers, I sense it's not the same case with them, romantic or otherwise.

"It's clear our fans want more behind-the-scenes content," Rena says, breaking into my musings. She and her assistant are here this morning, too, making sure we're focused on the Landsharks's brand and meeting their expectations.

"Agreed," my boss says then clicks to the next slide on the PowerPoint presentation filling the drop-down screen. "And you'll notice to combat the decrease in organic reach, our trick is to repost content multiple times throughout the day. We'll double those efforts this week with the Thanksgiving holiday to take advantage of PTO."

"On Friday, we're doing a live Twitter chat with the guys," I say, "again hoping to take advantage of people home from work. We'll kick it off with a picture of their favorite Thanksgiving food and segue into the Landsharks Love Toy Drive taking place next week. Finn would also like to visit the Children's Hospital in the coming weeks so I'm happy to arrange a group visit there."

Julie's son, Josh, left a big impression on Finn. As we left the park on Saturday he talked about both of her boys with reverence, as if he was remembering his own childhood with his brothers. I can somewhat relate in that I think of Jillian like a sister. I don't know what it's like to live under the same roof as a sibling, to have to fight for the bathroom or television or attention, but I do know what it's like to come to Jillian's defense, to laugh and cry with her, to tell her my secrets.

"Sounds good, Chloe. Thank you. We'll also run a special campaign for Landsharks Love," my boss says, taking my introduction to pull up the appropriate slide and elaborate.

"Perfect," Rena says.

Discussion continues on tone of voice, retweets, what

time of day posts are most effective, social monitoring, and a reminder about our main goal: gain team support.

The Monday meeting ends with donuts, coffee, and a chance to socialize. Before she leaves, Rena pulls me aside. "Could I speak with you for a minute?"

Oh, shit. She knows. She knows Finn and I crossed the professional line and I'm about to get replaced. Or reprimanded. Or both. I follow her out of the conference room, her assistant striding out of earshot. That doesn't bode well. I run my sweaty palms down the legs of my jeans. I'd rather be at the dentist getting a root canal than here.

"Finn called me this morning," she says.

"Oh?"

"He wanted to tell me he was enjoying this more than he thought he would and that you were easy to work with."

"That's good to hear."

"It is, considering I was worried he'd be difficult. But I also had a feeling you were a perfect match, so thank you for proving me right." She smiles.

My posture relaxes. "You're welcome."

"Finn also asked me for jerseys for two kids he recently met so I've got those in the car. Would you mind giving them to him the next time you see him?"

"I'm happy to. Let me say goodbye and I'll walk out with you." I spin around, letting out a relieved breath.

And once again Finn is at the forefront of my mind, his unexpected compliment to Rena docking deep in my bones. He thought about me more than once this morning. And thinks enough about my work ethic to warrant praise. He doesn't strike me as the kind of person to give false flattery, even with our hot-as-hell kiss to fall back on, so I'm more confused than ever about what to do with him. Finn falls under my Anti-Man campaign. (Not to be confused with *Ant Man*, the movie, which I loved.) He's not to be trusted. Not now. Not ever. No matter how easy it is for him to slip past my defenses.

"Happy friendsgiving!" I say to Jillian an hour later.

"Happy friendsgiving!" she reciprocates, greeting me outside the pop-up taco stand on Ocean Avenue in Santa Monica. "I am so happy you chose this place for our annual turkey outing."

"Me too. Spicy turkey tacos and an ocean view? What could be better?"

We link arms, do a little Laverne & Shirley bounce up and down (her mom introduced us to the late-seventies/early-eighties television show) and step to the counter. We place identical orders then carry our food to a bench on the grass, sitting side by side. I zip up my down vest to stave off the chill in the air, while puffy white clouds play peekaboo with the sun.

Our tacos are loaded with ground turkey, garlic, cayenne pepper, tomatoes, mozzarella, cilantro, and salsa. A dollop of sour cream completes the combination. Before we dive in, I take a picture and post it to Insta with the hashtags #friendsgiving #bff #turkeyvibes. We eat the first few bites in easy silence as we stare at the placid sea. We started this tradition five years ago at Jillian's request. I cried when she suggested it. She has a sister. A dad *and* a mom. Extended family nearby. And she requested my presence, and mine alone, for giving thanks to friendship.

"I think I just had a tacorgasm," Jilly says. "Please don't tell Robert."

I laugh. "I think the correct term is tacogasm, no 'r.'"

"Tah-may-toe, tah-mah-toe. This is seriously our best friendsgiving meal yet."

"Definitely." I bite into my second crunchy shell, which for the record is way better than a soft shell, and I have my own tacogasm.

All this *gasm* talk makes me think about you-know-who again, damn it. Between leaving work and meeting Jillian, I'd successfully made a mental grocery store list, sang to the radio, debated on apple pie versus pumpkin and decided on both, and talked my dad through using the new coffee machine I picked up yesterday as a surprise for him. He's been sleeping in, and our normal coffee pot is cold by the time he's ready to drink it, so I bought a single-serve coffee maker and different flavored coffees for him to enjoy. He never buys anything for himself, and wasn't exactly thrilled when I gave it to him—save your money, he always says—but too bad. It's a small thing given all he does for me. I pay very little rent. (I insisted on something.) We share the utilities and shopping duties. And weirdly, my dad likes to clean so besides being asked to keep things neat, I'm off the hook there.

"You're still staying with me and Michelle at the hotel the night before the wedding, right?"

"Of course." The wedding is less than two weeks away. Less than fourteen days for Finn to make good on his promise about my dress. I'm trying really hard not to freak out about it, but if Jilly wants to talk about the wedding, she may notice my nervousness, and the very last thing I want is her worried, too. Finn apologized for the delay and assured me my dress would be "good as new," which makes me wonder, is he buying me a new one? I lock my jaw in irritation. I can take care of my own problems, I don't need him to do it.

"We thought we'd order room service and watch *The Proposal*."

"Sounds perfect."

"What's not so perfect is I'm late."

I drop my taco and turn to my best friend. "Late as in *late*?" She nods. "How late?"

"Late enough."

"Should we go get a pregnancy test?" I try to decipher if Jilly is happy about this, but it's hard to tell. I know she wants kids. Eventually.

"Did one this morning."

"*And?*" She's killing me here, her face giving nothing away. It's not like she and Robert don't love each other like crazy. This is a good thing, just ahead of schedule.

"You're going to be a godmother."

"Oh my God! Jilly. Congratulations." I hug her so tight her "thanks" is muffled in my vest. When I release her, she's got a huge grin on her face.

"So much for best laid plans, huh?" she says. "Wedding at twenty-five. First baby at twenty-eight…"

I glance down at her stomach. "You've got a baby in there right now."

She rubs her belly. "I do. It's crazy. I haven't told Robert yet. I was hoping you could help me come up with a fun way to tell him tonight."

"I'd love to." I wipe the corner of my eye.

"Don't you dare cry," she reprimands, rubbing a finger over her eyelid.

"I'm not. It's dust or something." Something called love. I met this girl when we were ten and drafted onto the same softball team. When she was always put at the bottom of the batting order, I stood up to Coach and said that wasn't fair, that he needed to rotate the order. And when friends didn't know how to talk to me after my mom died, Jilly chatted about boy bands and young-adult novels and putting gummy bears on frozen yogurt to fill the awkward silence.

"I'm a little worried about how he's going to take it."

"Don't be. He loves you and he'd be happy even if you had an alien baby inside you."

"Chloe! Don't go putting images like that in my head."

"Sorry. You know what I mean. You guys are meant for each other. So, you got knocked up before the wedding. It just means you get to be a mom and dad for longer."

She sniffles. "That's a really nice thing to say."

I pick up my taco. "I should write Hallmark cards."

"You should." She resumes eating, too. "So, any ideas on

how I can tell him?" Jillian is a math teacher and is excellent with numbers, but when it comes to creative or artistic type things, she requires backup.

"Hmm… You could buy a pair of baby booties and tell him your family is growing by two feet."

"Mhmm," she says, her mouth full of taco.

"Or you could use body paint or lipstick on your stomach and write, 'baby on board.' Oh! Or better yet, write, 'congratulations, you're going to be a DILF.'"

"I like that. What else you got?"

I rack my brain for more ideas. I know I've seen social media posts with cute baby announcements.

"You could make homemade pizza for dinner and spell out 'you're going to be a dad' with pepperoni or olives since you and Robert love those toppings. Food always goes well with big news."

Jillian tosses her napkin into her empty taco box. "And then I could buy a bag of Sugar Babies for dessert."

"Love that. But you know, you could also go the simple route and we can hunt down a baby T-shirt or onesie that says 'I love daddy' on it. You could wrap it and tell him it's an early wedding present." This is more Jillian's speed, but she needed to at least consider some other ideas first.

"I think that's the winner."

Do I know my best friend or what? "Let's go shopping then." We stand and toss our trash before walking toward the shops on Third Street.

"I think I should buy a super sexy bikini for our honeymoon now, too, since next summer—" she silently counts off to nine with the fingers on one hand "—August probably, I'll be giving birth." She stops us in our tracks with a hand to my forearm. "Holy shit, Chlo, I'm having a baby before my next birthday."

"You are."

We resume walking. "I think I want to keep it a secret until Robert and I get home from Bora Bora. I mean not from him, *duh*. But from our parents and family. I'd like to enjoy the news just with him. And I don't want to take the focus off the wedding. You know how excited my mom is about it."

I do know. And I couldn't be happier for Jillian and her mom to share this incredible occasion. Sometimes, though, it's hard. Sometimes I don't like myself for the jealous, bitter feelings that press down on my chest.

For a fleeting moment, I miss my mom. I miss her so much I can't breathe.

"Chloe?" Panic fills Jillian's voice.

"Sorry," I force out. "Got emotional for a second. I think that's a good idea. It can be yours and Robert's secret."

"And yours."

"And mine." And that right there is why my spirits immediately return to normal. I have family, it's just different. I wrap my arm around her, our steps in sync, just like our periods. Although I guess that's no longer the case.

Our hunt for the perfect onesie proves difficult. It turns out adult tees rule the fashion scene in this area, so we do what every person does when in search of a must-have. We google it. *Ding, ding, ding.* Lots of cute baby outfits pop up on my phone screen.

"I really want to tell him tonight, though," Jillian says, noting we can order online from many different places. "There's no way I can keep it from him. I'm bursting at the seams as it is."

"Instead of 'bust a move' you'll be 'bust a seam,'" I say, cracking myself up. Jilly frowns. "What? All pregnant women stop fitting into their regular clothes." I playfully bump her hip with mine. "And you're going to be gorgeous. Hey, looks like Target carries what we need."

We drive to the superstore, talking nonstop about the wedding, the baby, the way life works out. Jilly can't resist buying a few baby things in addition to the onesie. I can't ignore a camel cable-knit sweater that reminds me of Sammy's fur. She and I will be twins.

Later that night I'm working on my laptop when Jilly texts me Robert is over the moon with the baby news. I smile down at my phone. Like there was any doubt. The two of them are peanut butter and jelly. Salt and pepper.

My phone peals with another text. This one from Finn.

Good night.

For a dangerous second, I wonder if he's the meatballs to my spaghetti and laugh out loud to extinguish the dangerous thought.

Chapter Fourteen
#CrushingOnYou

Chloe

THE HOUSE SMELLS like turkey, bacon, and spices that make my mouth water. My dad does Thanksgiving dinner like nobody's business. I make the salad and pies, and he cooks the rest. His fluffy onion and celery stuffing, and bacon mashed potatoes alone could give Wolfgang Puck a run for his money. Not to mention the turkey is so juicy you don't need a knife to cut it and his buttermilk biscuits melt in your mouth.

Welcome to my favorite holiday, everybody.

And no, I am not sharing any leftovers.

A football game plays on the television as we continue our backgammon challenge on the coffee table. It's a tradition that goes back to when my mom was alive. We've done our best to keep all of her rituals a part of our lives.

I roll the dice, land a pair of twos to win the game, and throw my arms in the air in victory. "Looks like I'm up two-to-one."

"For now," Dad says, smiling. He doesn't really care who comes out the winner in our best of five, but he's also never *let* me win.

We're setting up the small round pieces for the next game when the doorbell rings. I startle, suddenly nervous. Which is ridiculous. I knew he was on his way over. And it's just a turkey dinner with my dad, not a date or anything.

"I'll get it." I rise to my feet, cool as cucumber on the outside. The last thing I need is my dad noticing my crush on Finn. Yes, I said crush. It's grown full blown over the past two days. How? Let me count the ways for you:

1) More short, sweet texts, including one from Sammy that said she was *pawsibly* missing me.
2) That Finn is texting says a lot. With his dyslexia, I'd noticed he gets calls from his family and friends and does the same in return. I'm honored and flattered he's taken to a written exchange with me.
3) Hanging on the back of my closet door is my bridesmaid dress. It was delivered yesterday inside a garment bag, gorgeous as the day I first picked it up. Finn won't tell me the particulars so I've decided this is one gift to be grateful for and to shut up about the specifics and paying him back.
4) He hasn't pushed me on my dad. I haven't seen Finn this week because of doctors' appointments set up weeks ago. Finn's left me two voice messages checking in and offering to share his green smoothie recipe if my dad is interested in a healthy morning boost.

Burying my crush way, way back in the recesses of my

mind, I open the front door and burst out laughing. Not at Finn. Never at Finn. In olive-green slacks and a white collared shirt open at the neck, the sleeves pushed up to his elbows, he looks good enough to eat. His light brown hair is a little shorter than the last time I saw him and combed neatly. His strong jaw is clean-shaven. But Sammy is sitting beside him and around her neck is a bandanna decorated with cartoon turkeys and an orange pom-pom trim that is more funny than cute. Her adorable face is aimed up at me and she looks furious.

"Aw, Sammy. I'm sorry. I didn't mean to laugh at you."

"She's definitely mad at me," Finn says, glancing down at his puppy with obvious affection.

"I think she'll get over it pretty quickly."

"Hopefully. Happy Thanksgiving." He hands me a beautiful bouquet of sunflowers. (Add brings me my favorite flower to the crush list. I mentioned it to him once!)

"Thank you. Happy Thanksgiving. Come on in."

Sammy trots inside alongside Finn. "Wow, it smells great in here. Thanks again for having us."

"Of course. I wasn't going to let you have Thanksgiving alone." I close the front door and usher them into the family room.

"Hello, Finn," my dad says.

"Hi, Casey. It's good to see you. How are you?" He shakes my dad's hand.

"I'm great." My dad's standard answer is mostly true. He's struggling with some fatigue and sinus problems from his headaches, but otherwise his GCA is behaving. "This must be Sammy." He bends down to pet her.

"She's miserable in that bandanna," I say.

"She is." Finn unclasps her leash and takes the bandanna off from around her neck. Immediately her puppitude changes from gruff to friendly. "Sylvie assured me it was necessary until you saw it."

I open my free hand, palm up. "Seen and forever put in my memory. How about I hide it away while I put these in water?"

"Hide, toss in the trash. Either is fine with me." Finn and I share a smile like we're conspirators working the K-9 beat and we're dealing with a fashion emergency.

I listen to Finn and my dad talk baseball while I'm in the kitchen, the two of them falling into easy conversation. Obviously. I wonder if they've ever spoken off the field before today. Neither mentioned it, but then I haven't been super talkative about Finn to my dad and vice versa. Hearing their cheery voices, I spend a few extra minutes checking the turkey cooking in the oven and stirring the potatoes on the stove to give Dad and Finn time to yammer on.

I'm glad Finn is here. It killed me to think of him without his family, eating alone somewhere or ordering in. He mentioned Sylvie stocking his fridge before she left this morning for time with her own family, and that's okay for the rest of the week, but not today.

"Hey," Finn says entering the kitchen. "Anything I can do to help?"

Putting the vase of sunflowers on the dining table, I shake my head. "We've got some time before we eat so I thought we could head to the park."

"Great idea. You've got the jerseys?"

"I'll go grab them and give Julie the heads-up we're heading over there."

Finn signs the jerseys, we leash Sammy, and say bye to my dad who's elected to keep the couch warm. I slip a jacket on over my jersey dress. Today's Vans are navy to match my outfit.

"Julie sounded a little off," I say as we near the playground. "I hope everything is okay."

"Me, too. Thanks for keeping in touch with her. I've been looking forward to seeing Josh and Jesse again."

"Is it okay if I take pictures of the three of you with Sammy?"

"Absolutely."

The second the boys see Finn their faces light up. Jesse does a flying jump off the swing and Josh drops his gloved hand to his side to signal to his dad (the resemblance is unmistakable) he's done playing catch.

"Hi!" I wave hello.

Sammy tugs the leash toward Josh so we walk to him. He looks paler than he did last week and concern knots in my stomach.

"Hi, guys," Finn says to the boys before putting his hand out to their dad. "Hey, I'm Finn. Nice to meet you."

"Patrick," the man says. "And you, too. The boys can't stop talking about you and your dog. This is Sammy, I'm guessing?"

"See, Daddy?" Josh says. "Sammy really likes me."

She does indeed, ignoring everyone else while she brushes up against Josh's legs.

Julie joins us looking more tired than usual. The kids ask if they can play fetch with Sammy again and Finn nods. "I've got something for you first." He hands each boy a jersey.

"Thank you!" Josh says, immediately placing his glove on the ground and sliding the jersey over his head.

"Thank you!" Jesse agrees, taking time to check out the shirt. "And it's signed, too. No eating Jell-O when we wear these, Joshy."

"Or anything that can stain," Josh says. He hugs Sammy. "This is the best day ever."

He and Jesse pose for a few pictures with Finn and Sammy then take off for the middle of the field to play fetch.

"Thank you so much," Julie says.

"It's my pleasure," Finn says. "They're good kids."

"The best," Patrick says.

"If you don't mind me asking, is everything all right?" I ask tentatively. It's not like we're close friends and they owe me details about their family.

"I look that bad, huh?" Julie jokes. Her husband wraps an arm around her. "Josh has a chest infection. Antibiotics are helping, and the doctor assures us it isn't serious, but he's only seven and been through a lot, so even a sniffle feels monumental to me."

I nod in understanding, unsure what the right words are to say. I watch the boys play with Sammy. Jesse is doing most of the running, fetching the ball when Sammy stays right beside Josh rather than chase it down.

Finn can't take his eyes off the two of them. "Kids are resilient," he says, his response just right. "And I can tell Josh is a fighter. A quiet one, but one nonetheless."

"You're right. He is." Julie gives Finn an appreciative smile. "Do you have kids?"

"Not yet."

Not yet. Meaning Finn wants them. He's thought about a future outside of baseball. It surprises me, given he's so ultra-focused on his career. But then there are lots of major leaguers with families. The two don't have to be mutually exclusive. His dream girl is out there just waiting to have his babies.

The conversation veers to Thanksgiving dinner, extended family, and Black Friday shopping while your brain is on tryptophan overload.

"We should get going," Julie says. "Family will be arriving any minute. Boys," she calls out. "Time to go."

Josh and Jesse bring Sammy back without protest. They thank Finn again, give him fist bumps, and we go our separate ways. Or try to. After two steps, Sammy digs her paws into the grass and starts to whimper. She looks over her shoulder at Josh. He's looking over his shoulder at her.

Finn drops her leash and she takes off, stopping at Josh's feet.

We all freeze, taking in this somewhat surreal situation. Josh kneels to give Sammy a hug. "Bye, Sammy." Only she is having no part of goodbye, mewling when Josh stands to move away.

Finn strides over. I follow. "Boys, can I talk to your mom

and dad for a minute?"

Julie and Patrick look confused, but Patrick says, "Why don't you take Sammy for a short walk around the sandbox?"

The boys agree, the leash firmly in Josh's hand. Not that I think Sammy will go anywhere without him. She seems very in tune to him.

"Do you have any pets?" Finn asks.

"No," Patrick says.

"Keep Sammy."

"*What?*" Julie and Patrick say simultaneously.

My eyes are glued to Finn and the sincerity stamped across his face. He darts a quick glance to Sammy and the boys before resolution pulls his mouth into a tight smile. "There's something special between Sammy and Josh. I saw it last week and it's plain to see it's even stronger today."

Julie brings her palm up over her heart.

"Dogs can be very therapeutic and it's clear Sammy is supposed to be with your family."

"That's very generous of you, but we can't accept your dog," Patrick says.

"I'm not sure she was ever mine. I think I was the placeholder until she found her true owner."

I'm about to ugly cry right here in front of everyone. I blink and wiggle my nose to stave off the tears.

"I know this is a big deal," Finn continues, glancing at the threesome again. "A pet is a lot of time, work, and expense, and so my offer comes with everything you'll need for all of Sammy's life."

Julie shakes her head. "Finn, that's too—"

"Please." The one word is full of won't-take-no-for-an-answer, but there's a touch of vulnerability there, too, like their refusal would hurt more than anything else. "My gut tells me we shouldn't separate them."

Patrick and Julie share an uncertain look.

Finn threads his fingers through his hair. "I'm not the only one feeling their connection, am I?"

"No," I say in support. And because it's true.

"We..." Julies trails off.

"We don't know what to say," Patrick finishes.

"Say yes. Or at the very least say we can ask Josh and Jesse what they think. I'd like nothing more than to give Sammy to you today."

To Julie and Patrick, who barely know Finn, they probably see a man who is a superstar, a man who can have as many dogs as he wants, a man who is kind because he can afford to be.

All those things are true. But what *I* see is a man who, stripped of his last name, wealth, and stature, would still give his dog to a boy because deep down, Finn Auprince is the most noble person I know, plain and simple.

Jesse runs ahead of his brother and Sammy, rejoining us with, "Don't worry. Those two are fine together."

Julie starts to cry.

"What's wrong, Mommy?" Josh asks in a worried voice. Sammy rubs the top of her head against his hip. I think it's to comfort him.

"Nothing, sweetheart." She wipes at her cheek. "It's just..." Her voice wavers.

Patrick bends down to Josh's level. "It's just we've noticed how well you and Sammy get along and Finn would like to give her to us if you and your brother think that's a good idea."

Josh's jaw drops. It's cute as can be.

"What do you say?" Finn says. "Think you two can take care of her for me?"

Both boys shout "yes" then Josh wraps his arms around Finn's thighs in a tight hug. "Thank you."

Finn ruffles Josh's hair. "You're welcome." He lets them know he'll have everything Sammy needs delivered tomorrow and then he says a private goodbye to his dog, kneeling and whispering something in her ear.

I bump Finn's side on the walk back to my house. "That was beyond nice."

"It's a well-known fact I like to go above and beyond."

"Hmm, somehow I missed that in your bio."

"There's a lot not in my bio."

"True." I peek at him out of the corner of my eye. "Are you okay? You and Sammy were a pretty good match, too, you know."

"Not like that."

"No, not like that," I echo, noting he didn't answer my question. He'd grown more attached to Sammy than he's comfortable letting on.

Which leaves me to wonder what it would be like to mean that much to him, too.

Chapter Fifteen
#GreenLight

Finn

THE HOUSE SMELLS even better than when we left, and my stomach grumbles in anticipation of sitting down to eat. This is the first home-cooked Thanksgiving I've had in years, my family's usual MO being a restaurant at our hotel in Hawaii where we're served gourmet food that lacks the delicious simplicity of novice cooks. Truth be told, I prefer this, but don't tell my mother or grandmother.

"Where's Sammy?" Casey asks when Chloe and I walk into the kitchen. Dinner is laid out on the table in a really nice display and I'm grateful to be included here today.

I swallow the lump in my throat as we take a seat and I launch into the story. I miss Sammy already, but remembering the look on Josh's face, and the easy way Sammy stuck by his side, makes it easier to manage.

"And come March I'll be gone more than I'm home," I finish. "Sammy deserves full-time love and attention and now she'll have it." Not that my job influenced my decision. I only recalled my long absences after the fact.

"No doubt, you've made those boys very happy," Casey

praises.

"He very much did," Chloe says.

Chloe.

I sneak a glance at her and catch her sneaking one at me before her gaze drops to her plate. She's another reason the sting of giving Sammy away isn't so bad. I can't get her off my mind. She's in my every thought, making me smile. Making me think for the first time that she's a woman I don't want to let go of.

If only she was on board with getting caught.

"How's the rehab coming?" Casey asks.

"So far so good."

"Glad to hear it," Casey says. "Rumor has it the Landsharks are in active trade discussions rather than free agent negotiations."

"That's what I hear." I put my fork down, unable to take another bite.

"It looks like they're focusing on their starting rotation, inquiring on almost every starter available on the trade market," Chloe says. "Thank goodness. They have close to MLB's best one-two starting pitcher combination, but they're losing a couple of guys to free agency and Tommy John's surgery, so that leaves the back end of the rotation very unstable."

It's like she just told me a dirty story. Her love of the game is so fucking sexy.

"What?" she asks, looking at me funny.

Shit. It's a miracle I'm not drooling. "Nothing. Just thinking our catcher position is also a major need with

Boseman retiring."

"True. I read just yesterday that the Landsharks are a viable destination for Cavallero despite his high price tag. I hope you get him. He's phenomenal behind the plate *and* at bat, ending the season with a .323 batting average."

I can't help but grin at her. She is spectacular.

Casey pushes his plate away with a satisfied groan. "Looks like it's time I brought up the elephant in the room."

I erase my smile. *Stay chill.* He doesn't necessarily mean the crush you've got on his daughter.

Chloe pushes her chair back and stands. "If you say so."

I have no idea what is going on. Chloe's gaze flits briefly to me before she turns and walks to the fridge. She pulls out a cake. It's homemade from the looks of it, with white frosting. She brings it to the table and sets it down in front of me. On top of the cake, spelled out in tiny red candies, is *Second Place is still Red Hot.*

The sentiment is in reference to my second-place finish in the MVP award. The announcement was made yesterday. I laugh, overcome with gratitude. "You think so, huh?"

"Definitely," Chloe says.

"You had an outstanding year, Finn," Casey says. "Congratulations."

I'm not so sure a second-place finish deserves praise, but the fact that Chloe and her dad took the time to recognize it means more than I can say. In my head, the standing means I've got to work even harder during the upcoming season, and until then I need to jack up my workouts. I discreetly roll my shoulder back. I'm sore, Dwayne's words popping up in my head. *If we do too much too soon, you're going to reinjure yourself.*

"Thank you."

"FYI, those are red hot candies. Get it?" Chloe says, like candy is a foreign substance to me. She's not too far off the mark, but I don't live under a rock.

"I'm familiar with Red Hots. Nice touch, Webster."

"Webster?" Casey asks just as a phone rings from across the room. He stands to answer it, noting the caller before bringing the cell to his ear. "It's Aunt Becky," he tells Chloe. "Hey Becks. Happy Thanksgiving. I'm going to put you on speaker. Chloe's here and her friend, Finn."

"Happy Thanksgiving," Chloe half shouts.

"Happy Thanksgiving," Becky returns. "Did I catch you guys at an okay time?"

"There's never a bad time for you," Casey says. "How was your dinner?"

I recall Chloe saying her aunt lives in New Jersey, so it's three hours later there. I glance at all the food still on the table, thinking seconds could take place here in about an hour.

"It was interesting."

"Uh-oh. Why does that not sound very good?" Chloe asks.

"Well, I'm calling from the emergency room. I'm okay," she's quick to add. "Especially with the pain meds they gave me, but I broke my leg."

"Oh no," Chloe says.

Casey grimaces. "Shit, Becky. How did that happen?"

"Sliding into home."

My eyes widen. *Home plate?* I mouth to Chloe. She nods and whispers, "Annual turkey day softball game."

"Were you safe?" Casey asks.

"You bet your ass I was. We won five to four, and I'll most likely be getting a steal rod to remember it by."

"When?" Casey runs a hand up and down the side of his face.

"Not sure. The swelling is pretty bad. So, I was hoping maybe you could fly out here. I'm going to need help getting around for the next several weeks."

"I'll head out tonight if I can catch a flight. Otherwise ASAP," Casey says with zero hesitation.

"Thanks. I really appreciate it. Chloe, you should come, too."

"I can't. I'm working an assignment right now."

"Christmas, then. Let's plan on doing it here. What do you say?"

Chloe and her dad exchange a look. "Sounds good," Chloe says.

"You can't see me, but I'm smiling," Becky says. "Case, call me when you land and I'll let you know where I'm at."

"Will do."

"Okay, bye. Thanks again. Love you guys."

"Love you, too," Chloe and her dad say before he disconnects the call.

"What are the chances I get a flight tonight, huh?" Casey says to his phone. He's typing in an airline, I assume.

"Let me get you there," I offer.

Casey looks up in surprise.

"This is the busiest time of year for travel, right? My family has a private jet that can take you."

"No. Thank you, but I—"

"It would really make me happy to help," I interrupt. "I appreciate you having me for dinner and for the cake, and while I'm at it, thanks for not throwing me out of game three of the World Series when you had every right to."

"You do owe me for that," Casey says with a nod and smile before he turns his attention to Chloe. "I didn't even stop to make sure you're okay with me going."

"Of course, I am. Aunt Becky needs you. And she's got doctor friends if you need anything." Chloe rolls her bottom lip between her teeth. "Please make sure you pack all your medicine and don't forget to take it," she adds in a softer voice.

Casey reaches across the table and squeezes his daughter's hand. "A little giant cell arteritis isn't going to beat me, don't you worry."

Giant cell arteritis, I repeat to myself. I'll ask Siri about it on the way home. Chloe darts a glimpse at me to see if I caught those three little words before resting affection back on her dad and saying, "Okay."

"Finn," Casey says. "I appreciate your offer and will accept this once."

"You got it." I make a call and secure a red-eye flight per Casey's request. He sleeps like a baby on planes, he says. He's had enough practice, that's for sure.

"Did you know Chloe won a few softball awards in her

day?" Casey asks me.

"No, I did not."

"Dad."

"Plug your ears, sweet pea, it's about to get embarrassing." Fatherly pride is written all over his face while Chloe's cheeks turn pink. "Or better yet, I'll show you. Come on."

"Noooo," Chloe pleads. "This really isn't necessary. Finn does not want to see pictures of me in my softball uniforms."

"Sure, I do."

The three of us move into the family room. While talking with her dad earlier, I'd enjoyed looking at the framed school pictures of Chloe at different ages on the mantel. Sitting on the couch now, I notice a photo standing in what looks a place of honor on a side table. It's of Chloe with both her parents. She looks a lot like her mom.

Casey lifts up the top of the coffee table slash storage unit and produces a photo album.

"Just remember, Dad, payback's a bitch." Chloe plops down on the love seat adjacent to the sofa with her arms crossed and the corners of her mouth pulled down.

I don't feel a bit sorry for her. Her dad loves her and wants to brag. He runs his palm over the front of the book, nostalgia, I think, directing his actions today. I'm guessing he doesn't bust out the album on the regular.

He turns to the first page. "Chloe only played until she was thirteen. After that she was on the road with me so it made team sports impossible." He goes through the pages, telling stories with pride and adoration while Chloe slowly softens at his words. Soon she's sitting on the other side of him and the three of us are laughing and joking around—at her serious face, her pigtails, her refusal to tuck her shirt in. I share stories about my youth, too. I wasn't always the superstar I am now.

Actually, I was, but you get the idea. Sitting on this worn, comfortable couch after a fantastic meal shared with friends feels blissfully normal. While I always excelled on the field, off was a different story, so talking like this is gratifying.

"Okay, who wants cake and pie?" Chloe asks when we're finished. She places the album back in its hiding spot and then zeroes in on me with eyebrows raised in challenge.

I accept and eat both, complimenting the chef on her baking skills. Afterward, I help clean up and when it comes time to leave, I offer to drive Casey to the airport. Chloe takes the ride with us. She doesn't say as much, but I sense she's sad about her dad leaving with no set return date.

On the drive back to her house we rehash the day, constantly stealing glances at each other as we talk. Chloe's on her phone, too, reporting on the success of the photo she posted of me, Sammy, Josh, and Jesse. She types in my response to comments, and informs me I've received several proposals as well as baby daddy requests, whatever that means. I can't help but smile when she grumbles about the number of women hitting on me. Could it be my social media manager is jealous? If our roles were reversed, you can bet I would be.

"You know, you and I have yet to take a picture together," I say, turning down her street.

"That's because you're my client. It wouldn't really be appropriate."

"What about on *your* Instagram? We're friends, too, right?"

She turns her head to look straight at me. Her expression is hard to interpret. There's agreement in it, for sure, but there's also some mistrust or hesitancy, I think. She blinks—slowly—and when we reconnect I get the feeling whatever is going on inside her head is complicated.

"We are," she finally says, but I swear I hear more in her tone. *We are more than that.*

I park the car then hurry around to open her door. Her foot slips on the curb and I catch her, her nails taking purchase on the front of my shirt. For a beat we stay like that, the streetlight throwing shadows and casting a glow around us at the same time.

I take her hand on the walk to her front door. She wraps her fingers in mine with easy acceptance. *You're right, Webster. We're more than friends.*

"Thanks for today," I say, hoping she'll invite me in. I don't want to say good night. Not unless it's in her bed after I've touched every inch of her with my hands and mouth and we're skin to skin and so exhausted we can't keep our eyes open a minute longer.

She puts the key in the lock, looks over her shoulder at me.

And time freezes.

We've shared this knowing look a dozen times, and every time is hotter than the last. It's not a matter of *if* we slake our desire, but when, the constant thrum of sexual tension slowly building to a breaking point.

I've reached my limit. Has she reached hers?

"Just tonight," she says softly, reading my mind.

Thank fuck. "I'll take it."

Chapter Sixteen
#InScoringPosition

Finn

I FOLLOW CHLOE inside the house and the second the door shuts behind us, I'm on her, my body calling for hers like it's been starved for years. "Chloe," I whisper against her ear as my hands roam everywhere at once.

"Finn," she murmurs back, her grabby hands all over me as well.

Her smell overwhelms me as I kiss down her neck. I run my palms over her shoulders, sliding underneath her jacket and pushing it down her arms until it falls to the floor. I reach around to her ass, cup it, and bring her flush against me. I'm hard for her and I want her to feel it. To know that in a matter of seconds she turns me on like no one else.

We grind against each other like a couple of teenagers, my fingers finding the hem of her dress, the smooth skin of her thighs. I'm a second away from pulling the cotton up and over her head when I somehow register I'm acting like an animal and the entryway of her house isn't where I want her naked.

I let out a breath and get myself under control enough to

slow down and cradle her face. To count my favorite freckles, enjoy the parting of her full lips, absorb the dazzling shades of brown rimmed with soft, long lashes staring up at me with desire.

And then she smiles. It's crazy dizzying.

"Nothing in my life feels as good as your smile," I say, my heart beating louder than the words I've spoken. It's the truth. I've kicked ass on the baseball field, received standing ovations, won awards, made my parents proud, but this girl trumps all that. "Well, except for maybe our first kiss."

Her chest rises and falls. She wraps her arms around my neck. "Imagine what more kisses will do to you, then."

"Let's find out."

"What are you waiting for?"

Reality to set in? This insane, disorienting attraction to fizzle out? Doesn't happen.

I crash my mouth against hers. The kiss is immediately all encompassing. Lips, tongue, *feelings*. I said I'd take one night, but the truth is I'll fight for more. I'll show her how good we are together again and again until she's forgotten all about some silly curse.

She kisses me back with equal vigor, up on her tiptoes, her round, mouthwatering tits pressed against my chest. I release her face and lift her up, her legs wrapping around my waist, without breaking the kiss. She moans into my mouth when I slow the glide of my tongue against hers so I stay the course as I walk us down the darkened hallway hoping to find her bedroom.

"First door on your right," she says, slightly out of

breath. She rubs her nose against mine then pulls back to look at me. There's enough light from the entryway to take in every gorgeous detail of her flushed face.

Inside her room, a bedside lamp that was left on supplies enough incandescent light for me to see the bed and set her down on it. She kicks off her shoes, removes her socks, and scoots back. When she reaches the center, she pulls her dress up and over her head and tosses it to the side. Her barely there underwear is white with maroon polka dots and trim. Her bra is a simple black. I love that they don't match. I look my fill, from her neck to her feet, finding a few more freckles, a small scar on her side, and curves I can't wait to navigate.

I am one hell of a lucky man.

"Your turn," she says, not at all shy about my perusal.

I toe off my shoes, unbuckle my belt, and untuck my shirt. Her bottomless brown eyes stay on my hands as I work the buttons of my dress shirt. She licks her lips when the material falls away, squirms when I drop my slacks. My boxer briefs do little to hide how much I want her.

"Your turn," I say.

She reaches behind her back to unclasp her bra, letting the straps slip slowly over her shoulders. She stops the progression to torture me, no doubt, before removing the lingerie entirely and flinging it across the room.

I crawl up her body a split second later, supporting her back as I lay her flat while kissing lips that taste like peaches dipped in sugar. She runs her fingers through my hair before holding my head steady to deepen the kiss.

As good as it is mouth to mouth, I kiss down her neck, spending a little extra time behind her ear when she shivers. Sighs of pleasure follow my trail to her breasts. I cup one while taking the other in my mouth, licking and sucking on her nipple until it's hard. She arches her back, gathers the comforter in her hands.

"Finn." The breathless word is a straight shot to my dick. "That feels so good."

I move to the other breast, this time sliding a hand to between her legs, over the cotton, then underneath. She bucks her hips. I slip a finger inside her. "That does, too," she hums. "Please don't stop."

"Don't plan to," I say easing off her nipple so I can skim my lips lower, and lower still.

The scent of her skin, clean, warm, and intoxicating lingers in my nose and if I had to walk a straight line right now I'd fail spectacularly.

I do plan to make her come with my mouth, though. I kiss her hip then slide her underwear down her legs, tossing the small undergarment over my shoulder.

She pushes up onto her elbows to see what I do next. Under heavy lids she watches me kiss the inside of her ankle, her calf, behind her knee. I move to the other leg and kiss the inside of her thigh. I stop a hair's breadth away from her center. She spreads her legs, inviting me to feast.

Best Thanksgiving ever.

I bury my face and eat her out until she's writhing and vibrating, and her first orgasm rolls into a second release that has her thrusting against my chin, her heels digging into the mattress, and moans of pleasure filling the room. I don't let up until her body stills, her legs completely relaxing.

"Holy shit, you're good at that," she says.

I raise an eyebrow.

"Unbelievably good," she clarifies. "On a scale of one to ten—" she takes a second to consider her words "—a twenty-five."

Twenty-five is my jersey number.

"I'm about to rock your world a third time." I take off my boxer briefs at the same time I snag the one and only condom out of my wallet, kneel on the bed, and start to—

"Slow your roll there, stud," Chloe says, sitting up and covering my hand with hers. My dick jerks at the close proximity of her fingers. "It's my turn to look at you."

No problem. I raise my hands in surrender, giving her all access.

"I knew you'd live up to my imagination." She s-l-o-w-l-y rolls the condom down my shaft.

"You've surpassed mine," I admit.

That earns me a modest smile to add to my assorted collection. I want to be the reason she smiles every single day. I push the possessive thought out of my head to concentrate on right here, right now.

"Now lie down, Webster, arms over your head."

Chloe

I'VE NEVER LIKED being told what to do, but when Finn commands me to lie back down with my arms over my head, his giant, beautiful cock poised to come inside me, I don't hesitate.

Because I want nothing more than to be connected to him in the most intimate way possible. He's already touched and kissed me everywhere, made me feel like this is a bed of clouds. A place where the two of us are a world away from everyone and everything. He's plucked my heart out of despair so effortlessly, it doesn't matter whether I wanted him to or not. I was—I am—helpless against his charm.

He won't be mine forever, but he's mine right now.

And let me tell you, he is ALL THE THINGS.

His hard body covers my soft one as he laces one hand with mine. His other hand glides down my side, raising feel-good bumps on my skin.

"I want to go slow, but I'm not sure I'll be able to," he says, gazing down into my eyes with affection and enthusiasm and I'm completely gone for him.

"We have all night," I say.

"I don't have any more condoms."

"I do."

If I still had my panties on, they would have just disintegrated from the sexy curve of Finn's mouth. His fingers find my wet and ready entrance. He rubs and teases and then he slips inside me with one smooth thrust of his hips. For several glorious seconds we stay just like that. Perfectly still. Him deep inside me, stretching me. Filling me so completely, the sweet sensation is a kind of delicious pressure I've never felt before.

It's heaven.

And then he moves, pushing in and pulling out, his hips

rolling with expert precision. The energy surrounding us is both languid and hot as Hades. I don't want Finn to ever stop. I want him this close to me always.

The sound of our lovemaking fills the room and takes me to the edge over and over again. He kisses the side of my neck, my shoulder. Takes my nipple between his teeth, licks and sucks. My boobs have always been a big erogenous zone and the combo of Finn's mouth and surging cock has me falling into my third orgasm. I very loudly let him know how high he's taken me and then it's his turn.

"God, Chloe," he mumbles before he thrusts once, twice, three times the charm, and groans through his own release. He stills inside me once again so we can hold on to our connection a little longer before he rolls off of me and onto his back.

I lower my arms, exhausted in the best possible way.

He gets up and walks toward the bathroom. His ass is round, firm, and I have the sudden urge to bite it. To mark it. *Property of Chloe Conrad.* I've stared at his backside in baseball pants numerous times, unable to look away, but seeing him in his birthday suit is insanely better. I roll onto my side so as not to miss a second of his departure. He disappears into the bathroom, I hear some rustling and the sink being turned on, and then I'm blessed with his return.

Jesus, I can't believe he's real. Muscles, muscles and more muscles in collaboration with a face so handsome I have to glance away for a second to catch my breath.

He joins me back on the bed, lying on his side so we're looking at each other.

"Hi," I say.

"Hi."

"You hungry?" I don't know about him, but I've worked up an appetite.

"I could eat."

"Don't move." I pick his shirt up off the floor and put it on, buttoning just two middle buttons before I hurry to the kitchen. The starched cotton falls to the middle of my thighs and smells like Finn, a mix of man and clean laundry. I grab a few plates out of the fridge. The stuffing needs to be warm so I microwave it for two minutes. Turkey is delish cold. So is apple pie. I tuck napkins and a couple of forks into my hand, and snag the dish towel hanging on the oven door.

The main light is on in my room and Finn is sitting against my headboard wearing his underwear when I walk back in. I can't believe he's in my bed. I can't believe what we just did. My cheeks heat at the thought. I don't know why I'm feeling shy after the fact. Maybe because I've had a few minutes to think about it and I highly doubt I'm the kind of girl Finn normally hooks up with. His degree of cool and mine are on epically different levels.

Not that he's ever made me feel inadequate. Quite the opposite, actually.

"Here we go," I say, laying the dish towel and plates of food on the bed between us. I hand him a fork.

"Looks like you brought my favorites," he says. "Thank you."

"I may have noticed what you ate the most of."

He forks a piece of white meat turkey. "So, is this the

house you grew up in?"

I dig in to the apple pie. The next bite will be stuffing. The combo is better than chicken and waffles. "Yes. We moved here when I was three weeks old."

He looks around the room. "I'm going to take a stab and say blue is your favorite color."

"How observant of you," I tease. My bedding, the walls, the few pieces of framed artwork, are all in shades of blue. "What's your favorite?"

"Brown."

"Like dirt brown or dark chocolate brown?"

He dips his head and peers onto my eyes. "Somewhere in between."

Oh. I take a bite of stuffing, then apple pie, then stuffing. Keeping my mouth full seems wise at the moment. Otherwise, I might blurt out how much I like Finn and I'm trying really hard to do whatever we're doing without feelings getting involved.

Finn makes a face. "What are you doing?"

"Eating."

"I can see that, but it looks like you've got a unique system going on."

"Don't knock it till you try it."

"Okay." He puts his fork down, looks at me expectantly.

All right. I can feed him and keep my pulse from running out of control at the sexiness of it. I give him a piece of apple pie. While he chews, I scoop up a bite of stuffing. The cold pie and warm stuffing are best served one right after the other. Eat. Repeat.

"Not bad," Finn says when finished with four bites.

"Want more?" I wave a forkful of pie in front of him.

"No, thanks. I'm good."

I shrug and gobble it myself. We eat in pleasant silence, rarely taking our eyes off each other. "Have you ever been pants drunk?" I ask out of the blue.

"Depends. What is it?"

"It's when you get drunk at home by yourself in your underwear."

"Are you implying you'd like to get pants drunk with me right now?"

"I'm not in my underwear."

"No. You're in my shirt." He traces his finger along my collarbone and down to my cleavage. "And look sexy as hell. Is there a Women & Pie Instagram? Because I could take a picture of you right now and break the platform with the response."

"You do realize talk like that to a social media manager is like porn, right?"

He laughs. "I've thought the same thing when you talk baseball."

"Really?"

"Webster, your brain in combination with your body is a direct link to my dick."

"So, if I was to, say, tick off some of your stats, like your OBP was .460 this year, with seventy-nine RBIs and ten HBPs, you'd get excited by that?" I glance down at his lap. He's sporting some major league wood. "Mmmm. Seems so."

Faster than I can say Silver Slugger Award, Finn has the food off the bed and me spread out beneath him. "Condom?"

"In the drawer." I lift my chin toward my nightstand.

Finn wastes no time. His magic fingers touch me until I'm squirming with need and then he covers himself and slides home. This round is less hurried and more controlled. He moves inside me like a slow song is playing in the background. We kiss, we rub noses, we suck and kiss each other's necks. My hands wander over his shoulders, into his hair.

"Wrap your legs around me," he commands.

I do and he rolls onto his back, taking me with him so I'm on top and riding him, setting a new tempo. Controlling our rhythm. A pulsing and throbbing that ends with us coming at the same time.

"You're incredible," he says, looking up at me.

"You, too." I bend down to give him a kiss. It's just a peck, but I hope it conveys how wonderful tonight has been.

We crawl under the covers and talk more. About baseball, Finn's family, Sammy, and my bridesmaid dress. He finally confesses to buying me a new one and tells me about his cousin, Meredith. She assured him it was exactly the same measurements and I'd never know the difference. I stick my tongue out at him and announce I'm paying him back. He says the only currency he'll accept from me is kisses.

"Can I ask you something?" Finn whispers after a few minutes of cozy silence.

I'm tucked under his arm, my head on his chest. "Sure."

"Will you tell me about your dad's illness?"

My muscles tense, but only for a moment. It's a fair question. And after the day and night we've had together, a question I find myself content to answer. Finn is on the quieter side, a lone wolf who loves his family. He's stoic, funny, tough. He's an incredible athlete and not an egomaniac. His career is his first love, as evidenced by his insane work ethic and accomplishments and the fact that as far as I can tell, he hasn't had a serious girlfriend since making it to the majors. All this to say, I like him. A lot. And I trust him.

Which leaves me vulnerable.

Worried I'm setting myself up for heartache all over again. I can lie to myself all I want and say it won't bother me if Finn meets the girl of his dreams and fits her into his baseball life, but the truth is it would.

"He's going to be okay, right?" Finn asks when I've yet to say something.

"Yes," I answer, focusing on the present and trusting Finn with info about my dad.

He rubs the tips of his fingers lightly up and down my arm. "He mentioned arteritis at the dinner table. I'm guessing that has to do with inflammation of the arteries."

"Yes. The ones in his head near his temples. He was having severe headaches, scalp and jaw pain, and fatigue when he finally went to see a doctor. Left untreated it could have led to blindness."

"But you caught it early enough."

"We did. He's being treated with corticosteroid medications, but he's had two relapses, which means for him, the disease is chronic."

Finn shifts and raises my chin with the pad of his finger. When he looks into my eyes like he'd move heaven and earth for me and my family, my heart stops. "He's got this."

I press my lips together and nod. He does. My dad is strong. A fighter. And he's told me he wants another five years, minimum, before he retires from umpiring.

"And if there's anything I can do to help…specialists, new drug therapies, whatever you don't need now but might need later, just say the word."

"Thank you." I brush my mouth against his softly. Reverently. Then I lay my head back down on his chest.

The last thing to go through my mind before I fall asleep in his arms is that I'm in way over my head.

Chapter Seventeen
#WeekendUpdate

Chloe

FRIDAY MORNING, FINN brings me breakfast in bed. Scrambled eggs with turkey and onions and a buttermilk biscuit. We spend the day right where we are, on Twitter for his live Q&A, then listening to the rain outside, finding each other's ticklish spots, and having sex on repeat.

Saturday morning, I bring Finn breakfast in bed. It takes me sixty seconds to microwave the mini frozen pancakes, but I do cut up some strawberries to add on top. He shakes his head with a smile when I hand him his plate and mumbles something about a juice cleanse come Monday, but he eats everything—and asks for seconds. We venture out of my room to watch *Elf* on TV, play backgammon by the fireplace, and have sex on repeat.

Sunday morning Finn eats me for breakfast.

Chapter Eighteen
#HomerunDerby

Finn

I'M TOO OLD for this. Too old to be on the receiving end of my grandmother's third degree. She's like a bloodthirsty reporter who won't stop with the questions until she's been given the answers she wants. My only saving grace is Ethan is sitting next to me at a table in his restaurant and getting almost as much attention. He did just spend a week with her in Hawaii so it's not like she doesn't know what he's been up to.

Me, on the other hand? I've just come off one of the best weekends of my life and if my grandmother hadn't summoned me to join her for lunch today, I'd still be basking in the afterglow. It's fucking hard keeping the elation off my face, but give Grandma Rosemary a hint of something new and not even a magician could escape her interrogation.

Until I know what that something is between Chloe and me, my lips are sealed.

Ethan's chef delivers our lunch, salmon with some chutney mixture on top, roasted brussels sprouts, and mashed sweet potatoes. Tomorrow I'll start a cleanse and then return to my regularly scheduled meals with one exception. Hopefully that menu includes Chloe.

"Are you sick?" Ethan asks.

"What? No. Why?"

"Your face just turned colors. You're either sick or..." He trails off, a knowing smile making me fully aware I can't even think about Chloe or I'm going to get myself in trouble.

"Actually, I do feel a little out of sorts," I half lie. Chloe does have my focus out of whack. I'd done a shit job working out with Dwayne this morning, my brain on Chloe rather than training.

"Out of your shorts you mean," Ethan mumbles, then takes a bite of his food. I glare at him. Thankfully, our grandmother is a little hard of hearing.

"Chloe told me you gave Sammy away," she says, like she talks to her all the time.

"You talked to Chloe?"

Grandmother eyes me with a mix of affection and worry. "I think you might have a fever. I just said that, didn't I?"

"Right. I know. I'm just surprised."

"You of all people should know it's important to keep in touch with your social media manager."

I choke on a brussels sprout. "Since when are you on social media?"

"Since my surf lesson last week."

Ethan holds up his hand with a pained expression on his face. *Don't ask.*

"I'm on Insta as Musings from Grandma. Chloe didn't

tell you?"

"No, she didn't mention it."

"Must be some client-manager confidentiality thing. You should follow me."

I run a hand over the four-day scruff on my jaw, trying not to laugh, but also not sure how I feel about Chloe being in close contact with my grandmother.

"Oh shoot," my grandmother says. "I should have taken a picture of my food."

"No worries," Ethan says.

"I am worried about you," she answers.

I look at my brother. "Something going on?"

"Nothing important," he says to me before turning to our grandmother. "And you need to stop. Between you and Mom, I've had enough." He says this with respect, but there's some underlying irritation only Drew or myself would detect.

It's clear whatever it is, Ethan doesn't want to talk about it, but I'm not one for patience where my brothers are concerned. If something is going on, I need to know.

"Break it down into a sentence or two, and I won't bug you about it."

Ethan puts his fork down and sits back in his chair. "Last week while I was out of town, someone left a package for me. I had Charlotte open it and it wasn't something pleasant."

"He has a stalker," Grandmother says, trying to keep her tone even. It isn't the first time our family has been targeted by a fan or someone looking for a payout, and our security team always handles it, but it's never something to take lightly.

"I think that's taking it too far," Ethan says. "It was one time. Now, let's get back to Finn and Chloe."

"Finn *and* Chloe?" Our grandmother is sharp as a tack, so her feigned surprise doesn't fool anyone.

I still don't want to talk about it, though. "Looks like your Cardinals are headed toward a national championship," I say to Ethan to change the subject. Stanford is kicking football ass this season.

"Fingers crossed," Ethan says. "We're still on for Saturday's game, right?"

Shit. I forgot all about it. Stanford is playing one of their biggest rivalries, USC, and every year when the two teams play, Ethan, Drew, and I go to the game.

"I can't make it this time."

"You're breaking tradition? What for?"

I hate the disappointment I hear from my brother. He's right. This will be the first time in ten years that I don't make it.

"Or is the better question, who for?"

Yeah, I deserve that. I glance at my grandmother. She's stopped eating to put her chin in her hands and watch her grandsons like she's watching a tennis match at Wimbledon. "Don't mind me," she says.

Apparently, the topic of Chloe and me isn't going away anytime soon so I may as well get this over with. "I'm going to a wedding."

"Stag?" Ethan prods.

"No. Chloe invited me."

Ethan grins. "Tell us more. Friend of the bride or groom? Black tie? Church wedding? Where's the reception?" He's hilarious.

"You know you sound like a girl right now?" It's a weak retaliation, but whatever.

"I know you're trying to avoid answering any more questions."

As cool as I am about letting Ethan off the hook about things—the mysterious package for example—he doesn't always extend me the same courtesy. And he damn well knows I like to keep the peace, especially in front of our mom or grandma. "It's Chloe's best friend. I don't know the specifics, only that it's on Saturday night."

"Oh, you mean Jillian."

I stare at my grandmother.

She smiles at me with barely a wrinkle. "I follow Chloe on Instagram and saw them together. Don't you follow her? You really should if you plan to date her. Showing interest in someone's social media presence is crucial nowadays."

There's complete silence for all of one second before Ethan and I crack up. And just like that any brotherly tension between us disappears.

"What's so funny?" Grandmother takes another bite of salmon.

"You are," Ethan and I say at the same time.

"Well, obviously. Where do you think you boys get your sense of humor from? Your father can't tell a joke to save his life and your mother thinks mustaches are funny. She can't look at Tom Selleck without giggling. The man is a hottie."

There are some things you wish you could unhear, and your grandma calling someone a hottie is one of them. "This chutney is really good," I tell Ethan. "Everything is."

"Thanks. I'll let Louis know. I think it would be good on other types of fish as well."

"Like halibut."

"Or trout."

"Even swordfish."

"Okay, message received. No talking about hotties with my grandsons. But can we talk about something besides fish, please?" She pats the corners of her mouth with her napkin. "It is delicious, Ethan."

"What would you like to talk about?" he asks.

"How about my birthday? No one is telling me anything."

"That's because it's still months away and you're just supposed to show up," I say. Not that I know anything. My mom is in charge of the plans, along with Drew. Our baby brother got roped into that one.

My phone rings in my pocket. I pull it out without glancing at the caller. Only a few people have this number. "Hello?"

"Hi, Finn. It's Chloe."

"Hey." I almost forget where I am and add, "beautiful."

"Are you still at lunch?"

"Yes. Almost done, though. Are we still meeting at the stadium?"

"Yes, but they'd like you here a little earlier now. Is that possible?"

"Sure, I can leave here in five."

"Perfect. I'll see you soon. Bye."

I hang up and meet two sets of inquiring eyes head-on. "That was Chloe. I've got a shoot for Body Shield I need to get to sooner than I thought." Normally my agent handles this kind of thing, but Chloe approached Body Shield and the startup was thrilled to team up with me and the Landsharks for an online holiday campaign. A big portion of the profits will be going to children's charities.

"That's the new athletic apparel company, right?" Ethan asks.

"Right." I push my chair back to stand.

"Say hello to Chloe," my grandma says.

"I will." I move around the table to kiss her cheek and say goodbye then give Ethan's shoulder a quick grip. "Thanks for lunch. Louis, as usual, nailed it."

"Thanks. Talk to you later."

I enjoy the solitude of my car on the drive to the stadium. It gives me time to think about Chloe without prying eyes. I can't stop reliving the way she moved against me, the sexy sounds she made when she came, the taste of her on my tongue. The way she squeezed my cock when I was buried deep inside her, so warm and tight it felt like I'd died and gone to heaven. She is an unexpected diversion from my off-season regimen, one I should walk away from, but I can't.

I like her too much.

Have from the moment our cars collided. The second I laid eyes on her, there had been something familiar, something I couldn't put my finger on until she walked into the

Landsharks conference room a few days later and I learned who her dad was. I rarely look into the stands during games, especially when I'm up to bat, but one night last June, I remember glancing behind home plate and locking eyes with a woman wearing a Landsharks baseball cap. A jolt of awareness had practically knocked the bat out of my hands. I'd quickly turned away, shaken by the impact, and walked up to the plate where I'd proceeded to strike out. Casey was the home plate umpire. Chloe was that mysterious stranger.

Which is further proof I need to keep my head in the game and not on a relationship.

As I pull into the parking lot, I tell myself to stop enjoying Chloe so much. To put some distance between us by putting my focus—and discipline—back where it's been for the past dozen years. On being the best professional baseball player there is.

However, when Chloe greets me outside the equipment room, I forget I even play baseball. "Hi. Thanks for rushing over," she says, being very professional.

And dumbass that I am, I don't like it. I want sexed-up Chloe on her tiptoes kissing me hello. Until she darts her eyes down the hall and I see Rena fast approaching. There's no rule against Chloe and me getting together, but I understand keeping our personal interactions private.

"Hi. No problem. Hey, Rena."

"Hello, Finn. How are you? Thanks to Chloe, we've got everything set up already and we just need your body. We'll be doing…" She barely takes a breath as she runs down the schedule for the shoot with Chloe and me following her into the room. My pinkie finger lightly brushes Chloe's. She links our fingers for a brief moment, taking the edge off my desire. Things continue to happen with efficiency after that, and I lose track of Chloe. A couple of reps from Body Shield introduce themselves. The four-person production crew, too. I change into their clothing and am positioned in front of the equipment shelves. Shiny blue batting helmets fill most of the cubbies, with white arm guards, shin guards, and batting gloves stacked neatly, in the others. In the corner is a large rubber trash bin full of wooden bats.

Next, I sit in a folding chair with my glove on, elbows on my thighs.

I change my shirt, put on a Landsharks cap, grab a bat.

Sit. Stand. Smile. Look serious. Repeat. I've been photographed hundreds of times, as a pro ball player and as a quasi-celebrity with a famous last name, but it's never comfortable. Tension rolls down my spine, leaving an ache in my lower back.

Until I find Chloe, watching me. She's standing at the back of the room against the wall. Hair pulled up into a high ponytail. Off-white sweater over stone-washed blue jeans. Her generous pink lips glossy. If I were to kiss her right now, they'd taste like peaches.

Every nerve ending in my body relaxes. It's the weirdest thing. Like a layer of protection has fallen into place around me. In Chloe's gaze I find peace.

"Yes!" the photographer says. "Stay just like that."

The camera flashes several times before my view of Chloe is obstructed by the stylist stepping in front of me. "We'd like to do a few more without the hat," Mandy says to me.

"Okay." I remove my cap.

Mandy takes it, places it between her legs, and fusses with my hair. She's probably a couple years younger than me, pretty, and definitely likes to keep her hands busy. Not that she's been inappropriate, just thorough.

"I've been wanting to ask how you are," she says quietly. "Is your injury healed?"

"It's getting there, thanks for asking."

"I'm a big Landsharks fan."

"Appreciate it."

"Maybe when we're done here I could buy you a drink or something?"

"Sorry, but I've got plans after." I've found subtle rejection works better than a flat-out "no." Mandy is nice enough and obviously interested, and if it weren't for a blonde, brown-eyed girl I can't get off my mind, I'd probably take her up on her offer. But there's no one I want to be with more than Chloe. I can tell myself a million times over to keep my distance, but it doesn't make her any less appealing.

"Another night then?" Mandy asks.

"Actually, I'm seeing someone, so…"

"Oh. I thought you were single. My bad." She steps away, appraising my appearance before blending into the background.

I immediately latch on to Chloe again. She meets my gaze then looks away, her expression unreadable. I'm asked to focus on the camera so I do, anxious to get this over with. After a few more shots, we're done. I shake everyone's hand in thanks.

Mandy is talking to Chloe when I'm free to go.

"He is so dreamy," Mandy is saying. "I could stare at him for days. And did you see his body when he changed shirts? I asked him to go for a drink, but he's seeing someone. Lucky—"

"Hey," I interrupt. "Chloe, do you have a minute?"

"Sure. Mandy, it was nice meeting you."

"You, too."

I take Chloe's elbow and lead her out of the equipment room, down the hall, and into an empty office. I shut and lock the door.

"What are you doing?" she asks, light brown eyes the color of honeycomb nearly knocking me off-balance. Not because they're uncommonly pretty—which for the record they are—but because there's reservation in their depths.

"This." I step forward to kiss her and demolish any doubts she might have, but she halts my progression with a firm palm to my chest.

"Hang on there, Mr. Dreamy. You're seeing someone? I can't believe I—"

"You," I say, cutting her off. I take her wrist and kiss the soft underside where her pulse beats. "I'm seeing you."

"Oh."

"I'm a little hurt you thought otherwise, Webster. You know me. I'm not that kind of guy."

"I'm sorry. You're right. I just…we're not…"

"Dating?"

"Right. We're not doing that," she says like there is no

steam left for her to spar with but she wishes there was.

"We kind of are." I thread our fingers together, drop our arms.

"Finn, I told you—"

"I know what you told me, but we both know we want to rip each other's clothes off right now. Is it just sex you want from me? Okay, fine. But it's exclusive. I'm going to prove to you you're not cursed. Let's date and have fun and when spring training starts we say goodbye. Stay friends." I know myself well enough that come next season I will forgo anything that distracts me. I'd rather be up front with Chloe now than hurt her feelings later on.

"And you'll see, I will not be meeting my soul mate." *Because she's standing right in front of you. Are you really going to let her go in a couple months?*

Yes, I am. Because baseball is my life. I can't split my devotion. And Chloe deserves someone who will give her 100 percent all of the time. Right? My teammate, Mike, and his wife are blissfully happy. Their toddler is adorable. Mike's got it all, and neither his career nor personal life have suffered. But that doesn't mean the same would hold true for me.

Chloe gently shakes her head. "I don't think—"

I squeeze her hand. "Don't think. Just be with me. Have you ever casually dated?"

She thinks about that. "No, actually."

"So, let's give it a try. We're two mature adults. We can keep feelings other than friendship out of it."

"There's a name for this, you know. Friends with benefits. And I'm not sure I'm wired that way." She pulls her hand free. "My heart's been hurt too many times, Finn. I can't risk it again."

"I won't hurt you, I promise. That's why we're talking it through. Complete transparency." I cup her cheek. "If anything, you hold the power here, Chloe. I made it clear from the start I wanted to hang out with you. But if you really want to keep things strictly platonic, I'll abide by your wish." I was already fortunate enough to have spent three nights with her rather than the one she proposed.

"Is it me you don't trust or yourself?" I ask when she doesn't say anything. I'm pushing my luck, but I do so because I know she feels something for me. It's been communicated in her words, her body's response to mine, and in her everyday actions.

She swallows, the column of her neck giving away her apprehension. "Both."

Her honesty is a relief and a burden. Maybe she's stopped to think this through longer than I have, or maybe she hasn't, but either way, I can't let go of the chemistry between us.

"We have a wedding this weekend."

"Yes."

"And a long list of social media content to get across in the next two months, which means we'll continue seeing a lot of each other."

"Yes."

"I've got this thing at the end of the month I need a plus-one for."

She frowns. "Oh-kay?"

"Probably something next month, too."

"So, you're saying I'm easy?" She arches her brows and crosses her arms over her chest. It's damn cute.

"I'm saying this works. I'm saying you put the 'awe' in awesome. I'm saying I'm not looking for a relationship. I've got baseball records to break and a team I want to help get to the World Series again, and you're not looking for a relationship either, but we do like being together, so this is the perfect arrangement." I take her face in my hands. "Now please tell me I can kiss you before I lose my mind."

"On one condition."

"Name it."

"I steer this boat."

"Done," I say, before I devour her mouth, feeling so much more than I can ever tell her for fear she'll abandon ship.

Chapter Nineteen
#FiftyShadesOfFinn

Chloe

THERE ARE MOMENTS in your life that are surreal and tonight is one of mine. My very best friend and her new husband are standing on stage at their wedding reception and singing a love song to each other. Robert is strumming along on his guitar while Jillian serenades him—and all their guests—at the mic. I'm standing on the middle of the dance floor with other members of the bridal party swaying to the romantic lyrics while tucked inside Finn's arms.

My back is to his chest. My head leans on his shoulder. His lips graze my ear, and every time they do he whispers how beautiful I am, how sweet I smell, how incredible I feel, filling my head with dizzying delight. He's been extremely attentive all evening, his hand on my lower back, around my waist, and his fingers laced with mine under the table. We've kissed when no one's looking. We've laughed when someone says something funny. (Robert's family is a bunch of comedians. Literally.) We've stolen glances at each other too many times to count.

Wrapped up in Finn right now is equivalent to a warm

bath that leaves your skin silky soft and smooth, your body light, and your mind serene.

In mine and Finn's movie, this would be the moment when everything changed. When I stopped fighting my feelings for him and put off thinking about our precarious future until some distant time.

Up on stage, Robert and Jillian look into each other's eyes, sing the last verse of the song together, and then kiss. The crowd applauds like crazy and hollers compliments. I put my pinkie fingers in the corners of my mouth and give a high-pitched whistle, so happy for my best friend. The entire wedding has been flawless.

Once the accolades die down, the bandleader speaks into the mic. "Chloe Conrad, you're up!"

What? I look left, then right, like there must be some mistake. What am I up for?

"It's karaoke time!" Jillian shouts, while a member of the band wheels out a karaoke machine.

Oh no. No way, Jose. I am not singing. Jillian knows I suck at singing, but she's always said one of her favorite memories of the two of us was at a karaoke bar right after she met Robert. She wanted to impress him (because she has an amazing voice) and being the best friend that I am I went up on stage with her because she was super nervous. The two of us sang "Lean on Me."

Correction: she sang while I chirruped the words and plotted ways to get even with her.

"Get up here, best maid of honor ever!"

I hold my ground and shake my head, withdrawing into

Finn like maybe his size will hide me from the spotlight.

"Hey," he whispers against my temple, "what can I do?"

"Pretend you're me."

"I can't exactly do that, but how about I go up there with you?"

I spin around in his arms. God, even after several hours in his tux, he still smells delicious. "You'd go up there and sing with me?"

"Absolutely."

"*Can* you sing?"

"How about you find out?" He kisses me right on the mouth. Right in front of everyone. And I mean everyone, since the entire room is looking at me. This includes my dad, who flew in just for the wedding. If he'd been wondering about my relationship with Finn, he isn't any longer.

"Okay." I spin around and march up to the stage, Finn right behind me. "It's a duet or nothing," I say to Jillian.

She laughs and waves Finn and me up. "I love you, Chlo. And I know the perfect song for you two." She speaks to the band member finishing with the karaoke machine—a big blue screen for lyrics atop a large black boom box, for lack of a better description. The rest of the band steps off the stage for a break.

"We're good to go," the band guy says.

"Have fun!" Jillian gives me a quick hug before she and Robert step off the stage. They stand front and center on the dance floor, ready to watch the Chloe and Finn Show.

It's not that I'm shy. And it doesn't bother me to stand in front of an audience. My problem is I only like to do things I'm good at. I get that karaoke doesn't require a good singing voice and is about fun more than anything else, but that doesn't make this any easier. To make matters worse, the videographer has his camera poised to immortalize the entire performance.

"I've got you," Finn says, bringing my attention to him. "*We've* got this."

The band guy hands a microphone to me and one to Finn. "Push this button here when you're ready." He points to a big round silver button. "Adjust the volume here." His hand moves to a large dial. "I'll get you started to make sure everything is working."

It's then that I notice the song on the blue screen. "Don't Go Breaking My Heart" by Elton John. I dart a glance down to Jillian. She gives me two thumbs-up.

"Ready?" Finn asks. He took off his tuxedo jacket some time ago and his white dress shirt molds to his chest and biceps. The top two buttons are open, sexy as sin. I guess if I'm going to be humiliated, there's no one better to have by my side. Everyone—even the men—will be watching the handsome pro baseball player from a famous family rather than me.

"As I'll ever be," I say.

The music starts, loud and clear through the stage speakers. Every muscle in my body stiffens. Finn, though? He's loose, his arms swinging slightly in time with the beat. I imagine being on a baseball field with fifty thousand fans watching you and hoping you hit a home run makes this a piece of cake. He smiles at me, his eyes sparkling, and my body responds. Relaxes.

He sings the first verse and holy mother trucker. Is there nothing this man can't do? He nods to the screen. Oh yeah, it's my turn. I sing the next verse. He grins at me like I've got a boat-ton of Grammy awards sitting on a shelf at home. I relax further.

We go back and forth, and before I know it, we're gesturing to go along with the lyrics, eyes locked on one another. Then Finn puts his arm around me and together we belt out, "Who-who!" And the crowd goes wild. At least I think they do. I'm so in tune with Finn, mesmerized by his talented voice and grateful he's up here with me, that everyone else in the room falls away.

Finn holds his mic in front of me to sing into.

I hold my mic in front of him.

We follow the prompts on the screen, singing our own lines and collaborating on the refrain. I forget that I can't sing. My voice grows louder, stronger. Who cares if I can't carry a tune? This is so fun I may want to sing another song.

Finn and I get totally into it. Our hips swing, our arms. He gestures to his heart. I put my thumbs and index fingers together to make a heart shape. We are rocking this song like we've sung it together a million times. In my head, anyway.

I can't believe I'm saying this, but I'm sad when the song comes to an end. Finn and I take a bow to a massive round of applause.

Jillian is the first to greet us when we step down from the stage. "That was fantastic!" She gives me a hug. "Thanks for being a good sport."

"Of course." I'd swim through piranha-infested waters for her and she knows it. *Wait until I get you back at my wedding, though.* Whoa. Where did that thought come from?

Finn and I accept compliments and praise as we walk toward our table holding hands. His warm, slightly callused fingers make me feel good all the way to my toes.

"Nice job, you two," my dad says stopping us midstride. He takes a quick glimpse at our hands, keeps his expression neutral.

"Thanks, Dad. It turned out to be a lot of fun."

"I'm glad. And you didn't sound half bad."

"It helps when paired with someone who can sing."

"I'm sure," Dad says. "I came over to say goodbye. I've got a plane to catch so I'm leaving now." He reaches out to shake Finn's hand. "Finn, good to see you again. Thanks for watching out for my daughter."

"My pleasure," Finn says. "She's watching out for me, too."

"I've no doubt. Mind if I borrow her for a minute?"

"Not at all. Have a safe trip." Finn lets me go, and my dad and I step away.

"I bought you a plane ticket for Christmas," he says. "I'll email you the itinerary. Your aunt's healing slower than we'd like so I'll be staying with her until then. My plan is to fly back home with you on the twenty-seventh."

"Sounds good. Thank you. I'll give you a call tomorrow morning. Make sure you got in okay."

He wraps me in a side hug. "I love you, sweet pea."

"Love you, too."

"So...you and Finn."

"It's nothing serious." I'm lying a teensy bit, but it's to myself, too, so it doesn't count.

"Good. I like the man, but he's got a demanding job. One he's strongly dedicated to."

"You don't need to tell me. It's one of the things that makes him the great person he is."

"You've crushed on a lot of baseball players over the years."

"How would you know that?"

He gives me a look.

"Well, you don't need to worry. I've got this." I smile for emphasis. "You're doing okay in the colder weather, right?"

"I'm fine. You don't need to worry, either. Now give me a hug so you can get back to the party."

My dad's hugs always reassure me. We say goodbye, and I keep eyes on him until he's out of sight. I'm a grown woman with her own life, but I miss my dad a lot when he's not in the same city as me. Just knowing he's close, even if we don't see each other, is preferable to him being across the country. And with his illness... I blink the thought away. He can't—he won't—stop living his life the way he wants, and that's a good thing.

Standing on the periphery of the room, I take in the reception. Candles, flowers, people laughing and talking. The gorgeous three-tiered white buttercream and fondant cake. Robert's brother taking a turn at karaoke.

And then I see Finn. He's seated at our table, looking at his phone. His chiseled jaw is smooth, his nose straight with a slight upward slope near the tip. The hair on top of his head is standing up in messy sophistication; the sides are neat. He presses his shoulders back, holds the position, then relaxes. It's not the first time I've seen him stretch that way. He worked out hard this week. I know because I watched one morning. Dwayne is relentless. Meticulous. I rubbed lidocaine cream all over Finn's upper back and neck afterward.

Funny story… I made the mistake of kissing the smooth skin between his shoulder blades right after I'd finished and my lips went numb and prickly! Yep, that medicated cream works well. For approximately thirty minutes when it comes in contact with your mouth. Finn thought it hysterical. I grumbled and made faces at him, but it *was* pretty funny, so eventually I cracked up, too, and tried to kiss him on the mouth so he could feel the same sensation there. He avoided mouth-to-mouth contact, but kissed me in other places.

A waitress stops by the table. The same one who served us dinner. She hands Finn a piece of paper. He signs it with his usual geniality. She slips the autograph into the pocket of her black pants and moves on. Finn continues to scroll through something on his phone. He's like a unicorn when it comes to his cell, barely on it, so whatever he's checking out must be important.

Okay, creeper, quit staring at him and walk back to the table.

I'm not quite there when Finn turns his head. He watches me approach. I watch him watch me. I've never been so at ease with eye contact before. So secure in not looking away.

"Hello, handsome," I say, taking my seat beside him. "Whatcha doing?"

He turns his phone to me. On the screen is one of the selfies we took earlier tonight. We're making funny faces, our heads canted toward each other. And when I say funny, I mean I look ridiculous making fish lips and scrunching my nose, while Finn looks hot as hell sticking his tongue out a la Mick Jagger.

Basically, Finn looks hot no matter what he does.

"I'm trying to decide which picture I like best," he says.

"And?"

"I can't. I like them all."

"You know you don't have to flatter me to get me to go home with you, right?" I walk my fingertips up his arm.

"Care to go now? The sooner I get you in bed, the longer I can express my admiration for certain parts of you."

"Which parts exactly?" I rub his shirt collar between my thumb and fingers, tugging on the material to expose more skin at his neck.

He kisses me softly on the mouth, making my lips tingle. "That part." He kisses the side of my neck. More tingles. "That part." He splays his hand around my waist. Yep, tingles erupt there, too. Let's just call me tingly all over. "This part." His other hand touches down on my thigh. "This part."

My senses spin out of control at the low, sexy timbre of his voice. "So, lots of this and that," I say softly.

"And then lots more." He bends his head so his warm breath fans the side of my face. "I want to sink into you over and over again, worship your nipples until raw pleasure spreads everywhere and you come so hard you see stars."

Said nipples now strain against my dress. My panties are wet with anticipation. If I wasn't the maid of honor, I'd drag Finn to the restroom for a quickie to quench this thirst we have for each other. But my duty is to Jillian for a little while longer.

"After the cake cutting. And bouquet toss. And garter thing. Then we can go," I say. I wrap my arms around his neck and touch his nose with mine. "So, another hour. Two, tops."

"Thank God it's not more than that. Three would have put me over the edge," he teases.

Lord, I like this guy. We have a quick make-out session, keeping it PG.

The cake is cut.

The bouquet is thrown. Remember how I mentioned I'm the only single friend Jilly has? Well, on Robert's side of the family there are several single ladies and they form a wall worthy of an NFL defensive line, their arms shooting up when the throw is made, and the tallest woman catches the prize. Not that I would have tried for it. Not really.

The garter is removed by the groom's teeth to hoots and hollers and his brother is the lucky recipient of the toss.

The sexiest man alive, AKA my date, asks if he can take me home now.

We say our goodbyes and given the late hour hit zero traffic and pull into Finn's garage in no time. "Last one upstairs is a rotten egg," I call out, hurrying out of the car.

My high heels are on the floor of the passenger seat, so I lift up my skirt and easily make a run for it.

"Oh, it's on," Finn counters.

I bump him out of the way so I can pass through the doorway into the laundry room first. I'm not delusional, I know he lets me lead, and when I look over my shoulder at him, his playful mug confirms it.

He pursues me for all of three seconds before taking the lead.

We can't have that, can we?

"Ow!" I cry out. (Side note: before my dad home-schooled me, I was in every drama performance possible at school.) I limp to the kitchen counter to lean on it for fake support.

Finn puts on the brakes, spins around. "Shit. Did you twist your ankle?" He rushes over and lifts me up onto the counter like I weigh nothing. "Let me see."

I wasn't expecting that, so I adjust my ill-thought-out plan. "Maybe get me some ice?" I say, neither confirming nor denying I hurt my ankle. Maybe I like to chew on ice. Maybe I want to put it down his shirt. Or his pants. Who knows?

"Sure." He steps around the counter toward the fridge. With his back to me, I stealthily hop down and run for the stairs. "Gotcha!" I shout after a head start.

Now before you get mad at me for pulling such a stunt, remember Finn is a professional athlete who can run a six-minute mile, while even if a pack of skunks were chasing my ass, I'd maybe run a nine-minute one.

"Oh, you want to play dirty, do you?" Finn calls after me.

"Only with you!"

I'm halfway up the stairs when Finn scoops me up. "Hey, put me down!"

"When I'm good and ready." All my wiggling is useless against his strong hold. "Looks like it's a tie," he says when we get to the top.

I go limp in his arms. He laughs.

"What am I going to do with you?" he jests.

I sigh in dramatic fashion. "Punish me, I guess."

He stops in his tracks, narrows his eyes. "What exactly are you saying?"

"Take me to your Red Room, Mr. Auprince," I tease.

"What?" Finn's pinched eyebrows and twisted mouth are adorable. I think he's clueless, not repulsed by the idea.

"Fifty Shades of Grey?"

"I have no idea what you're talking about."

"You are shitting me. Everyone's heard of Christian Grey."

"Oh, you mean the character from *League of Extraordinary Gentlemen*." He resumes walking down the hall.

"No, goofball! That's Dorian Gray."

"I know. I'm just messing with you."

I swat him in the chest.

He drops me on his bed. Traps me between his arms. It's a nice trap. I could survive in this trap for a very long time. "However, besides the title, I truly am unfamiliar with *Fifty Shades of Grey*."

I'm not really that surprised. Finn doesn't follow a lot of pop culture, and probably none at all during baseball season. "The Red Room was where Christian Grey showed his true sexual proclivities. Lots of pain *and* pleasure."

"It was a book and a movie, right?"

"Right."

"And are you telling me your proclivities lean that way?"

"Pleasure, yes."

He tips his head down, takes my earlobe between his teeth. He bites just hard enough for me to feel the sweet sting between my legs. "And pain?"

"A minute ago, I would have said 'no way' but that felt pretty good."

"Yes to nibbles then," he says, his voice husky. "Anything else?"

I stare up at him. There's nothing I won't do with this man. The realization hits me hard. I've never given up full control to my previous partners. "I don't know, but I'd be willing to try things. If you wanted to."

"There's nothing I want more than to make you feel…" he grazes his teeth along my neck, and electricity sparks up and down my limbs "…like I can't get enough of you. You are magnificent, Chloe, incredibly soft and strong, delicate and vibrant. Did I tell you how gorgeous you are in this dress?" He drags down the zipper on my side.

I feel his affection in my bones. I'm melting, lost in Finn Land. "You did. You look gorgeous, too," I whisper to him.

He pulls down the bodice of my gown. I wriggle to help, freeing my arms and then combing my fingers through his hair when he flicks his tongue over one rigid nipple, then the other.

"I have an idea." He tows the rest of my dress down my body, leaving me in only a lacy thong. His eyes rake over my body, hungry. Eager.

"What's that?" I get to my knees. Finn stands at the foot of the bed so I undo a button on his shirt. Move down to the next one.

"We could watch the movie and anything you want to try, we can try."

I concentrate on his buttons. "I have a better idea."

"What's that?" he echoes.

"I could read the book to you." I finish the last button.

He tilts my chin up with his knuckle. We lock eyes. "I'd like that."

"Should we start tonight? I think I saw you have an iPad."

"After." He works his belt off, then starts on his tuxedo pants. His socks and shoes go, too.

My jaw drops. "You went to a black tie wedding commando? How did I not notice this?"

His grin, in combination with the devilish twinkle in his eyes, is on a level that defies any word I may come up with to describe how freaking sexy he is. I scan down his muscular torso, stopping at the now very hard evidence.

"After what?" I ask, remembering what I meant to ask.

"I do you my way," he says, flipping me onto my stomach, where he proceeds to touch and kiss every inch of exposed skin. His fingers slip under my panties, stroke me just right. I grind against his hand, unbidden.

"Finn."

He rips off my thong like he has laser vision, the dainty material simply falling apart. All I know is the only thing between me and the bed now, is Finn's mouth. He tastes me from behind, lifting my hips just enough to give him access, and it is heaven. His clever tongue flicks and licks and when I feel the pad of his finger at my rim, I come so hard I see the stars he promised.

My heart is still pounding when I hear him open a foil packet. His hands find my waist to ease me toward the edge of the bed. My legs fall to the floor so I'm leaning over, my booty in the air. His tip finds my wet and ready entrance and with one smooth thrust, he buries himself. He drives into me, every surge of his hips better than the last, hitting a spot inside me that's been untouched until now.

His hands roam and rub my sweetest spots. One kneads my breast. The other taps between my legs. I fall into my second orgasm. More intense. More powerful.

Finn's release follows, gripping my hips, inhaling sharply, then letting it go.

He kisses my shoulder blade. "I'm going to grab a quick shower. Come join me."

Quick does not happen. Instead, we wash each other's bodies from head to toe. Shampoo each other's hair—Finn is excellent at bubbly scalp messages. Talk about the wedding. And then tender turns to desperate. Finn somehow produces a condom and takes me against the shower wall while I straddle his hips, his sculpted legs easily holding my weight.

Mind-blowing pleasure finds me once again. The sounds of our lovemaking echo off the tile walls. We pant. Moan. Strain against one another as our slick bodies make a slapping noise that is erotic and wild and passionate.

We come together, my nails digging into his shoulders. He has one palm on my ass, the other around the side of my neck. Eyes locked on one another, we stay like that until our very last tremors have stilled.

A little while later, I read to Finn in bed.

I get a warm, mushy feeling in the middle of my chest as he listens attentively.

I fall harder for him.

I wonder how in the world I'm going to come out of this with my heart intact.

Chapter Twenty
#BasesLoaded

Finn

I SIT ON Chloe's bed, waiting for her to come out of the bathroom. Her suitcase is packed for her trip back east and we've got about an hour this morning before I have to drive her to the airport. I bought her a scarf since it's freezing in New Jersey, and after squealing with happiness at the sight of it, she ducked out of the room to try it on. It's not her Christmas gift—that she'll get when she returns a week from today. I'm planning to whisk her away to Big Sur.

I lace my fingers behind my head and look around the bedroom I've got memorized. Seven days without her is going to suck. We've been inseparable the past couple of weeks. My days are better when she's in them, my new routine going as follows: workout with Dwayne, work with Chloe on social media tasks, walk hand-in-hand on the beach with Chloe, goof around with Chloe at each other's houses, watch Netflix with Chloe, have sex with Chloe, listen to Chloe read, have more sex with Chloe, fall asleep with Chloe in my arms.

As you can see, there's a lot of Chloe.

Six weeks ago, I would have thought you were high if you said I'd be spending this much time with the same woman. Now, I can't imagine my life without her. I don't want to. Somehow, I've got to convince her to make this a permanent deal.

"What do you think?" she says.

My gaze snaps up from the foot of the bed to the bathroom doorway. Chloe stands there, hand on her hip, in nothing but the maroon scarf artfully placed around her neck and chest and a tiny pair of white underwear. I think I fucking love her, that's what I think.

All that killer bare skin has my dick instantly pressing against the zipper of my jeans.

"Get over here and I'll show you," I say.

She saunters toward me, sliding the scarf into a different configuration. I look everywhere at once, up her toned legs to her stomach, her pert dark pink nipples, her lush mouth, her smiling eyes. She stops just out of reach.

"I'm going to wear it every day. I love it."

"And I'll think of you wearing it—like this—every day."

"That's what I was hoping for."

"Mission accomplished." I scoot to the edge of the bed, plant my feet on the floor, and palm her ass to haul her between my legs. Making love to her is exactly how I hoped we'd spend our time before leaving for the airport. I kiss along her rib cage, enjoying the way her muscles tense under my mouth. Her skin is like a sunny day in spring, her scent feminine, fun, and forever in my memory.

She places her hands on my shoulders. "I do take hijacking your mind seriously."

I look up at her. "Yeah?"

"Uh-huh."

"I've got a secret for you."

"Okay."

"You're stuck in my mind no matter what you do." The closer I get to spring training, the baseball side of my brain says this could be a big problem, but right now I'm not on the field. Right now, I lower my head to bite and suck the skin near her belly button so she'll have my mark on her when she leaves. I soothe it with a kiss and then admire my work.

She examines the blemish then giggles. "No one's ever done that to me before."

No one's ever touched her many of the ways I have. *Thank you,* Fifty Shades. It's on my agenda to scope out other erotic novels she can read to me.

"Get on the bed," I instruct.

She doesn't hesitate, jumping onto the mattress with gusto. The way she responds to me is unlike anything.

I'm about to strip when the doorbell rings.

"Are you expecting someone?" I ask.

"No." Indecision pulls her brows together. Answer the door or ignore it? It's most likely a salesperson selling something we don't need.

It rings a second time.

"Damn it. I better see who it is." She zips into the bathroom to pull on her clothes in record time, replying, "No, that's okay," when I ask if she'd like me to answer it.

We walk to the front door together. She opens it.

"Leo?" Chloe says to the man standing on her front porch.

Leo? Ex-boyfriend Leo? What the hell is he doing here?

"Hi, Chloe." His eyes shift from Chloe to me then back to her.

"What are you doing here?" she says.

My thoughts exactly.

"I was hoping we could talk. Do you have a few minutes?" Something in his voice tells me the talk isn't about the weather, and I clench my fists.

Chloe and I agreed we were exclusive, but we're not official, which means she can talk to whatever douche she wants without my input. I put my hand on her waist, reminding her I'm here, and that she should shut the door in this guy's face so we can pick up where we left off in her bedroom.

Instead she says, "Is everything okay?"

I'm guessing if he says yes, she'll say adios. If he says no, she'll talk to him. She's got a big heart. And she's curious by nature. *Shit.* This guy doesn't deserve her time, but glancing at her out of the corner of my eye, I see the wheels turning.

"Can I come in?" he asks. "I'd like to talk to you privately."

"I was just getting ready to leave for the airport," she says.

"Going back east for Christmas with your aunt?"

I feel Chloe visibly soften under my hand, the reminder that Leo knows her well a strong argument for giving him a few minutes. They share a past. One where she thought he was going to put a ring on her finger. I want to bash this guy's face in for hurting her at the same time I want to thank him. His loss was my gain.

Chloe is not cursed. She just hadn't met me yet.

She looks up at me with an unreadable expression that just about kills me. "Do you mind?"

Hell yes, I mind. "No." I take a step back, dropping my arm. Hating that I'm no longer touching her.

"This needs to be quick," she says to Leo as she allows him entry.

"I can do quick," he says, his voice way too pleased for my liking. He struts in like he owns the place—raising the hairs on the back of my neck—and barely acknowledging me.

Chloe wraps her arms around herself. This isn't easy for her, and me being a jealous prick won't help. I take the high road, because the last thing I want is for her to feel any kind of pressure from me, too.

"I'll wait in your room." I kiss her cheek; glad Leo is paying attention when I do so. The small amount of satisfaction is short-lived, however, when I hear the next words to come out of his mouth.

"I broke things off with Adele," he says.

"*What?*" is Chloe's response.

I lean against her open bedroom door. The small house affords me easy listening. I tell myself if they wanted complete privacy, they'd take it outside.

"I was an idiot, Chlo. Beyond stupid to mess up what you and I had. I love you. I never stopped loving you and I want you back."

Silence.

I picture *my* Chloe with her gorgeous face scrunched in disbelief. She certainly won't believe this jackass, will she?

"I don't know what to say."

I press my fist to my chest, completely unprepared for the blaze of helpless anger that squeezes my lungs. Her immediate response was supposed to be: "Too bad, loser, I'm in love with someone else now."

Yeah, I want her to love me.

"Say we can get back together."

"What about all those things you said to me the night we broke up?"

"They were true at the time, I guess."

"You guess? Leo, you told me you'd fallen for someone else. That it was love at first sight and some other crap. You broke my heart when I thought you were going to propose to me."

The only reason I don't hurl myself down the hall to fight for what's mine is Chloe sounds pissed more than anything else. There's no forgiveness or tremble in her voice to indicate I need to worry.

"I, uh, was," the dickhead says.

Silence.

Again.

Fuck.

"But then you met Adele," Chloe says evenly.

Leo lets out a very audible breath. "Yes."

"Where's Adele now? Why did you break things off?"

"Is that really important?" Leo asks. "I want you back, baby, and I'm prepared to get on my hands and knees to beg you if that's what it takes. I miss you."

"You did notice there's someone here with me, right?"

"Is he your boyfriend?"

"No, not exactly."

The truth has never made me want to throw up as much as it does right now.

"Then I don't see the problem."

"The problem is I can't trust you. Among other things."

That's my girl. She can trust me all the way to Mars and back.

"You can," Leo whines. "The thing with Adele was just a blip in our relationship and I promise you it won't ever happen again."

There's some shuffling—of feet, I think. Maybe the brushing of a couch cushion.

"Why are you looking at me like that?" Leo asks.

"She broke up with you, didn't she?" Chloe asserts.

He doesn't answer.

"Oh my God. She did. She dumped you and so you come running back to me, thinking I'll take you back? Well guess what? That is never going to happen. I don't want you. I don't want anything to do with you. Adele did me a favor. I didn't see it then, but I do now. I'm too good for you, so you can take your apology—wait a second, you didn't even say you were sorry—you can take your pathetic ass out the door and please don't come back."

"Chlo—"

"It's over, Leo."

I punch my fist in the air in victory. Although, victory isn't really the appropriate word. I'm happy as hell Chloe didn't overlook what her ex did, but the win is bittersweet. I have no idea what it's like to be in either one of their shoes, but I know the woman who's managed to snare my heart and while she handled the faceoff with Leo like a champ; she's no doubt hurting inside. No one likes to be reminded of betrayal.

The sound of the front door scraping open reaches my ears. "Goodbye," Chloe says.

"I'll call you—"

"No." It's the most unshakable "no" I've ever heard.

I can't stay hidden any longer. I walk down the hall and catch Leo leaving with his tail between his legs. Chloe shuts the door with a resounding thud.

I'm there when she turns around. I give her a second to catch her breath before I've got her pinned against the door, my mouth on hers. It's not our usual kind of kiss. She parts her lips almost begrudgingly when my tongue darts out for more. In the back of my mind, I think about stopping. Instead, I kiss her harder, asserting some primal masculine urge to claim her as mine without words.

She lashes her tongue against mine in retaliation. Her nails dig into my back. The kiss is punishing, yet satisfying. I'm happy to take her frustrations, her pain, her anger, and swallow them. I may not know much about being a boyfriend, but I'm a damn good teammate, and Webster is my team captain.

I have no idea how long we duel—it could be seconds, it could be minutes. Chloe backs off first. Her lips are gorgeously swollen, her cheeks flushed. She steps around me. "We should get going," she says. In the same tone she might say, "Pick up your socks, would you?"

The drive to the airport passes in relative silence. It's not exactly awkward, more like reserved, which for the record, feels just as shitty. We've never held back from each other.

I pull up to the drop-off for American Airlines, glad to see there aren't a ton of cars vying to get in and out. I turn off the engine.

"Thanks for the ride," Chloe says.

"Call me when you get in, okay?"

"I will."

"Hey." I take her hand. "In case I haven't told you enough, you're incredible and I appreciate everything you've done for me." Her gaze moves out the windshield. "I talked to Rena yesterday and she's very happy that my number of followers is up, way more than Mike and Giancarlo's, which you know, I had no doubt would happen. I mean, look at them and then look at me," I say to lighten the mood and hopefully get her eyes to meet mine again.

She twists her mouth into a wry smile and looks at me. Hard. I wish I knew what she was thinking. "You are pretty easy on the eyes."

"Right back at you."

"Grab my bag for me?"

"Absolutely." I hop out of the car, meeting her at the trunk. When she wraps her arms around me in goodbye, I hold on for an extra few seconds. Her body molds to mine like it was made for me, and me only.

"See ya," she says, turning and rolling her suitcase behind her.

I wave and watch her walk away until she's out of sight. There's so much I want to say to her when she gets back. Climbing into the driver's seat, I hope waiting was the right move.

And I hope the sudden surge of unease in the pit of my stomach is nothing to worry about.

Chapter Twenty-One
#TheHeartWantsWhatTheHeartWants

Chloe

THE DEFINITION OF 'hard and fast' is: fixed, definite, strict, rigid, inflexible, ironclad, binding, and a few other similar words. The term originally applied to a ship that had come out of the water either by dry-docking or running aground, and therefore was unable to move.

I used to agree with this description. After Leo broke up with me, I made the hard and fast rule of no more dating. No more men.

Then Finn came along. And now when I think 'hard and fast' I think about sex. With him. When he's so desperate to come inside me that he can't control himself. *I* do that to him. I hold power over him I've not held over my previous boyfriends.

It's part of the reason why it was easy to look Leo right in the eye and say "no" when he practically begged me to get back together.

The entire time I was in New Jersey I thought about what it meant for that strange turn of events. Was I no longer cursed? Was the curse something I made up to make myself feel better? Because the universal truth still applied—my boyfriends dumped me to be with someone else. How many times can a person try at love before courage and hope are dismantled to dust?

Sitting against my headboard, I roll my head to the side and look out my bedroom window. It's bright out, but raindrops trickle down the glass. It's the second passing shower in as many hours, which is not unusual for December in SoCal. Dad and I have come home a day early. Aunt Becky is doing well and we both wanted to sleep in our own beds. Dad especially, after so many weeks away. I didn't tell anyone I was back. I walked into the house, straight to my bedroom, plopped a green coconut bath bomb into the tub and soaked until I turned into a prune. Then I put on jammies and climbed into bed with my laptop. The great thing about my job is I can be online from anywhere without anyone knowing my location unless I want them to.

There's something else I can't get off my mind. Finn's last words when he dropped me off at the airport. He had to have overheard my conversation with Leo. Our house is small. Yet he didn't say anything. Not that I wanted to talk about it, but still. He could have acknowledged it, right? Instead, he complimented me on our working relationship. It caught me completely off guard. Have I read all of his signals wrong? Is it only sex for him? I didn't think so, but I've been wrong before. Multiple times.

And if I'm right and we have something special? Then there's a part of my brain that is waiting for him to drop the breakup bomb on me. Tell me he met the real love of his life. More than any of my other boyfriends, Finn's betrayal would devastate me the worst because…because I love him the hardest. I didn't mean to fall for him. I didn't even try. Everything is just so easy with him. My heart reached for him the moment he said, "Small world, huh?" in the Landsharks conference room at our official first-meet.

Which brings me to the other part of my brain that says—no, *knows*—Finn is first and foremost a baseball player. He's dedicated to his career above all else, which is something I greatly admire. I feel the same. I love my job. I'm great at it. Social Media Manager Chloe is effortless. It's off-the-clock Chloe that is harder for me to trust.

Can I trust off-the-field Finn?

"Chloe?" my dad says through the closed bedroom door.

"Come in," I call out.

He peeks his head around the door before fully entering. Since I hit puberty after my mom passed away and needed his help with my period, he's always been careful about barging in on me. "This package just arrived for you. It's from Finn."

I put my laptop to the side and accept the box. "Thanks."

"I thought our early return was top secret," he says.

"It is. I guess he wanted it to be here waiting for me." The outside of the box says *Best Cookie Ever Bakery*.

Dad sits on the edge of the bed. "You okay?"

"Yeah."

He studies me like he knows I'm lying. I've never been able to get anything past him. "I didn't bug you while we were at your aunt's house, but we're on our home turf now, so spill."

If I don't come clean, he'll keep pestering me. "Leo came to see me," I say, starting from there. I tell him about our entire conversation. And I tell him about how Finn and I left things after a somewhat awkward car ride to the airport. As I talk, he rubs the new beard on his chin. He decided that No Shave November should roll through December, too. It's taken me a while to get used to it.

"I've told you all along you're not cursed," he says lovingly. "Some bad luck, yes. But thank God for that, because none of those boys were good enough for you."

"You loved Leo."

"No. But I would have, for you."

I can't believe my ears. "I thought—"

"Faked it."

"Dad!" Since when does my father surprise me? Since never.

"I had a feeling it wouldn't last so there was no need to voice my concerns. Not that you would have listened to me anyway." The beard hides the lines around his mouth, but I can still make out his indulgent smile.

"Since when are you an expert on dating?"

"I may be rusty, but I remember exactly how it felt when I started dating your mom."

My mom and dad were college sweethearts. They met when my dad coached her powder-puff football team during a Greek Week event. Mom was a receiver and when a girl on the other team tripped her and my dad didn't call it, she threw the football at his chest. He was immediately smitten. "How come you haven't dated? It's been a long time since Mom passed." It's a question I've wanted to ask for a while. My dad is only fifty-four.

"Who says I haven't?"

"*What?*" Okay, Surprise Dad has got to knock it off.

He shrugs like it's no big deal. "Your aunt set me up with one of her friends."

"I can't believe you didn't tell me."

"I'm telling you now."

"How was it?"

"Terrible," he says with conviction, so I lean over and hug him. "But you know what your mom always said."

"In order to grow you have to step out of your comfort zone," we say together.

"I wish she was here," I say softly.

"Me, too. Every day." His chest rises and falls. "She'd be so proud of you, Chloe."

"Why was the date terrible?" I ask, steering the conversation back to him so I don't start to cry.

"We had nothing in common. And then she told me she hated baseball."

I make a face. "What was Aunt Becky thinking?"

"That she'd torture her baby brother." He looks down at the floor, lost in thought, before raising his eyes back to me. "You know, just because I've chosen to be alone, doesn't mean I want you to be."

"I know. But..." I squeeze my eyes shut for a second. "I'm afraid if my heart is broken one more time, it won't ever be fixable."

"You're talking about Finn."

I nod. "Neither of us was looking for a relationship, but it happened anyway and now I'm scared he'll hurt me, just like everyone else has."

"I wish I could promise you that won't happen, but I can't. Life throws us curve balls, sweet pea, but if you've got the right fielder ready to catch what you have to give, then it's worth getting up to bat."

I suck in my bottom lip. It's the first time my dad has spouted advice with a baseball metaphor and I wonder if he was saving it until the right person came along. "Like maybe a certain center fielder?"

He arches his brows. *You said it, not me.*

"I don't need to make a decision about anything yet. We're still working together for another month and after that…"

"He'd be an idiot to let you go."

"Thanks, Dad."

"Anytime." He kisses my forehead. "I love you."

"Love you, too." As soon as he closes my bedroom door, I open the box from Finn. Inside is another box, this one an upscale white, and nestled inside on top of silver tissue paper are six large sugar cookies, three Xs and three Os. They're decorated with either red or white icing. A notecard is included on top telling me each month I will receive a Box of Sweetness containing a half dozen handmade cookies.

Finn bought me a cookie subscription box! I grin from ear to ear. *Nice timing, Mr. Auprince.*

I lift a cookie up and find there's a small envelope tucked into the side of the box. I open it and find a note from Finn. *Chloe, Roses are red, violets are blue. Cookies are sweet, but not the things I want to do to you. Finn*

I crack up. That is the most ridiculous poem ever, and I love it. If you looked up Finn Auprince in the dictionary it would read: sexy, athletic, smart, kind, hardworking, caring, determined, confident. He's the kind of guy every girl has dreams of being with. And he's never given me a reason to doubt him.

The cookie is delicious. I eat a second one and then grab my phone to call him. All of a sudden, I'm dying to see if he's up for company tonight. Two can play the not-so-sweet game. My shoulders sag when he doesn't answer. It's eight o'clock on a Friday night. He's probably out to dinner or something, so I hang up.

Maybe I'll drive over to his house. Surprise him when he gets home by being naked in his bed or naked in front of the fireplace.

I like that plan. I know where he hides his spare key and I've missed him a ton this past week. I slide off the bed to change clothes, twisting around to grab my iPhone when it pings with an alert. I've got it set to notify me when Finn or any of his teammates are mentioned. I do this with all my clients, removing the alert when my contract is complete.

I've never once had my heart sink at a notification before, though. I blink several times to be sure I'm not seeing things.

Nope. The photo of Finn with some gorgeous woman on

his arm is right there in living color. She's smiling—actually it's more like a sexy simper, as if she knows she can have any man she wants—at Finn and he's returning the admiration. Another notification sounds, and another. My phone lights up with news of Finn at The Surfeit Hotel.

I wasn't aware of any event at his brother Drew's hotel, not that I'm privy to everything on Finn's social calendar. He's free to do whatever he wants. And it's not like he knew I'd be back home tonight. But the cocktail attire and the sparkly lights in the background rub me the wrong way. It looks very date-like and my fragile heart suffers another punch.

I'm cursed.

And shattered.

Again.

Deep breath, Chloe. It might not be anything. Finn isn't the kind of guy to lie or cheat. He said we were exclusive. He wouldn't go back on his word without being up front with me if his feelings had changed. The problem is, while my head can rationalize he's with famous and beautiful people all the time, and this woman may be just an acquaintance, my heart is freaking the fuck out.

This is Finn's life. He's mega-wealthy, highly regarded, worshipped by baseball fans and non-fans across the country. What if? What if he does meet someone else he likes better than me? He's made me no promises. In a couple of months, he'll be on the road more than he's home. Sleeping in hotel rooms. Fending off female fans. I've seen them—women who stake out the lobbies and bars of team accommodations, hoping to hook up with a player.

When it comes to Finn, my heart leads my head. It makes me sick to my stomach that right now jealousy overrules trust, but given my history, who could blame me? I've been jilted over and over again. I can't bear for it to happen one more time. The only safe place for my heart is with me. I've got dreams and goals and those are what I need to focus on. I can't go wrong if I commit to myself.

I crawl back into bed and reach for my laptop to send an email to Rena. I need some time to lock down my feelings before I see Finn. It's still the holidays so I'm hoping I can push things to after the new year. By then I should be able to explain to him that I'd like to continue our working relationship, but nothing more.

Opening my email, I find a new message from my boss—make that two messages—flagged as important. I open the first one. She's got a one-week job she wants me on with Hayden Clemons. *Huh.* Hayden is another pro baseball player and pretty damn close to Finn's equivalent on the field. He's a year younger than Finn, I think, and plays for the Landsharks' biggest rival—and the team that won the World Series. It's a little odd that she wants me for this last minute, but I'm not going to argue. The gig requires I leave for Sacramento, Hayden's hometown, on Sunday. I won't need to make up some excuse to Rena now, as my boss has already let her know this is a project for Major League Baseball.

I reread that last part. Hayden is chairing this special MLB event, a three-day toy swap where kids can trade or donate sports equipment they received for the holidays. Anyone who brings a gift will get their picture taken with Hayden. Working with Finn is huge, but working with Major League Baseball is a BFD. It's a dream of mine I thought would take years to make a reality. Excitement charges past all the other emotions I'm feeling. This could be a big step in my career. A game changer.

The second email includes my flight and hotel info. I kick my feet, making the sheets rustle. This is really happening.

This is another new beginning—just when I needed it most.

Finn

ALL I WANT is to be home. I dread nights out like this, but Drew reminded me I owed him one and he requested payment tonight. The more "celebrities" hanging out at his hotel, the more media coverage and word of mouth. Why he needs me, I don't know. There are a dozen people more famous than me at his upscale bar to celebrate Ryan Seacrest's birthday. Flashbulbs have been blinking for the past hour, the food and drink flowing. But ten more minutes and I'm out of here. Drew won't notice, given he's got a woman looking at him like she wants to do a lot more than just sit on his lap.

My only saving grace is my friend, Hannah. She's been attached to my hip while we catch up on life. She works with my cousin in fashion design and does some modeling on the side. Her brother and I played high school ball together so

I've known her forever. Am I a little put-off by her sudden flirting? Yeah, but I can handle it and not flirt back.

"So, do you have plans for New Year's Eve?" Hannah asks, escalating her interest by putting her hand on my thigh. "If not, I'd love to ring in the new year with you."

I swivel in my barstool so her hand falls away. "I do have plans." They aren't confirmed, but I plan to be with Chloe in Big Sur through the first of the year.

"Oh?" Disappointment surrounds the single syllable. "With anyone I know?"

"No," I say, taking a sip of my drink. Even if she did know Chloe, it's not anyone's business but mine, and I'd like to protect my relationship with her for as long as possible.

Hannah narrows her eyes at me. "You're being awfully secretive."

"Just keeping it private for now."

"So, it's someone special."

"Yes." Being away from her this past week has only made it more so. I knew I'd miss her, but not like this. Not like my heart forgets a beat every hour of every day we've been apart. It's scares me as much as it excites me.

"*Phew.*"

I frown in confusion.

"I thought I was losing my touch. I've been flirting with you for the past half hour and you've given me nothing. I'm relieved to know it's not me."

"You were flirting?" I deadpan.

She gives me a push in the upper arm, my left upper arm. A slight sharp pain fires off in my shoulder. I've been working out like a fiend and am more sore than normal, but fear creeps into the back of my mind that it's more than regular soreness. I'm used to a quick recovery, not this lingering ache.

"Shut up," she scoffs.

"And since when you do you flirt with me, anyway?"

"I don't know. Boredom?"

"Gee thanks."

"Like your ego needs any stroking. You're hands down the best-looking and sexiest man in this room, and you couldn't care less, which just ups your appeal." She twirls a strand of hair around her finger. "You sure this girl is special enough to pass me up?"

I laugh. "Sorry, Han. I'm positive." If Chloe were in town I would not be sitting here without her. "There's a guy three o'clock, though, who can't take his eyes off you. How about I head home and give him space to make his move?"

She casually inclines her head in his direction. "I wouldn't be opposed to that."

I kiss her cheek. "See you around. Happy New Year."

"Happy New Year. Good luck with your girl."

"Thanks." I don't put a lot of stock in luck, but in this case, I may need it. No matter how hard I work to convince Chloe we should be together, it's ultimately up to her. Of course, I don't give up on things I want.

The valet brings my car around and the first thing I do is look around for my phone. I patted my pockets earlier with no luck, but thought I brought it with me. Ah. There it is. On the floor under my seat. I tap the screen and find dozens of notifications.

All of them focused on a couple pictures of me and Hannah, taken inside the hotel right after we said hello. I'm too tired to decipher everything being said, but the few words that do catch my eye tell me the subject is my love life. And that subject is racking up thousands of likes. Bloody hell. Two pictures curated by someone other than my social media manager are collecting way more attention than they should.

I dial Chloe. Has she seen them? I need to explain. I need to hear her voice, that vibrant and melodic timbre I love just as much as the sound of my bat hitting a home run. The call goes to voicemail as I realize belatedly that it's three hours later back east and she's probably asleep. "Hey, Chloe, I know it's late there, but I wanted to say hello anyway. Call me tomorrow before your flight… Miss you," I tack on because I really fucking miss her and I want her to know it before she hits the friendly skies.

When I get home, the house feels emptier than usual. Too quiet. Too bleak. I love this place, seriously love the solitude it affords me, so I'm not sure what's up with my sudden glum mood. I stop in the kitchen for a glass of water and find Sylvie left me a peanut butter and jelly sandwich on the counter. My mood immediately lifts. I marvel at how cognizant she is of my routine. PB&J has been my go-to nightly snack as of late. She probably knows what time I take a dump every day, too.

I down my sandwich and then trudge upstairs ready to hit the sack. Yeah, I know. It's barely ten o'clock on a Friday night and I'm going to bed. But sleep is important to maintain my killer physique. Muscles like mine need proper rest. Don't get me wrong, if Chloe were here I'd be all over her, exercising one particular muscle to great length and sleeping later.

A solid eight hours will do me good, though.

And a run tomorrow morning before Dwayne shows up to kick my ass.

Then before I know it, the hot blonde I'm in love with will be back in my arms. I fall asleep to the surety of our impending reunion.

Big mistake.

Chapter Twenty-Two
#DownForTheCount

Finn

"Dude, you're scowling so hard your face is gonna get stuck," Giancarlo says to me. "And what good do you think it's doing, anyway? Clemons can't see it. Only me and Mike can, and it's messing with our vibe, so knock it off."

He's right. Glaring at an Instagram picture of Clemons and Chloe on my phone isn't accomplishing anything. It's Thursday night, there's a hockey game on my big-screen TV, and my two teammates are here to enjoy themselves. (Although they were highly amused when I grumbled about the injustice of the Chloe-Clemons situation.)

I place the phone on the coffee table and slide it out of reach.

"Was that so hard, smiley face?" Mike asks.

I dial back my irritation. It isn't Mike or Giancarlo's fault Chloe got assigned to a project with Clemons. "Nope. Who wants another beer?"

They both do, so I grab three bottles out of the fridge. Another plate of Sylvie's homemade tamales too.

I can't remember the last time I was drunk, but tonight seems like a good idea. I'm pining for a girl whose left me one measly message in the past five days, and it pisses me off that I'm letting it get to me. It's not like I won't see her again. And I'm genuinely happy she's doing work she's excited about. But seeing her smile alongside Clemons's smug grin is like a fastball to the solar plexus. I can't breathe, the wind completely knocked out of me.

I replay her message in my mind. She called when I was in the shower on Saturday morning.

"Hi, Finn. Sorry I missed you. I'm sure you'll hear from Rena, but I'll be out of town for the next week on a special MLB project. I'm super excited about it as it's been a dream of mine to work directly for them. So, I guess I'll see you next year. Crazy, huh? Take care. Bye."

Take care is something you say to an acquaintance, not the man who's been balls deep inside you.

After leaving her a couple of voice messages, I gave up. Those times I've said I go after what I want until I get it? I'm not feeling it so much anymore. I've got my pride and I get the sense Chloe is pushing me away. I'm not sure of her reasons, and that doesn't sit well with me, but that makes her reticence even more bothersome. Confusion isn't a color I like to wear. She's been hot and cold with me from the start, though, hasn't she? Not to be cruel. To protect herself. And I get it. I did the same as a teenager to keep my dyslexia a secret, and I still do it now on occasion.

"Yes!" Giancarlo shouts, snagging my attention.

The Kings have scored a goal to take the lead three to

two with ten minutes left in the third period. The crowd goes crazy. Los Angeles fans are the best. I bring my beer to my mouth as the game goes to commercial.

"Oh, hey, I'm supposed to invite you to dinner at our house next weekend," Mike says to me. "Layla wants to set you up with another friend of hers."

Giancarlo throws the last bite of his tamale at him. "Hey, why doesn't she ever set me up?"

Mike catches the piece of tamale with ease and pops it in his mouth. "Because you're all about 'variety is the spice life' shit, and Lay wants to see all her friends married."

"Ah. True." He settles back into the couch, while I choke down my drink.

Mike slaps me on the back. "Was it something I said?"

He damn well knows it is. The last time Layla set me up with one of her friends, the woman had our wedding planned before we'd finished dinner.

"Not interested," I rasp.

"Swear to God this girl's different. She's an investment banker. Owns her own home. Runs half marathons and eats tofu. Interestingly, she said the same thing when Lay brought up your name."

I didn't see that coming. "No shit?"

"No shit."

"Why are you bringing it up then?"

"Because, *duh*, you two would be perfect for each other." He grabs another tamale.

Not true. I've met the woman perfect for me.

The game fires up again on the TV, but my teammates

are looking at me like I've got a baseball bat coming out both ears.

"What?" I say.

"You have?" they ask at the same time. Mike's got a smug look on his face, while Giancarlo wears surprise like a clown just rode into the room on a unicycle.

Damn it. "I said that out loud?"

"You sure as hell did," Mike bellows. He turns to Giancarlo, puts his hand out, palm up. "Pay up, player."

Giancarlo groans in defeat as he pulls his wallet out of his pocket, fishes out a hundred-dollar bill, and slaps it down on the coffee table.

"What is happening?"

Mike tucks the bill away. "We made a little wager about you and Chloe."

"Me and Chloe?"

"Nice try, Romeo. I can read you like a flashing neon sign and after our lunch at the stadium a few weeks ago, I knew you were in deep with her. Giancarlo said I was crazy, so we made a bet."

I rub the back of my neck. "How exactly could you tell?"

"First off, you blush every time you say her name."

"No, I don't."

"Go look in the mirror, dude." This from Giancarlo who's now studying me like he can't believe he didn't see it sooner.

"And second, you're happy."

"I'm always happy," I argue. Minus a few games in the World Series and my epic collision with the back fence.

"Not this kind." Mike shakes his head once. "Trust me, I know. I was in your shoes once. The combo of a happy dick and a happy heart is lethal."

"So is a punch in the face if aimed right."

Mike laughs. "If that isn't a confirmation, I don't know what is. Try to deny it all you want, but you're not fooling anyone."

I lean forward, elbows on my knees. It's not that I want to deny it, or that I hadn't thought these guys would find out eventually. I've been caught off guard, is all, so I voice my biggest concern. "Think I'm fooling Chloe?" Because one wrong move could send her running even farther away, if she hasn't already decided to. She's into me, no doubt. Maybe she even loves me back. But that doesn't mean she's willing to take a chance on us when she believes she's cursed.

"Why would you want to?" Mike asks.

"She's playing hard to get, for good reason."

"A douche for an ex?" Giancarlo takes a drag on his beer.

"More than one, actually."

"Ouch." Mike puts his hand under his chin in thought. "Okay, I see your concern, but she's a smart girl. She knows something."

"Go! Go! Go!" Giancarlo shouts at the TV screen, his body lifting off the couch and angling forward. "Damn. I can't believe he missed that breakaway." He sits back down, tips his bottle back until it's empty. Then he burps.

After that we stop talking to watch the rest of the game. I'm twisted up in goddamn knots for the first time in my life, and I hate it. It's unlike me to be unsure of myself, so while the guys cheer on the Kings, I remember what's always been most important to me. Baseball. It's uncomplicated, fulfilling, and never leaves me in doubt. It's what I'm best at. Chloe distracted me in the best possible way, but no more.

"Fetch!" I tell Sammy, tossing the ball across the field. She's grown since I last saw her. Joshua has, too. He's taller, put on a few pounds. His mom says he's the happiest she's ever seen him, thanks to his four-legged best friend.

He's standing on my left; his brother Jesse is on my right. We're at the park across the street from their house. It's Saturday morning. The sun is shining, but the smell of chimney smoke fills the air.

"See how good she is now?" Josh says when Sammy brings the ball right back and drops it at our feet. He picks up the toy and throws it again.

"You've taught her well."

"We're doing puppy school and our teacher says Sammy is one of the smartest dogs she's ever seen," Jesse says with pride.

"She's an A-plus student," Josh adds.

I know about the training. I've made sure the Davidson family has everything they need where Sammy is concerned. My mom was upset with me when I told her I'd given Sammy away—until she heard the reason why. I've never lost Mom points and gained them back so fast in my life.

"Except she likes to eat our shoes." Josh pets her head

and then lobs the ball again.

She catches it midair, returns it, chases down a pitch from Jesse, returns it. I wonder who will tire first, Sammy or the boys.

I look down at the boys' feet. Sure enough, the rubber toe of Josh's sneaker has a chunk missing. "I can see that. Have your feet grown since I last saw you?"

"Yep. I'm a size one now," Josh says. "No more baby shoes for me."

"I'm a size four." Jesse lifts his leg to show me.

I remember my mom buying me and my brothers shoes almost every month, our feet grew so fast. Monday morning I'll have a box of new shoes in their sizes and a few sizes up delivered to their house. It's my fault, after all, their shoes are being eaten.

The boys talk nonstop as we play with Sammy. They tell me what Santa brought them, what movies they've watched, how when they go back to school it won't be long before baseball season starts. For me either. In just six weeks I'll be taking the field with my team for our first full-squad workout. Two weeks after that I'll be in Arizona for our first spring training game. I close my eyes for a second to picture the emerald-green grass, the snow-white bases, the scoreboard. I can't wait to get back out there. My fingers tingle thinking about wearing my glove on the regular.

"All right, guys, it's time I walk you home." I haven't decided yet if I'm going to stop by Chloe's. Rena told me her flight from Sacramento was landing this morning, and it's walking distance to her house, but given our relationship has cooled off, maybe it's best to leave the ball in her court.

Josh skips ahead with Sammy. He's got the ball in his hand so Sammy is trying to snag it out of his palm. Her playfulness gets to him and he throws the ball. The kid has a good arm and the ball sails toward the street.

Sammy takes off running for it. I see a car turn the corner. My pulse picks up as my stomach sinks. "Sammy, no!" I shout. She doesn't listen.

I give chase, passing Josh who has started to run, too. "Stay here," I command, grateful when I glance over my shoulder to find he and Jesse are huddled together, stricken looks on their almost identical faces.

Don't do it, Sammy. Don't run into the street. The car continues, albeit at a slow speed, but whatever tons of metal it weighs is no match for a thirty-pound dog. "Sammy! Stop!"

She slows for one thundering heartbeat before the ball bounces and she can't help but follow it. *Shit.* I'm closing the gap, closer…closer. She's just about within reach. The ball rolls into the street. Sammy stops at the curb, *thank fuck*, but a split second later she's on the asphalt. The car puts on its brakes, screeching toward a stop. I lunge off the sidewalk, catch Sammy's fur in my fingers and yank. She yelps as I crash to the ground with her in my arms. The smell of burned rubber stings my nose.

There's another thing that stings. Although *sting* isn't the right word, not by a long shot. Scathing pain radiates in my shoulder and across my collarbone. *Not again. Please God, not again.* The last thing I remember is Sammy licking my face.

WHEN I WAKE up my eyelids feel too heavy for my face. My throat is parched. The bed I'm lying on is comfortable as hell, though. There's a vitals cart to my left. Looks like I've got a steady heart rhythm and normal blood pressure. That's reassuring. And at the foot of the bed and to my right is my entire immediate family, staring at me like I've woken from a year-long coma. That isn't so reassuring.

"Hello, darling," my mom says.

I try to sit up. Pain hurtles through my neck and shoulders, my upper chest. A whimper slips through my pursed lips. I've got a goddamn sling on my left arm again.

"Don't move." Ethan puts his arm across my body. "I'll bring the bed up for you."

I squeeze my eyes shut as the events of earlier flood my memory. "Is Sammy okay? Josh and Jesse? The driver of the car?"

"Everyone is fine," my mom says. "The Davidsons are in the waiting room. The boys told us what happened and they feel terrible but we assured them it wasn't their fault."

"I passed out." It's really more of a statement than a question but my dad answers it anyway with, "Yes."

"Did I fracture my clavicle again?"

"Yes," Drew says. "Let me go grab the doctor so he can tell you what's up."

I turn my head to the side, away from everyone, and stare out the window. I want to scream at the top of my lungs. I want to punch a goddamn hole in the wall. I want to be left alone to wallow in misery.

The hospital suite I'm in is huge. I recognize the private VIP room from when my grandma had minor surgery last year. I'm on the sixteenth floor with an ocean view in the distance. No one will have access to me unless we want them to, and my privacy is guaranteed, every staff member on this floor here because they signed a confidentiality agreement.

"Mr. Auprince."

I roll my head to a neutral position. I hate that the man wearing light blue scrubs with graying hair and an easy smile is familiar to me. After the team doctor treated me back at the end of October, I was referred to this fine man, renowned orthopedic surgeon John Bell.

"Dr. Bell. It's really not good to see you." I'm serious and I don't care if I sound like a dick. The weight of my situation is settling in further, and I want everyone out of this room so I can be mad at the fucking world in private.

"Agreed," he says. "I won't beat around the bush. You've suffered another fracture. It involves several fragments this time and given your occupation, I recommend we do surgery. At this point, a surgical repair with a plate and screws will lead to a better long-term outcome than non-surgical healing. X-rays taken when you arrived showed there was some slight scar tissue forming. Were you still having pain before this accident?"

"A little, yes."

"With your permission, I'd like to schedule surgery for Monday."

"How much recovery time am I looking at?"

"Three to four months."

I swallow the bile coming up my throat. I'll miss Opening Day and the Japan series opener. We're scheduled to kick things off with two games against Oakland at the Tokyo Dome. "If we don't operate?"

"You risk improper alignment, which could make it tough to get full strength back in your arm."

My mom puts her hand atop mine. I look into each family member's eyes, not for help with a decision. It sucks, but it's a no-brainer to go the surgery route. I'm seeking reassurance, that whether or not I walk back onto a baseball field, they won't think any less of me. Ethan and Drew are rocket scientists in business with the utmost respect from our father. Drew is carrying on in the hotel world, and to an extent, Ethan is too, with restaurants in our families' hotels in addition to Royal. Not that my dad has ever made me feel inferior because of my calling. It's just that baseball is *my* legacy and if I have to cut my career short, where does that leave me?

"Let's do it," I tell Dr. Bell, seeing nothing but respect reflected back at me from my family.

"Great. I'll notify the Landsharks of the plan. Make sure we're on the same page. I'd like you to stay here until then to keep your arm and shoulder isolated as much as possible."

"Okay. Thanks."

"Knock, knock." A nurse walks into the room flanked by Josh and Jesse. "These two need to go home but wanted to see you first."

"Dad and I have a thing," Mom says. "We'll stop back

tomorrow." She kisses my cheek, Dad gives me a warm smile, and then they walk out with Dr. Bell, leaving room for my new visitors.

"Hi, Finn. Are you okay?" Josh asks.

"Absolutely. You don't need to worry about me, not at all."

They nod. "Thanks for saving Sammy. You're like a real-life superhero," Josh says.

Drew groans. "Aw man. Seriously? We will never hear the end of that."

I give the boys a genuine smile. "Keep taking good care of her, okay?"

"We will," Jesse says, then they wave goodbye and follow the nurse out. Once they're out of eyesight I tell my brothers they don't need to stay. I don't like pretending I'm okay when I'm anything but.

"And let you mope in private? I don't think so," Ethan says from an armed chair across the room. He points the remote at the flat-screen TV hanging on the wall.

"See if they get the E! channel here. There's a *Keeping Up with the Kardashians* marathon this weekend," Drew says, pulling up a chair. "We know that's Finn's favorite show."

"Don't you fucking dare," I say.

Drew laughs, which pisses me off further. Why are they torturing me like this? *You'd do the same thing if one of them were lying in a hospital bed. It's called brotherly love.*

Fine. I'll lie here and ignore them. I've got better things to think about than worrying about what's on television. I forgot to ask the doctor what the surgery is like. How long does it take? How long will I be under? When can I go home? Will I be in a sling like last time? I'm guessing yes, but for how long? I need to talk to my coach and management personally before they put me on the injured list. Guarantee them I'll be back stronger than ever. There's no other option. Baseball is my life.

"Hey, so we were able to keep a lid on your…" Ethan trails off until our eyes meet. "Accident. And no one publicly knows you're here, but is there anyone special you want us to get in touch with?"

"Like a certain blonde, brown-eyed beauty?" Drew suggests with a know-it-all cock of his eyebrow.

I glance at the wall clock. It's midafternoon. Chloe's home now, and if I'm being honest, nothing would make me happier than to see her. But after two weeks apart, and the lack of communication, she doesn't need to be made aware of my condition. She'll no doubt find out from Rena eventually. At that point, we can resume a working relationship. Moving forward, I've got to give everything I have to rehab. If I do that, maybe, just maybe, I'll beat the doctor's timeline and be on the field for Opening Day.

"No," I say.

"No?" Drew pulls a shocked face before turning his attention to Ethan. "You said they were definitely screwing."

Ethan and I lock gazes. "No, I said there was definitely something more going on," my brother clarifies.

"So?" Drew asks. "What's going on?"

"Nothing is going on," I say.

My brothers know me better than anyone, though, so it's

no surprise when Drew says, "You left off the 'not anymore' part." Then his brows knit together. He studies me. "And the part where that bothers you."

I give him a blank look. I don't want to admit the power Chloe has over me. No woman has ever captured my attention the way she has. Made me willing to compromise my time to be with her, to be what *she* needed. It never occurred to me to protect myself. That what she wanted from me would end before I was ready.

"I'm getting over it," I say, circumspect, hoping that appeases them.

"It?" Ethan asks.

"Jesus, can we stop talking already?" I close my eyes, ready to take a nap—or at least fake it.

"You love her," Drew says, straight-out, no doubt at all. Perceptive jerk.

I lift my good arm and give him the finger. He and Ethan laugh and then talk about me like I'm not in the room. I tune them out. It's not the first time I've brushed off their snooping, and it won't be the last. Brotherly love and all that.

As I drift off to honest sleep a few minutes later, I am conscious of one thing: the disconcerting truth is I haven't fooled anyone about my feelings for Chloe. Well, no more. As of right now, any personal sentiments I have toward her are dead and buried.

Chapter Twenty-Three
#LoveDefinitely

Chloe

AFTER BASICALLY TWO weeks away from home, it feels good to know I'm staying put for the foreseeable future. I'm fried from living out of a suitcase, so the first thing I do after I walk through the front door is my laundry. When done, I inhale the ocean-fresh scent from dryer sheets and put all my clothes away. It's the neatest my closet and dresser have been in months. I'm pretty excited to open a drawer tomorrow morning and get dressed.

Dad's watching a basketball game out in the family room while the lasagna he made us for dinner cooks in the oven. A minute ago, he shouted it would be ready in thirty. That gives me time to take a long, hot shower.

This past week in Sacramento has left me tapped out. Being responsible for the posts MLB and Hayden Clemons shared on various social media outlets took extra brain power. For the MLB accounts because I stressed over every image and accompanying text being perfect. And for Hayden because 1) he's demanding 2) he's selfish (although with the kids he was great) and 3) he kept hitting on me. His ego is the size of Australia and he couldn't understand why I kept turning him down. Umm, because you're so not my type with a side of jackass? I can't believe sportscasters continually put him in the same box as Finn. There is no comparison. Not on the field and most definitely not off.

Finn.

I stand under the hot spray of water in my small shower. I haven't been in touch with him all week. He left me a couple of voice messages, but I never got back to him. Guilt ate at me every day, and I started dialing him back at least a dozen times before I chickened out. I listened to his deep, sexy voice over and over again, hating myself for being a jerk, but so unsure about what to say to him that I chose to remain silent. *Miss you*, his last message had said. God, I missed him, too.

So much so, that I've stalked him online. There's been nothing since the night I saw him with *Hannah Mills*. That's the gorgeous woman's name. I did a little more digging and discovered besides modeling, she works with Finn's cousin Meredith. Meaning she and Finn are probably friends. Soooo, maybe I overreacted.

No maybe, I absolutely did.

Jelly Nellys of the world, raise your hand. I'm officially one of you now, jealousy having invaded my body without my permission.

Time has set me straight, but the courage to speak to Finn has lagged. Leaving myself vulnerable *again* is difficult. We can all agree a broken heart is the worst kind of break. But something interesting did happen while I was up north.

With each passing day, my heart didn't feel broken. It felt full. And I realized despite it being trampled on *four times*, I wasn't done with love. My gut or intuition or whatever it is people sense deep in their core finally woke up to tell me this time is different. Finn is different. Having time away to feel what it would be like without him helped me see I want it all. The career *and* the man.

If he still wants me.

An unpleasant voice in the back of my mind reminds me I've ghosted him the past week, and I may have blown my chance.

I step out of the shower and throw on black leggings and my new MLB sweatshirt. I've still got a few minutes before dinner so I check my emails. I open one from Rena that came in just a few minutes ago.

The first sentence guts me. It steals every doubt, all my hesitation, and sends my pulse spiraling out of control.

Finn's been in some kind of accident and is in the hospital. He's having surgery on Monday... I don't bother to read the rest. I couldn't even if I tried, the words blurring as emotion burns behind my eyelids. Without any uncertainty, I call him. Why didn't I phone him sooner, or at least the minute I landed? Why did I have to play it safe?

The call goes to voicemail. I hang up and try again. Same result. Shit. Shit. Shit. I need to talk to him. Need to know he's okay. Whatever bravado I hid behind this past week vanishes, and an entirely new kind of fear invades my body. I'd trade everything, do anything, to guarantee Finn is whole and healthy and able to run back onto the baseball field when the season starts.

I stare at my phone—who else can I call? Grandma Rosemary! She'll know the details and talk me down from this ledge.

"Hi, Rosemary. It's Chloe."

"Hello, sweetheart. How are you?"

"Going out of my mind. I was out of town and just heard Finn is in the hospital. He isn't answering his phone."

"No need to worry. He's in good hands." She goes on to tell me he saved Sammy from being hit by a car and once again landed the wrong way, only this time the fracture is more serious. I bite down so hard on my bottom lip I'm surprised I don't draw blood. I'm worried about Finn, but also Josh and Jesse. They must have been terrified. I make a mental note to stop by and see them after I see Finn.

"He's grumpier than a grizzly who forgot to hibernate," Rosemary continues.

"I'm sure he is."

"Maybe you can cheer him up."

"I'd like to try." Mission Make Finn Smile accepted.

She tells me which hospital he's in and wishes me luck. My hands shake as we say goodbye, Finn's circumstances sinking in deeper. Anytime someone is put under anesthesia, it's a big deal. There are risks no one wants to talk about, but are there nonetheless. What if he has an unknown allergy to one of the medications? What if they operate on the wrong shoulder? What if he wakes up and has amnesia? What if his heart stops beating while he's on the table?

I'm freaking out, but love does that to a person.

I stumble out of my room, hopping and putting on my Vans at the same time. "Dad, I've got to run out. Finn's in the hospital." I break into a cold sweat as I give him the quick lowdown. This isn't anything life-threatening, I *know* that. But I also know Finn, and how hard he's worked to be the elite athlete he is. And the huge mental toll an injury can take.

"Want me to go with you?"

"It's okay. Keep some lasagna warm for me."

"How about I give you some to go. Hospital food is the worst."

"Great idea. Thanks." Finn has to be happy to see me if I come bearing a home-cooked meal. Suddenly, memories wash over me and I have to hold on to the wall for support. Vague recollections of my mom in the hospital and the bland, monotonous food she got zero enjoyment out of. I'd bake her favorite pie and sneak pieces in to her inside my backpack.

Hospitals are not my favorite places.

I hug my dad tightly before I go. "You're feeling good, right?" I ask even though it was the first thing I asked him when I got home. His outward appearance is the best I've seen in a while, but he's excellent at hiding how he feels on the inside.

"Yes. I promise I'll tell you otherwise."

"Voluntarily?"

He makes a chuffing sound. "Yes."

I kiss his cheek. "Thank you."

An hour later with Tupperware in hand, I hurry into the

lobby of the hospital. Right away I dislike the smell, not that it's bad. It's just so sanitary, and that implies measures haven been taken to guard against disease and infections. It means there are sick people here. Loved ones who are facing much more difficult diagnoses than a fractured clavicle. The furniture is upscale, the décor sparse. I forgot to ask Rosemary what room Finn is in, so I make a beeline for the reception desk.

"I'm sorry but Mr. Auprince is on the VIP floor and the only visitors allowed are those on the approved list," a very stern-looking forty-something woman says politely.

"Do you have the list?"

"Of course."

"I'm sure my name is on it. Chloe Conrad." Rosemary didn't mention I'd have any difficulty getting to Finn.

"I'm sorry. It's not."

My heart sinks. "Could you check again, please?"

She gives me a withering look, but takes a second glance at her computer screen. "It's not here."

I think about pleading with her. Promising her I'd be welcome and this is just some sort of oversight. Instead, I spin around and walk out the sliding glass door into the cool fresh evening air. The entry is flanked by beautiful flowering shrubs and inviting wooden benches. I sit on one. There are two reasons why my name isn't on that list. The first is Finn doesn't want to see me. The thought kills me, mostly because it's my own fault. I kept my distance this past week and that wasn't very nice of me. The second is Finn doesn't want to see anyone and there is no list outside of his immediate family. That possibility is almost worse. It means he's hurting and pushing away the people who love him.

"Chloe?"

I startle at the deep male voice and lift my head to see Finn's brother walking out of the hospital. "Drew. Hi."

"Hi. Are you here to see Finn?" Surprise flavors his low-pitched question.

"I was hoping to, yes, but my name isn't on the magic list."

Drew runs a hand over his jaw. "Yeah. Sorry about that. Privacy is always an issue we have to be careful with."

"I understand, but do you think…" I trail off, not sure I have the right to ask for his help.

"You want me to take you up to see him." It's a guarded statement and the reticence stings.

I jump to my feet. It's time to show everyone I'm here to love Finn with nothing less than everything I have. He's stitched in my heart, my soul, my future. "I would love that."

Drew regards me, his hand holding his chin. "But do you love him?"

I want Finn to be the first person I say the actual words to, so I respond with, "I promise," hoping that earns me Drew's trust.

"That's good enough for me. Come on. The guy is being a complete ass. If the sight of you doesn't cheer him up then nothing will."

My cheeks heat. "Finn's talked to you about me?" We pass the reception desk where a man is getting a visitors' pass, but I guess I don't need one with Drew as an escort.

"Sort of." Drew leads me past the main elevators, around a corner to a smaller lift and presses a code into the waist-high numbered panel. The door slides open. "Is that lasagna?" He nods to the Tupperware while pushing the button for the sixteenth floor.

"Homemade," I say cheerily, wondering what he meant by 'sort of.'

Crazy appealing light blue eyes observe me. Drew is gorgeous—almost as hot as Finn. "You know," he says playfully, "I'm a lot more fun than Finn. How about I steal you for a night to show you."

I laugh. "You try and steal all your brother's girl…" I cut off since I'm not his girlfriend. I'm a girl. And his friend. And we've had sex. And laughed together. Had fun together. Learned from each other. Spent a lot of time together. Had amazing sex together. (That bears repeating.)

"He's never had anyone to steal before."

"Oh. Right."

"He had a serious girlfriend in high school, but back then I was the little brother and not half as charming as I am now." He winks at me.

Finn's high school girlfriend. The girl who crushed his heart with cruel words to her friends, making Finn feel used and unintelligent. My unexplained silence while I was in Sacramento was unkind, too, and I'll do whatever it takes to make it up to him.

The elevator door glides open. Drew puts his arm out to hold it in place. "It's not too late," he says around a smile.

"Cranky Finn or Lovable Drew. I know which option gets my vote." His teasing is cute.

I step into the hallway. "I'm kind of head over heels for Cranky," I tell him, saving the L word for Finn, but putting my feelings out into the universe. A giant hell hole doesn't swallow me. The ceiling doesn't crash down. All good signs my renewed confidence is leading me down a safe path.

"Make sure you tell him that."

"I thought I'd fill him in now."

"Excellent plan." He pulls his arm back, the elevator shutting him inside for the ride back to the first floor. "Welcome to the family."

Family. How I've longed for more of that. "Oh hey! Which room?"

"Two," he says right before he disappears and I'm staring at the steel door.

My heart pounds as I walk down the swanky corridor. Wood-paneled walls, fancy tiled floor, the smell like fresh air rather than disinfectant. I pause outside Finn's room to take a deep breath before I step inside.

His bed is a million miles away from the doorway—that's how huge the space is. There are four upholstered chairs in various positions around the room, a square table, an armoire, giant flat-screen TV, and a large window. Tears of joy press against the backs of my eyelids at the sight of him. He's within touching distance for the first time in two weeks.

I walk closer, relieved to find him alone so I can cheer him up the way I practiced on the drive over. His eyes are closed, long lashes resting almost to the tops of his cheekbones. A blanket covers him up to his waist. His smooth, muscles-for-miles torso is bare save for a sling on his left arm.

He's beautiful.

"Finn?" I whisper. If he's deep asleep I'll take a chair and wait for him to wake up.

His eyes fly open. "Chloe?"

"Hi." I'm at the side of the bed now.

"I told Drew I didn't want any visitors." The hard tone of his voice stings inside and out.

Those tears of joy? They turn to grief. I'm an idiot. I take a step back. Finn has every right to turn me away.

Something must show on my face because before I can flee, Finn grabs my wrist, his mouth twisting in discomfort before he says, "Wait."

I'm not sure if his unease stems from the way he spoke to me or the pain in his shoulder, but I stop nonetheless.

"I'm sorry," he adds. "I'm in a crappy mood and didn't mean to take it out on you."

"Are you sure that's all it is?" It's time to girl-up and face our music. It's time he knows he's the love song in my head I play on repeat. He's my last boyfriend, the one I'll fight tooth and nail to keep. Any other woman who thinks she might have even a chance with him, is going down by any means necessary. I'm not above a cat fight to keep the best thing that's ever happened to me. "Because I wouldn't blame you if you were pissed at me. I do still owe you a phone call. Or three."

He tugs me closer before dropping my arm. His gaze

dips to the container in my hands. "That's true, but I see you brought me food."

Not the response I was expecting, but I'll gladly play this Finn's way. At least he's not kicking me out.

"My dad's lasagna. We thought you might like something good to eat, but I'm guessing on this floor they serve lobster if you want it."

"I love lasagna."

"Are you hungry now? It's still a little warm."

"Hand it over." His lighter tone is euphony to my ears. He winces as he shifts, though, accepting the food in his free hand.

"I'll go grab you a fork."

"There's silverware inside the tray there." He nods to the other side of the bed and a wood tray on wheels. Sure enough, there's a drawer with enough utensils for a party. "Have you eaten?" he adds.

"Not yet. I uh..." I peek at him out of the corner of my eye. "I rushed over here once I heard what had happened."

Tenderness, and dare I think forgiveness, flares in his baby blues. "Grab two forks then."

I get situated on the bed, my hip meeting his, and to make it easier for him, I hold the lasagna so he can fork bites with minimal stress to his injury.

We eat in almost-easy silence, stealing glances at each other, until the entire thing is gone. "I'll bring you more tomorrow," I say. "If you want."

There it is. The opening lines to our future, Finn. Please take them and continue our story toward a happily ever after.

He swallows thickly. "I want."

Yes! "Me, too."

"But I want my career back on track, too."

I nod and wait for him to add something about putting me second or not having enough time for both.

"I'll be honest, I'd given up on us."

I nod again because I'm not quite ready to speak without my voice cracking.

"You've been pretty unavailable the past two weeks and I didn't like that. I didn't know what to think."

"I'm sorry about that. I was wrong to shut you out, but when I left for New Jersey I wasn't sure of your feelings for me, and then when I saw the picture of you with Hannah Mills, I thought the worst. About you and about myself. FYI, I googled her and I know it was nothing." I pause to catch my breath. "Still, when I got the job in Sacramento, I was relieved I had something else to focus on. I buried myself in work so I wouldn't have to deal with these intense feelings."

He raises an eyebrow. "Go on."

"You're my favorite person ever," I blurt out. "When I look at you it's like nothing else exists but the two of us. I'm sorry I made you think differently. It won't happen again."

One side of his mouth curls up. "What do you know. You're my favorite, too." He laces our fingers together. "I want it all, Webster. The career, the girl, and so much more."

"Yeah? How much more?"

"I'm not going to scare you off, am I?"

"No." I shake my head. "But..."

"But what?"

"That doesn't mean I'm not scared. Because I am. More than I've ever been before. I tried really hard not to fall in love with you, and it didn't work. I'd rather have all two hundred and six of my bones break than have my heart broken again, so you better not even think about it. My dad told me to find a heart big enough for my love and I pick yours and give you mine. No takebacks. I—"

His hand swiftly moves to the back of my head and he tugs my mouth to his. His lips aren't like sugar, they're better. He fastens us together with a kiss that reaches everywhere inside me. It's passionate. Earnest. Unlike all our other kisses, this one promises *more*. His tongue slips between my lips, tasting and possessing and stealing all the breath out of my lungs.

"I love you, too," he murmurs, resting his forehead against mine.

We stay like that for several beats, until he pulls back. Lines crease the corners of his eyes, telling me he's in pain. More kissing will have to sit tight until post-surgery when he's feeling better.

"I will never break any part of you. You put the kind of meaning in my life that only comes around once in a lifetime. Those other guys? They were just so you'd know what true love feels like—with me."

I nod. And blink. And swallow the emotion lodged deep in the back of my throat, in my bones, in the special place in my heart that's been waiting for Finn. He's right. All my experiences led me to here. "So, we're doing this," I finally say, quietly but surely.

"You bet your gorgeous ass we are. No takebacks."

Chapter Twenty-Four
#GrandSlam

Three weeks later…
Finn

I BRUSH MY thumb over Chloe's full bottom lip, relishing how soft the skin is against my harder fingertip. My other hand grips the smooth slope of her waist with minimal discomfort as she rides my dick. Not that I'd stop if it hurt. Hell no. This is our first time since my surgery and no amount of pain is ending this before we orgasm.

"Chloe," I growl, when she slows her movements. "Don't you dare stop."

"Am I hurting you?"

"Only if you stop."

"I thought this would be the least painful position."

"It is." Damn this woman and her concern. I shoot my hips up, taking over our rhythm, each thrust a desperate desire to feel her squeezed tight around me.

"Oh my God," she moans. "Finn…"

That's more like it. Her palms press into my stomach as she impales herself on my cock over and over again. Her ass slaps my thighs. Her breasts bounce. Her cheeks and neck flush.

I'm so far gone for this incredible woman, I'm seconds away from blowing my load in embarrassingly quick time. Did I mention she's riding me bare? We had the talk last week, she's on the pill, and I'll tell you right now, Chloe is my forever.

She bucks against me, the hot, slick feel of her without any barrier between us pure heaven. She swirls her hips and Jesus Christ, heat flashes through me, drawing my balls up. The base of my spine tingles.

I groan. She hums. Looks down at me with such admiration while clenching my dick like she can't get enough, that stars flash in my vision.

"I'm not going to last much longer," I say.

"Me either."

We move in sync, the sounds and smell of our lovemaking filling my bedroom. *Our* bedroom. Chloe doesn't know it yet, but things are about to change. I hope.

"Love you," I mumble. So damn much it's scary. It gives me insight into Chloe's fears and I've done everything I can to set her mind at ease. There's only one thing left to…

"Fuck," we say at the same time. And then she's panting and purring, and pulsing around my cock, milking me for everything I've got. A shudder rolls through my body and my own release crashes over me. I spill inside her, making every part of her mine.

"I love you, too," she says once we've calmed down. She bends over to kiss me, nice and slow, our tongues in a mellow duel for dominance before she lifts off me and rolls onto her back beside me.

"That was…" I trail off because there are no words to describe what just transpired between us. It was love and like and heat and passion and awesome and intimate.

Chloe turns to her side, props her head in her hand. "Amazificent."

I grin. "Tell me Webster, what does that mean?"

"It means amazing and magnificent."

My grin widens. "That works."

"How are you feeling?" She lightly traces her finger along my collarbone and the small keepsake scar.

"I don't want to talk about my injury today."

"What do you want to talk about?"

"I thought you'd never ask."

"Uh-oh. Can I grab something to eat first? I'll run down to the kitchen and be right back." She doesn't give me time to answer. She rolls off the bed, picks up my T-shirt to slip over her head, and makes a quick stop in the bathroom—yelling "I'm sticky!"—before striding out of the room.

She's going to be sticky again in a couple of hours. I carefully get out of bed and use the bathroom to clean myself up, too. The guy in the mirror looks damn happy as he pulls on sweatpants.

Getting back in bed, I arrange the pillows against the headboard and wait. I haven't exactly planned what to say, but winging it has worked so far. Chloe doesn't expect practiced speeches or elaborate gifts. Which isn't to say I don't plan on spoiling her every chance I get. Today, for example, I'm going big.

I need to seal the deal before she moves from being my social media manager to the Landsharks social media manager. That's right. She's been promoted, leaving the company she works for to work full time for the Landsharks organization. Next stop is the MLB she says. I say her brain is one of her best features and she can do whatever she sets her mind to.

Our lives will be hella busy come spring, but we've talked through every scenario, mostly so she doesn't worry. I don't want my girl doubting me for one second.

She strides back into the room with a plate of food. Sylvie now buys Chloe's favorites, too. And from the looks of it, Chloe's piled many of them onto her dish.

"What? I brought you something, too." She sits down next to me with her legs crossed in her lap, wiggling until she's situated just right.

"The banana?"

"Yep. Here you go." She hands me the fruit.

"Thanks… What are you doing?" I ask, making a face.

"Dipping string cheese in Nutella." She looks up at me. "Do not yuck my yum. It's delish. Here, try some." She waggles the cheese in front of me, knowing full well there's no chance I'm tasting that combo.

God, I love eating in bed with her.

"What's that noise?"

Shit. Calvin's early. Or more likely I'm late, too caught up in Chloe to notice the time. I inwardly smile. Before Webster, I was selfish with my time. Happy to be alone and abide by no one's schedule but my own. Not anymore. She's brought balance to my world, on most days at least. She accepts there are times when I'm wrapped up in *my* end goal: being the best pro baseball player I can be.

"It sounds like a helicopter," she says, turning her head to glance out the window.

"It is."

She narrows her eyes at me. "Is there a helicopter landing on your baseball diamond?"

"Yes."

"Please tell me you are not having deliveries made like this."

I laugh. More in love than ever with this down-to-earth, smart, kind human being. "No delivery." I put my banana aside. Her plate, too. And gather her hands in mine. "Chloe, you know how we've talked about a certain amount of risk involved in falling in love and that there are no guarantees?"

"Yes," she says cautiously.

"And how you're still not 100 percent certain I'm not going to bump into my soul mate at the gas station?"

That earns me a speck of a smile. "Yes."

"I have a solution."

"Oh-kay."

"The helicopter is waiting for us. It's going to fly us to Vegas." I release her hands, slide off the bed, and get down on one knee.

Her hand flies to her mouth.

"Chloe Webster Conrad, you are the love of my life. You turned my world upside down from the moment we met. Your laugh is my favorite sound. Your smile is my favorite sight. The wild berry shampoo stuff you use on your hair is my favorite smell."

She giggles.

"You're the one person I can't live without. And I want to be the one person you can't live without. Will you elope with me?"

"You want to marry me right now?"

"Yes."

"Are you sure?"

"I've never been surer of anything in my life."

Her big, beautiful eyes grow glassy. "What about your family? Are you sure they—"

"They love you. But even if they didn't. I do, and that's all that matters. I love you more than I thought possible. More than any other human and more than my favorite sport. Your strength is my strength. Your dreams are my dreams. I want to keep growing closer and discovering new things to love about each other. Which for the record will be much easier for me than for you." She giggles and wipes at the tear sliding down the side of her cheek. "You've trusted me with your heart, Chloe, and I promise to cherish it and keep it safe for the rest of my life. So, what do you say? We Vegas bound?"

"YES!" She tackles me, knocking me over and kissing my entire face. Her reaction takes the sting out of my shoulder. We roll on the floor for a minute, exchanging 'I love you' over and over again.

Once we're upright, we get properly dressed, throw some clothes into a bag, and grab our toothbrushes. "I'll need to buy a dress when we get there," Chloe says.

"Done."

"Can we do the full cheesy package?"

"Whatever you want."

She runs her hands down her jeans, lost in thought for a moment. "I'd like to call my dad and tell him."

I take her in my arms. "He's going to be there waiting for us. When I snuck by the house to ask him for your hand in marriage, I also told him about my plan and invited him to be our witness. I thought you'd like him there."

She cups my face in her hands and gazes at me with such unconditional faith and love that I know without a doubt our marriage will be both fantastic and incredible. "Thank you."

"You're welcome."

"That's not really fair to your parents, though."

"All I care about in this moment is you." I cover her hands and bring them to my chest, where my heart is still beating more pronounced than usual. "Besides, I'm pretty sure once they find out the good news, my mom will want to throw us a reception. Will you be okay with that? I'm cool to skip it."

She rises onto her tiptoes and kisses me. "I know you are. But if your family wants to celebrate with us, then I'll go along with whatever your mom wants." A flash of sadness pulls her head down, making me think she misses her own mom especially hard right now.

"Hey." I take her chin between my thumb and index finger, bringing her eyes back to me. "Can I tell you a secret?"

"Always," she says softly.

"My mom is beyond excited to have you for a daughter. I hinted at some big news coming her way soon, and her face lit up with happiness. Having three sons, she's eager to even the playing field, so to speak."

"Daughter-in-law," she corrects.

"Daughter," I respond firmly. "She'll never replace your mom, but she will treat you like one of her own and love you just as fiercely as she loves my brothers and me."

"Stop making me cry!" She wraps her arms around my waist and tucks her head under my neck.

I keep us rooted to our spot, rub her back. I've thrown a lot at her in the past twenty minutes.

"I love you," she says. "And I'm going to cherish you and cheer for you and—" she looks up at me with narrowed eyes "—you want kids, right?"

"I do. I always thought I'd have them after I retired from baseball, but if you want to start now, I won't say no."

"That's good because I'd like a big family."

"How big we talking?"

"Four?"

I brush a stray hair off her forehead. "Done."

"Wow, are all our discussions going to be this easy?" she teases.

"Doubtful, but that's a good thing because then we can have make-up sex."

She shakes her head. "You think sex will settle our fights?"

"Have you seen what I'm packing? I know it will."

"Oh my God." She swats me in the arm with a grin before her expression turns serious. "You're the love of my life, too, you know. You've given my heart a home. And I will cherish your dreams and your strengths, and make you green smoothies without scrunching up my nose, and give you babies I hope are miniature versions of you. Because, Finn, you are everything I thought I'd never have."

"Every day," I say. "I will love you every single day more than I did the day before."

"Every day," she mimics. "I will love you every single day more than I did the day before."

"Looks like the only thing we're cursed with is love."

"Someone had to get stuck with you." She shows off her beautiful smile. "And luckily that someone is me."

"I knew you were stuck on me the night you hit my car."

"More like the other way around."

I grab our duffel, put it over my good shoulder. "True."

"Wait. What?"

"You had me before you even said 'hello,' Webster. Now let's go. We've got a wedding to catch." I kiss her square on the mouth then take her hand, feeling like *I'm* the luckiest guy on the planet. Hashtag Walk Off Home Run.

The End

The American Royalty series

Book 1: *Heartthrob*
Finn's story
View the series here

Book 2: *Sweet Talker*
Ethan's story

Book 3: *Hotshot*
Drew's story
Coming soon

Available now at your favorite online retailer!

More books by Robin Bielman

Falling for Her Bachelor
The Palotays of Montana

Once upon a Royal Christmas
The Palotays of Montana

Available now at your favorite online retailer!

About the Author

Robin Bielman is the USA Today bestselling author of over fifteen novels. When not attached to her laptop, she loves to read, go to the beach, frequent coffee shops, and spend time with her husband and two sons.

Her fondness for swoon-worthy heroes who flirt and stumble upon the girl they can't live without jumpstarts most of her story ideas. She writes with a steady stream of caffeine nearby and the best dog on the planet, Harry, by her side. She also dreams of traveling to faraway places and loves to connect with readers. To keep in touch, sign up for her newsletter on her website! www.robinbielman.com

Thank you for reading

Heartthrob

If you enjoyed this book, you can find more from all our great authors at TulePublishing.com, or from your favorite online retailer.

CPSIA information can be obtained
at www.ICGtesting.com
Printed in the USA
FSHW020314230419
57429FS